Room 6.

PUFFIN BOOKS

Editor: Kaye Webb

THE LOST PRINCE

There was once a boy called Marco Loristan (that wasn't his real name, but he didn't know that) and he lived in a poor, dingy street in London with his father and their one devoted servant, Lazarus.

Marco's father was a patriot, fiercely devoted to a small unfortunate country named Samavia. Long ago Samavia had had a wicked king whose own people had murdered him, wishing to put in his place his young son, a good and noble, kind and courteous prince. But the prince had vanished, and ever since the once splendid little kingdom had been like a bone fought for by dogs, bullied by stronger countries and shaken by internal fights.

Years ago, when Marco was only a little boy, his father had made him swear, sword in hand:

> '*The sword in my hand – for Samavia!*
> '*The heart in my breast – for Samavia!*
> '*The swiftness of my sight, the thought of my brain,
>   the life of my life – for Samavia!*'

And now they were still involved in plots and secret councils for the sake of Samavia, still moving secretly from capital to capital, still poor and proud, and still hoping that one day a Lost Prince might come home to rule his people.

The waiting had been long but a change was coming now—young Marco was to cross Europe with his friend The Rat, disguised as beggar boys, to bear the great message that the salvation of Samavia was at hand!

This stirring, deeply romantic adventure story is by ter known for *The* oth in Puffins.

gn by Philip Gough

FRANCES HODGSON BURNETT

The Lost Prince

Illustrated by
Michael Whittlesea

PENGUIN BOOKS

Penguin Books Ltd, Harmondsworth, Middlesex, England
Penguin Books Australia Ltd, Ringwood, Victoria, Australia

—

First published 1915
This shorter version published by William Heinemann 1966
Published in Puffin Books 1971

—

Shortened version copyright © William Heinemann Ltd, 1966
Illustrations copyright © William Heinemann Ltd, 1966

—

Made and printed in Great Britain
by Richard Clay (The Chaucer Press) Ltd,
Bungay, Suffolk
Set in Linotype Baskerville

Contents

CHAPTER 1

The New Lodgers at No. 7 Philibert Place

THERE are many dreary and dingy rows of ugly houses in parts of London, but there certainly could not be any row more ugly or dingier than Philibert Place. There were stories that it had once been more attractive, but that had been so long ago that no one remembered the time. It stood back in its gloomy, narrow strips of uncared-for, smoky gardens, whose broken iron railings were supposed to protect it from the surging traffic of a road which was always roaring with the rattle of buses, cabs, drays, and vans, and the passing of people who were shabbily dressed and looked as if they were either going to hard work or coming from it, or hurrying to see if they could find some of it to do to keep themselves from going hungry. The brick fronts of the houses were blackened with smoke, their windows were nearly all dirty and hung with dingy curtains, or had no curtains at all, the strips of ground, which had once been intended to grow flowers in, had been trodden down into bare earth in which even weeds had forgotten to grow. One of them was used as a stone-cutter's yard, and cheap monuments, crosses, and slates were set out for sale, bearing inscriptions beginning with 'Sacred to the Memory of'. Another had piles of old lumber in it, another exhibited second-hand furniture, chairs with unsteady legs, sofas with horsehair stuffing bulging out of holes in their covering, mirrors with blotches or cracks in them. The insides of the houses were as gloomy as the outside. They were all exactly alike. In each a dark entrance passage led to narrow stairs going up to bedrooms, and to narrow steps going down to a basement kitchen. The back bedroom looked out on small, sooty, flagged yards, where thin cats quarrelled, or sat on the coping of the brick walls hoping that sometime they might feel the sun; the front rooms looked over the noisy road, and through their windows came the roar and rattle of it. It was shabby and cheerless on the brightest days, and on foggy or rainy ones it was the most forlorn place in London.

At least that was what one boy thought as he stood near the railings watching the passers-by on the morning on which this story begins, which was also the morning after he had been brought by his father to live as a lodger in the back sitting-room of No. 7.

He was about twelve years old, his name was Marco Loristan, and he was the kind of boy people look at a second time. In the first place, he was a very big boy – tall for his years, and with a particularly strong frame. His shoulders were broad and his arms and legs were long and powerful. He was quite used to hearing people say, as they glanced at him, 'What a fine, big lad!' And then they always looked again at his face. It was not an English face or an American one, and was very dark in colouring. His features were strong, his black hair grew on his head like a mat, his eyes were large and deep set, and looked out between thick, straight, black lashes. He was as un-English a boy as one could imagine, and an observing person would have been struck at once by a sort of *silent* look expressed by his whole face, a look which suggested that he was not a boy who talked much.

This look was specially noticeable this morning. The things he was thinking of were of a kind likely to bring to the face of a twelve-year-old boy an unboyish expression.

He was thinking of the long, hurried journey he and his father and their old soldier servant, Lazarus, had made during the last few days – the journey from Russia. Cramped in a close third-class railway carriage, they had dashed across the Continent as if something important or terrible were driving them, and here they were, settled in London as if they were going to live for ever at No. 7 Philibert Place. He knew, however, that though they might stay a year, it was just as probable that, in the middle of some night, his father or Lazarus might waken him from his sleep and say, 'Get up – dress yourself quickly. We must go at once.' A few days later, he might be in Petrograd, Berlin, Vienna, or Budapest, huddled away in some poor little house as shabby and comfortless as No. 7 Philibert Place.

He passed his hand over his forehead as he thought of it and watched the buses. His strange life and his close association with his father had made him much older than his years, but he was only a boy, after all, and the mystery of things sometimes weighed heavily upon him, and set him to deep wondering.

In not one of the many countries he knew had he ever met a boy whose life was in the least like his own. Other boys had homes in which they spent year after year; they went to school regularly, and played with other boys, and talked openly of the things which happened to them, and the journeys they made. When he remained in a place long enough to make a few boy-friends, he knew he must never forget that his whole existence was a sort of secret whose safety depended upon his own silence and discretion.

This was because of the promises he had made to his father, and they had been the first thing he remembered. Not that he had ever regretted anything connected with his father. He threw his black head up as he thought of that. None of the other boys had such a father, not one of them. His father was his idol and his chief. He had scarcely ever seen him when his clothes had not been poor and shabby, but he had also never seen him when, despite his worn coat and frayed linen, he had not stood out among all others as more distinguished than the most noticeable of them. When he walked down a street, people turned to look at him even oftener than they turned to look at Marco, and the boy felt as if it was not merely because he was a big man with a handsome, dark face, but because he looked, somehow, as if he had been born to command armies, and as if no one would think of disobeying him. Yet Marco had never seen him command anyone, and they had always been poor, and shabbily dressed, and often enough ill-fed. But whether they were in one country or another, and whatsoever dark place they seemed to be hiding in, the few people they saw treated him with a sort of deference, and nearly always stood when they were in his presence, unless he bade them sit down.

'It is because they know he is a patriot, and patriots are respected,' the boy had told himself.

He himself wished to be a patriot, though he had never seen his own country of Samavia. He knew it well, however. His father had talked to him about it ever since that day when he had made the promises. He had taught him to know it by helping him to study detailed maps of it — maps of its cities, maps of its mountains, maps of its roads. He had told him stories of the wrongs done its people, of their sufferings and struggles for liberty, and, above all, of their unconquerable courage. When they talked together of its history, Marco's boy-blood burned and leaped in his veins, and he always knew, by the look in his father's eyes, that his blood burned also. His countrymen had been killed, they had been robbed, they had died by thousands of cruelties and starvation, but their souls had never been conquered, and, through all the years during which more powerful nations crushed and enslaved them, they never ceased to struggle to free themselves and stand unfettered as Samavians had stood centuries before.

'Why do we not live there?' Marco had cried on the day the promises were made. 'Why do we not go back and fight? When I am a man, I will be a soldier and die for Samavia.'

'We are of those who must *live* for Samavia – working day and night,' his father had answered; 'denying ourselves, training our bodies and souls, using our brains, learning the things which are best to be done for our people and our country. Even exiles may be Samavian soldiers –I am one, you must be one.'

'Are we exiles?' asked Marco.

'Yes,' was the answer. 'But even if we never set foot on Samavian soil, we must give our lives to it. I have given mine since I was sixteen. I shall give it until I die.'

'Have you never lived there?' said Marco.

A strange look shot across his father's face.

'No,' he answered, and said no more. Marco, watching him, knew he must not ask the question again.

The next words his father said were about the promises. Marco was quite a little fellow at the time, but he understood the solemnity of them, and felt that he was being honoured as if he were a man.

'When you are a man, you shall know all you wish to know,' Loristan said. 'Now you are a child, and your mind must not be burdened. But you must do your part. A child sometimes forgets that words may be dangerous. You must promise never to forget this. Wheresoever you are, if you have playmates, you must remember to be silent about many things. You must not speak of what I do, or of the people who come to see me. You must not mention the things in your life which make it different from the lives of other boys. You must keep in your mind that a secret exists which a chance foolish word might betray. You are a Samavian, and there have been Samavians who have died a thousand deaths rather than betray a secret. You must learn to obey without question, as if you were a soldier. Now you must take your oath of allegiance.'

He rose from his seat and went to a corner of the room. He knelt down, turned back the carpet, lifted a plank, and took something from beneath it. It was a sword, and, as he came back to Marco, he drew it out from its sheath. The child's strong, little body stiffened and drew itself up, his large, deep eyes flashed. He was to take his oath of allegiance upon a sword as if he were a man. He did not know that his small hand opened and shut with a fierce understanding grip because those of his blood had for long centuries past carried swords and fought with them.

Loristan gave him the big bared weapon, and stood erect before him.

'Repeat these words after me sentence by sentence!' he commanded.

And as he spoke them Marco echoed each one loudly and clearly.

'The sword in my hand – for Samavia!

'The heart in my breast – for Samavia!

'The swiftness of my sight, the thought of my brain, the life of my life – for Samavia.

'Here grows a man for Samavia.

'God be thanked!'

Then Loristan put his hand on the child's shoulder, and his dark face looked almost fiercely proud.

'From this hour,' he said, 'you and I are comrades at arms.'

And from that day to the one on which he stood beside the broken iron railings of No. 7 Philibert Place, Marco had not forgotten for one hour.

CHAPTER 2

A Young Citizen of the World

H E had been in London more than once before, but not to the lodgings in Philibert Place. When he was brought a second or third time to a town or city, he always knew that the house he was taken to would be in a quarter new to him, and he should not see again the people he had seen before. Such slight links of acquaintance as sometimes formed themselves between him and other children as shabby and poor as himself were easily broken. His father had never forbidden him to make chance acquaintances. He had, in fact, told him that he had reasons for not wishing him to hold himself aloof from other boys. The only barrier which must exist between them must be the barrier of silence concerning his wanderings from country to country. Other boys as poor as he was did not make constant journeys, therefore they would miss nothing from his boyish talk when he omitted all mention of his. When he was in Russia, he must speak only of Russian places and Russian people and customs. When he was in France, Germany, Austria, or England, he must do the same thing. When he had learned English, French, German, Italian, and Russian he did not know. He had seemed to grow up in the midst of changing tongues which all became familiar to him, as languages are familiar to children who have lived with them. He did remember, however, that his father had always been unswerving in his attention to his pronunciation and method of speaking the language of any country they chanced to be living in.

'You must not seem a foreigner in any country. It is necessary that you should not. But when you are in

England, you must not know French, or German, or anything but English.'

Once, when he was seven or eight years old, a boy had
asked him what his father's work was.

'His own father is a carpenter, and he asked me if my
father was one,' Marco brought the story to Loristan. 'I
said you were not. Then he asked if you were a shoemaker,
and another one said you might be a bricklayer or a tailor
— and I didn't know what to tell them.' He had been out
playing in a London street, and he put a grubby little
hand on his father's arm, and clutched and almost fiercely
shook it. 'I wanted to say that you were not like their
fathers, not at all. I knew you were not, though you were
quite as poor. You are not a bricklayer or a shoemaker,
but a patriot — you could not be only a bricklayer — you!'
He said it grandly and with a queer indignation, his black
head held up and his eyes angry.

Loristan laid his hand against his mouth.

'Hush! hush!' he said. 'Is it an insult to a man to think
he may be a carpenter or make a good suit of clothes? If I
could make our clothes, we should go better dressed. If I
were a shoemaker, your toes would not be making their
way into the world as they are now.' He was smiling, but
Marco saw his head held itself high, too, and his eyes were
glowing as he touched his shoulder. 'I know you did not
tell them I was a patriot,' he ended. 'What was it you said
to them?'

'I remember that you were nearly always writing and
drawing maps, and I said you were a writer, but I did not
know what you wrote — and that you said it was a poor
trade. I heard you say that once to Lazarus. Was that a
right thing to tell them?'

'Yes. You may always say it if you are asked.'

So Loristan answered him, and from that time if, by
any chance, his father's means of livelihood were inquired

into, it was simple enough and true enough to say that he wrote to earn his bread.

In the first days of strangeness to a new place, Marco often walked a great deal. He was strong and untiring, and it amused him to wander through unknown streets, and look at shops, and houses, and people. He did not confine himself to the great thoroughfares, but liked to branch off into the side streets and odd, deserted-looking squares, and even courts and alley ways. He often stopped to watch workmen and talk to them if they were friendly. In this way he made stray acquaintances in his strollings, and learned a good many things. He had a fondness for wandering musicians, and, from an old Italian who had in his youth been a singer in opera, he had learned to sing a number of songs in his strong, musical boy-voice. He knew well many of the songs of the people in several countries.

It was very dull this first morning and he wished that he had something to do or someone to speak to. London as he saw it in the Marylebone Road seemed to him a hideous place. It was murky and shabby-looking, and full of dreary-faced people. It was not the first time he had seen the same things, and they always made him feel that he wished he had something to do.

Suddenly he turned away from the gate and went into the house to speak to Lazarus. He found him in his dingy closet of a room on the fourth floor at the back of the house.

'I am going for a walk,' he announced to him. 'Please tell my father if he asks for me. He is busy, and I must not disturb him.'

Lazarus was patching an old coat, as he often patched things – even shoes sometimes. When Marco spoke, he stood up at once to answer him. He was very obstinate and particular about certain forms of manner. Nothing would have obliged him to remain seated when Loristan

or Marco was near him. Marco thought it was because he
had been so strictly trained as a soldier. He knew that his
father had had great trouble to make him lay aside his
habit of saluting when they spoke to him.

'Perhaps,' Marco had heard Loristan say to him almost
severely, once when he had forgotten himself and had
stood at salute while his master passed through a broken-
down gate before an equally broken-down-looking lodging-house – 'perhaps you can force yourself to remember
when I tell you that it is not safe – *it is not safe!* You put
us in danger!'

It was evident that this helped the good fellow to control himself. Marco remembered that at the time he had
actually turned pale, and had struck his forehead and
poured forth a torrent of Samavian dialect in penitence
and terror. But, though he no longer saluted them in
public, he omitted no other form of reverence and ceremony, and the boy had become accustomed to being
treated as if he were anything but a shabby lad whose coat
was patched.

'Yes, sir,' Lazarus answered. 'Where was it your wish to
go?'

Marco knitted his black brows a little in trying to recall
distinct memories of the last time he had been in London.

'I have been to so many places, and have seen so many
things since I was here before, that I must begin to learn
again about the streets and buildings I do not quite remember.'

'Yes, sir,' said Lazarus. 'There *have* been so many. You
were but eight years old when you were last here.'

'I think I will go and find the royal palace, and then I
will walk about and learn the names of the streets,' Marco
said.

'Yes, sir,' answered Lazarus, and this time he made his
military salute.

Marco lifted his right hand in recognition, as if he had

been a young officer. Most boys might have looked awkward or theatrical in making the gesture, but he made it with ease, because he had been familiar with the form since his babyhood. He had seen officers returning the salutes of their men when they encountered each other by chance in the streets, he had seen princes raising the quiet, recognizing hand to their helmets as they rode through applauding crowds. He had seen many royal pageants, but always only as an ill-clad boy standing on the edge of the crowd. An energetic lad, however poor, cannot spend his days in going from one country to another without, by mere everyday chance, becoming familiar with the outer life of royalties and courts. Marco had stood in continental thoroughfares when visiting emperors rode by. He knew where in great capitals the sentries stood before palaces. He had seen certain royal faces often enough to know them well, and to be ready to make his salute when particular quiet and unattended carriages passed him by.

'It is well to know them. It is well to observe everything and to train one's self to remember faces and circumstances,' his father had said. 'If you were a young prince or a young man training for a diplomatic career, you would be taught to notice and remember people and things as you would be taught to speak your own language with elegance. It is as practical for one man as another – for a poor lad in a patched coat as for one whose place is to be in courts. As you cannot be educated in the ordinary way, you must learn from travel and the world. You must lose nothing – forget nothing.'

It was his father who had taught him everything, and he had learned a great deal. Loristan had the power of making all things interesting to fascination. To Marco it seemed that he knew everything in the world. They were not rich enough to buy many books, but Loristan knew the treasures of all great cities, the resources of the smallest towns. Together he and his boy walked through galleries filled with the wonders of the world, the pictures before which through centuries an unbroken procession of eyes had passed uplifted. Because his father made the pictures seem the glowing, burning work of still living men whom the centuries could not turn to dust, because he could tell stories of what they felt and suffered and were, the boy became as familiar with the old masters – Italian, German, French, Dutch, English, Spanish – as he was with most of the countries they had lived in. They were not merely old masters to him, but men who were great, men who seemed to him to have wielded beautiful swords and held high, splendid lights. His father could not go often with him, but he always took him for the first time to the galleries, museums, libraries, and historical places which were richest in treasures of art, beauty, or story. Then, having seen them once through his eyes, Marco went again and again alone. He knew that he was gratifying a wish of his father's when he tried to train himself to observe all things and forget nothing. These palaces of marvels were his schoolrooms, and his strange but rich education was the most interesting part of his life. In time, he knew whether this masterpiece or that was in Vienna, in Paris, in Venice, or Munich, or Rome. He knew stories of splendid crown jewels, of old armour, of ancient crafts, and of Roman relics dug up from beneath the foundations of old German cities. Any boy wandering to amuse himself through museums and palaces on 'free days' could see what he saw, but boys living fuller and less lonely lives would have been less likely to concentrate their entire minds on what they looked at, and also less likely to store away facts. Having no playmates and nothing to play with, he began when he was a very little fellow to make a sort of game out of his rambles through picture-galleries, and the places which, whether they called themselves museums or not, were store-houses or relics of antiquity. There were always the blessed 'free days', when he could climb any marble steps, and enter any great portal without paying an entrance fee. Once inside, there were plenty of plainly and poorly dressed people to be seen, but there were not often boys as young as himself who were not attended by older companions. Quiet and orderly as he was, he often found himself stared at. The game he had created for himself was as simple as it was absorbing. It was to try how much he could remember and clearly describe to his father when they sat together at night and talked of what he had seen. These night talks filled his happiest hours. He never felt lonely then, and when his father sat and watched him with a certain curious and deep attention in his dark, reflective eyes, the boy was comforted and content. Sometimes he brought back rough sketches of objects he wished to ask about, and Loristan could always relate to him the full, rich story of the thing he wanted to know. They were stories made so splendid and full of colour in the telling that Marco could not forget them.

CHAPTER 3

The Legend of the Lost Prince

As he walked through the streets, he was thinking of one of these stories. He had heard it first when he was very young, and it had so seized upon his imagination that he had asked often for it. It was a part of the long-past history of Samavia, and he had loved it for that reason. Lazarus had often told it to him, but he had always liked best his father's version, which seemed a thrilling and living thing. On their journey from Russia, during an hour when they had been forced to wait in a cold wayside station and had found the time long, Loristan had discussed it with him. He always found some such way of making hard and comfortless hours easier to live through.

'Fine, big lad – for a foreigner,' Marco heard a man say to his companion as he passed them this morning. 'Looks like a Pole or a Russian.'

It was this which had led his thoughts back to the story of the Lost Prince. He knew that most of the people who looked at him and called him a 'foreigner' had not even heard of Samavia. Those who chanced to recall its existence knew of it only as a small fierce country, so placed upon the map that the larger countries which were its neighbours felt they must control and keep it in order, and therefore made incursions into it, and fought its people and each other for possession. But it had not been always so. It was an old, old country, and hundreds of years ago it had been as celebrated for its peaceful happiness and wealth as for its beauty. It was often said that it was one of the most beautiful places in the world. A favourite Samavian legend was that it had been the site of the Garden of Eden. In those past centuries, its people

had been of such great stature, physical beauty, and strength, that they had been like a race of noble giants. They were in those days a pastoral people, whose rich crops and splendid flocks and herds were the envy of less fertile countries. Among the shepherds and herdsmen there were poets who sang their own songs when they piped among their sheep upon the mountainsides and in the flower-thick valleys. Their songs had been about patriotism and bravery, and faithfulness to their chieftains and their country. The simple courtesy of the poorest peasant was as stately as the manner of a noble. But that, as Loristan had said with a tired smile, had been before they had had time to outlive and forget the Garden of Eden. Five hundred years ago, there had succeeded to the throne a king who was bad and weak. His father had lived to be ninety years old, and his son had grown tired of waiting in Samavia for his crown. He had gone out into the world, and visited other countries and their courts. When he returned and became king, he lived as no Samavian king had lived before. He was an extravagant, vicious man of furious temper and bitter jealousies. He was jealous of the larger courts and countries he had seen, and tried to introduce their customs and their ambitions. He ended by introducing their worst faults and vices. There arose political quarrels and savage new factions. Money was squandered until poverty began for the first time to stare the country in the face. The big Samavians, after their first stupefaction, broke forth into furious rage. There were mobs and riots, then bloody battles. Since it was the King who had worked this wrong, they would have none of him. They would depose him and make his son king in his place. It was at this part of the story that Marco was always most deeply interested. The young Prince was totally unlike his father. He was a true royal Samavian, bigger and stronger for his age than any man in the country, and as handsome as a young viking god.

More than this, he had a lion's heart and, before he was sixteen, the shepherds and herdsmen had begun to make songs about his valour, and his kingly courtesy, and generous kindness. The people in the streets sang them too. The King, his father, had always been jealous of him, even when he was only a child whom the people roared with joy to see as he rode through the streets. When he returned from his journeyings and found his son a splendid youth, he detested him. The people began to clamour and demand that he himself should abdicate; he became insane with rage, and committed such cruelties that the people ran mad themselves. One day they stormed the palace, killed and overpowered the guards, and burst in upon the King as he shuddered green with terror and fury in his private room. He was king no more, and must leave the country, they vowed, as they closed round him with bared weapons. Where was the Prince? It was him they wanted for a king. They began to shout aloud his name, calling him in a sort of chant in unison, 'Prince Ivor – Prince Ivor – Prince Ivor!' But no answer came. The people of the palace had hidden themselves, and the place was utterly silent.

The King, despite his terror, could not help but sneer.

'Call him again,' he said. 'He is afraid to come out of his hole!'

A savage fellow from the mountain fastnesses struck him on the mouth.

'He afraid!' he shouted. 'If the Prince does not come, it is because thou hast killed him – and thou art a dead man!'

This set them aflame with hotter burning. They broke away, leaving three on guard, and ran about the empty palace rooms shouting the Prince's name. But there was no answer. They sought him in a frenzy, bursting open doors and flinging down every obstacle in their way. A page, found hidden in a closet, owned that he had seen

His Royal Highness pass through a corridor early in the morning. He had been softly singing to himself one of the shepherds' songs.

And in this strange way out of the history of Samavia, five hundred years before Marco's day, the young prince had walked. For he was never seen again.

In every nook and cranny, high and low, they sought him, believing that the King himself had made him prisoner in some secret place, or had privately had him killed. The fury of the people grew to frenzy. There were new risings, and every few days the palace was attacked and searched again. But no trace of the Prince was found. He had vanished as a star vanishes when it drops from its place in the sky. During a riot in the palace, when a last search was made, the King himself was killed. A powerful noble who headed one of the uprisings made himself king in his place. From that time, the once splendid little kingdom was like a bone fought for by dogs. Its pastoral peace was forgotten. It was torn and worried and shaken by stronger countries. It tore and worried itself with internal fights. It assassinated kings and created new ones. No man was sure in his youth what ruler his maturity would live under, or whether his children would die in useless fights, or through stress of poverty and cruel, useless laws. There were no more shepherds and herdsmen who were poets, but on the mountainsides and in the valleys sometimes some of the old songs were sung. Those most beloved were songs about a Lost Prince whose name had been Ivor. If he had been king, he would have saved Samavia, the verses said, and all brave hearts believed that he would still return. In the modern cities, one of the jocular cynical sayings was, 'Yes, that will happen when Prince Ivor comes again.'

In his more childish days, Marco had been bitterly troubled by the unsolved mystery. Where had he gone – the Lost Prince? Had he been killed, or had he been hidden away in a dungeon? But he was so big and brave, he would have broken out of any dungeon. The boy had invented for himself a dozen endings to the story.

'Did no one ever find his sword or his cap – or hear anything or guess anything about him ever – ever – ever?' he would say restlessly again and again.

One winter's night, as they sat together before a small fire in a cold room in a cold city in Austria, he had been so eager and asked so many searching questions, that his father gave him an answer he had never given him before, and which was a sort of ending to the story, though not a satisfying one:

'Everybody guessed as you are guessing. A few very old shepherds in the mountains, who like to believe ancient histories, relate a story which most people consider a kind of legend. It is that almost a hundred years after the prince was lost, an old shepherd told a story his long-dead father had confided to him in secret just before he died. The father had said that, going out in the early morning on the mountainside, he had found in the forest what he at first thought to be the dead body of a beautiful young huntsman. Some enemy had plainly attacked him from behind and believed he had killed him. He was not quite dead, and the shepherd dragged him into a cave where he himself often took refuge from storms. Since there was such riot and disorder in the city, he was afraid to speak of what he had found; and, by the time he discovered that he was harbouring the Prince, the King had already been killed, and an even worse man had taken possession of his throne, and ruled Samavia with a blood-stained, iron hand. To the terrified and simple peasant the safest thing seemed to get the wounded youth out of the country before there was any chance of his being discovered and murdered outright, as he would surely be. The cave in which the Prince was hidden was not far from the frontier, and while he was still so weak that he was hardly

conscious, he was smuggled across it in a cart loaded with
sheepskins, and left with some kind monks who did not
know his rank or name. The shepherd went back to his
flocks and his mountains, and lived and died among
them, always in terror of the changing rulers and their
savage battles with each other. The mountaineers said
among themselves, as the generations succeeded each
other, that the Lost Prince must have died young, because
otherwise he would have come back to his country and
tried to restore its good, bygone days.'

'Yes, he would have come,' Marco said.

'He would have come if he had seen that he could help
his people,' Loristan answered, as if he were not reflecting
on a story which was probably only a kind of legend. 'But
he was very young, and Samavia was in the hands of the
new dynasty, and filled with his enemies. He could not
have crossed the frontier without an army. Still, I think
he died young.'

It was of this story that Marco was thinking as he
walked, and perhaps the thoughts that filled his mind
expressed themselves in his face in some way which attracted attention. As he was nearing Buckingham Palace,
a distinguished-looking, well-dressed man with clever eyes
caught sight of him, and, after looking at him keenly,
slackened his pace as he approached. An observer might
have thought he saw something which puzzled and surprised him. Marco didn't see him at all, and still moved
forward, thinking of the shepherds and the Prince. The
well-dressed man began to walk still more slowly. When
he was quite close to Marco, he stopped and spoke to him
– in the Samavian language.

'What is your name?' he asked.

Marco's training from his earliest childhood had been
an extraordinary thing. His love for his father had made
it simple and natural to him, and he had never questioned the reason for it. As he had been taught to keep

silence, he had been taught to control the expression of his face and the sound of his voice, and, above all, never to allow himself to look startled. But for this he might have started at the extraordinary sound of the Samavian words suddenly uttered in a London street by an English gentleman. He might even have answered the question in Samavian himself. But he did not. He courteously lifted his cap and replied in English:

'Excuse me?'

The gentleman's clever eyes scrutinized him keenly. Then he also spoke in English.

'Perhaps you do not understand? I asked your name because you are very like a Samavian I know,' he said.

'I am Marco Loristan,' the boy answered him.

The man looked straight into his eyes and smiled.

'That is not the name,' he said. 'I beg your pardon, my boy.'

He was about to go on, and had indeed taken a couple of steps away, when he paused and turned.

'You may tell your father that you are a very well-trained lad. I wanted to find out for myself.' And he went on.

Marco felt that his heart beat a little quickly. This was one of several incidents which had happened during the last three years, and made him feel that he was living among things so mysterious that their very mystery hinted at danger. But he himself had never before seemed involved in them. Why should it matter that he was well behaved? Then he remembered something. The man had not said 'well behaved', he had said 'well *trained*'. Well trained in what way? He felt his forehead prickle as he thought of the smiling, keen look which set itself so straight upon him. Had the man spoken to him in Samavian for an experiment, to see if he would be startled into forgetting that he had been trained to seem to know only the language of the country he was living in? But he had not forgotten. He had remembered well and was thankful that he had betrayed nothing. 'Even exiles may be Samavian soldiers. I am one. You must be one,' his father had said on that day long ago when he had made him take his oath. Perhaps remembering his training was being a soldier. Never had Samavia needed help as she needed it today. Two years before, a claimant to the throne had assassinated the reigning king and his sons, and since then, bloody war and tumult had raged. The new king was a powerful man, and had a great following of the worst and most self-seeking of the people. Neighbouring countries had interfered for their own welfare's sake, and the newspapers had been full of stories of savage fighting and atrocities, and of starving peasants.

Marco had late one evening entered their lodgings to find Loristan walking to and fro, a paper crushed and torn in his hands, and his eyes blazing. He had been reading of cruelties wrought upon innocent women and children. Lazarus was standing staring at him with huge tears running down his cheeks. When Marco opened the door, the old soldier strode over to him, turned him about, and led him out of the room.

'Pardon, sir, pardon!' he sobbed. 'No one must see him, even you. He suffers too horribly.'

He stood by a chair in Marco's own small bedroom, where he half pushed, half led him. He bent his grizzled head, and wept like a beaten child.

'Dear God of those who are in pain, assuredly it is now the time to give back to us our Lost Prince!' he said, and Marco knew the words were a prayer, and wondered at the frenzied intensity of it, because it seemed so wild a thing to pray for the return of a youth who had died five hundred years before.

When he reached the palace, Marco was still thinking of the man who had spoken to him, even as he looked at the majestic grey stone building and counted the number of its storeys and windows. He walked round it that he might make a note in his memory of its size and form and its entrances, and guess at the size of its gardens. This he did because it was part of his game, and part of his training.

When he came back to the front, he saw that in the great entrance court within the high iron railings an elegant but quiet-looking closed carriage was drawing up before the doorway. Marco stood and watched with interest to see who would enter it. He knew that kings and emperors who were not on parade merely looked like well-dressed gentlemen, and often chose to go out as simply and quietly as other men. So he thought that, perhaps, if he waited, he might see one of those well-known faces which represent the highest rank and power in a monarchical country, and which in times gone by had also represented the power over human life and death and liberty.

'I should like to be able to tell my father that I have seen the King and know his face, as I know the faces of the Czar and the two Emperors.'

There was a movement among the tall menservants in the scarlet liveries, and an elderly man descended the steps attended by another. He entered the carriage, the other man followed him, the door was closed, and the carriage drove through the gates, where the sentries saluted.

Marco was near enough to see distinctly. The two men were talking as if interested. The face of the one farthest from him was the face he had often seen in shop-windows and newspapers. The boy made his quick, formal salute. It was the King; who, as he smiled and acknowledged the greeting, spoke to his companion.

'That fine lad salutes as if he belonged to the army,' was what he said, though Marco could not hear him.

His companion leaned forward to look through the

window. When he caught sight of Marco, a singular expression crossed his face.

'He does belong to an army, sir,' he answered, 'though he does not know it. His name is Marco Loristan.'

Then Marco saw him plainly for the first time. He was the man with the keen eyes who had spoken to him in Samavian.

CHAPTER 4

The Rat

M A R C O would have wondered very much if he had heard the words; as it was he turned towards home wondering at something else. A man who was in intimate attendance on a king must be a person of importance. He no doubt knew many things not only of his own ruler's country, but of the countries of other kings. Few had known anything of poor little Samavia until the newspapers had begun to tell them of the horrors of its war – and who but a Samavian could speak its language? It would be an interesting thing to tell his father – that a man who knew the King had spoken to Marco in Samavian, and had sent that curious message.

Later he found himself passing a side street and looked up it. It was so narrow, and on either side of it were such old, tall, and sloping-walled houses that it attracted his attention. It looked as if a bit of old London had been left to stand while newer places grew up and hid it from view. This was the kind of street he liked to pass through for curiosity's sake. He knew many of them in the old quarters of many cities. He had lived in some of them. Another thing besides its queerness attracted him. He heard a clamour of boys' voices, and he wanted to see what they were doing. Sometimes, when he had reached a new place and had had that lonely feeling, he had followed some boyish clamour of play or wrangling, and had found a temporary friend or so.

Half-way to the street's end there was an arched brick passage. The sound of the voices came from there – one of them high, and thinner and shriller than the rest. Marco tramped up to the arch and looked down through the passage. It opened on to a grey flagged space, shut in by the railings of an ancient graveyard behind a church which turned its face towards some other street. The boys were not playing, but listening to one of their number who was reading to them from a newspaper.

Marco walked down the passage and listened also, standing in the dark arched outlet at its end and watching the boy who read. He was a strange little creature with a big forehead, and deep eyes which were curiously sharp. But this was not all. He was a hunchback, his legs seemed small and crooked. He sat with them crossed before him on a rough wooden platform set on low wheels, on which he evidently pushed himself about. Near him were a number of sticks stacked together as if they were rifles. One of the first things that Marco noticed was that the boy had a savage little face marked with lines as if he had been angry all his life.

'Hold your tongues, you fools!' he shrilled out to some boys who interrupted him. 'Don't you want to know anything, you ignorant swine?'

He was as ill-dressed as the rest of them, but he did not speak in the Cockney dialect. If he was of the riff-raff of the streets, as his companions were, he was somehow different.

Then by chance he saw Marco.

'What are you doing there listening?' he shouted, and at once stooped to pick up a stone and threw it at him. The stone hit Marco's shoulder, but it did not hurt him much. What he did not like was that another lad should want to throw something at him before they had even exchanged boy-signs. He also did not like the fact that two other boys took the matter up by bending down to pick up stones also.

He walked forward straight into the group and stopped close to the hunchback.

'What did you do that for?' he asked, in his rather deep young voice.

He was big and strong-looking enough to suggest that he was not a boy it would be easy to dispose of, but it was not that which made the group stand still a moment to stare at him. It was something in himself – half of it a lack of irritation at the stone-throwing. It was as if it had not mattered to him in the least. It had not made him feel angry or insulted. He was only rather curious about it. Because he was clean, and his hair and his shabby clothes were brushed, the first impression given by his appearance as he stood in the archway was that he was a young 'toff' poking his nose where it was not wanted; but, as he drew near, they saw that the well-brushed clothes were worn, and there were patches on his shoes.

'What did you do that for?' he asked, and he asked it merely as if he wanted to find out the reason.

'I'm not going to have you swells dropping in to my club as if it was your own,' said the hunchback.

'I'm not a swell, and I didn't know it was a club,' Marco answered. 'I heard boys, and I thought I'd come and look. When I heard you reading about Samavia, I wanted to hear more.'

He looked at the reader with his silent-expressioned eyes.

'You needn't have thrown a stone,' he added. 'They don't do it at men's clubs. I'll go away.'

He turned about as if he were going, but, before he had taken three steps, the hunchback hailed him.

'Hi!' he called out. 'Hi, you!'

'What do you want?' said Marco.

'I bet you don't know where Samavia is, or what they're fighting about.' The hunchback threw the words at him.

'Yes, I do. It's north of Beltrazo and east of Jiardasia, and they are fighting because one party has assassinated

King Maran, and the other will not let them crown Nicola Iarovitch. And why should they? He's a brigand, and hasn't a drop of royal blood in him.'

'Oh!' reluctantly admitted the hunchback. 'You do know that much, do you? Come back here.'

Marco turned back, while the boys still stared. It was as if two leaders or generals were meeting for the first time, and the rabble, looking on, wondered what would come of their encounter.

'The Samavians of the Iarovitch party are a bad lot and want only bad things,' said Marco, speaking first. 'They care nothing for Samavia. They only care for money and the power to make laws which will serve them and crush everybody else. They know Nicola is a weak man, and that, if they can crown him king, they can make him do what they like.'

The fact that he spoke first, and that, though he spoke in a steady boyish voice without swagger, he somehow seemed to take it for granted that they would listen, made his place for him at once. Boys are impressionable creatures, and they know a leader when they see him. The hunchback fixed glittering eyes on him. The rabble began to murmur.

'Rat! Rat!' several voices cried at once in good strong Cockney. 'Arst 'im some more, Rat!'

'Is that what they call you?' Marco asked the hunchback.

'It's what I called myself,' he answered resentfully. ' "The Rat." Look at me! Crawling round on the ground like this! Look at me!'

He made a gesture ordering his followers to move aside, and began to push himself rapidly, with queer darts this side and that, round the enclosure. He bent his head and body, and twisted his face, and made strange animal-like movements. He even uttered sharp squeaks as he rushed here and there – as a rat might have done when it was being hunted. He did it as if he were displaying an accomplishment, and his followers' laughter was applause.

'Wasn't I like a rat?' he demanded, when he suddenly stopped.

'You made yourself like one on purpose,' Marco answered. 'You do it for fun.'

'Not so much fun,' said The Rat. 'I feel like one. Everyone's my enemy. I'm vermin. I can't fight or defend myself unless I bite. I can bite though.' And he showed two rows of fierce, strong, white teeth, sharper at the points than human teeth usually are. 'I bite my father when he gets drunk and beats me. I've bitten him till he's learned to remember.' He laughed a shrill, squeaking laugh. 'He hasn't tried it for three months – even when he was drunk – and he's always drunk.' Then he laughed again still more shrilly. 'He's a gentleman,' he said. 'I'm a gentleman's son. He was a master at a big school until he was kicked out – that was when I was four and my mother died. I'm thirteen now. How old are you?'

'I'm twelve,' answered Marco.

The Rat twisted his face enviously.

'I wish I was your size! Are you a gentleman's son? You look as if you were.'

'I'm a very poor man's son,' was Marco's answer. 'My father is a writer.'

'Then, ten to one, he's a sort of gentleman,' said The Rat. Then quite suddenly he threw another question at him. 'What's the name of the other Samavian party?'

'The Maranovitch. The Maranovitch and the Iarovitch have been fighting with each other for five hundred years. First one dynasty rules, and then the other gets in when it has killed somebody as it killed King Maran,' Marco answered without hesitation.

'What was the name of the dynasty that ruled before they began fighting? The first Maranovitch assassinated the last of them,' The Rat asked him.

'The Fedorovitch,' said Marco. 'The last one was a bad king.'

'His son was the one they never found again,' said The Rat. 'The one they call the Lost Prince.'

Marco would have started but for his long training in self-control. It was so strange to hear his dream-hero spoken in this back alley in a slum, and just after he had been thinking of him.

'What do you know about him?' he asked, and, as he did so, he saw the group of vagabond lads draw nearer.

'Not much. I only read something about him in a torn magazine I found in the street,' The Rat answered. 'The man that wrote about him said he was only part of a legend, and he laughed at people for believing in him. He said it was about time that he should turn up again if he intended to. I've invented things about him because these chaps like to hear me tell them. They're only stories.'

'We likes 'im,' a voice called out, 'becos 'e wos the right sort; 'e'd fight, 'e would, if 'e was in Samavia now.'

Marco rapidly asked himself how much he might say. He decided and spoke to them all.

'He is not part of a legend. He's part of Samavian history,' he said. 'I know something about him too.'

'How did you find it out?' asked The Rat.

'Because my father's a writer, he's obliged to have books and papers, and he knows things. I like to read, and I go into the free libraries. You can always get books and papers there. Then I ask my father questions. All the newspapers are full of things about Samavia just now.' Marco felt that this was an explanation which betrayed nothing. It was true that no one could open a newspaper at this period without seeing news and stories of Samavia.

The Rat saw possible vistas of information opening up before him.

'Sit down here,' he said, 'and tell us what you know about him. Sit down, you fellows.'

There was nothing to sit on but the broken flagged pavement but Marco had sat on flags or bare ground often enough before, and so had the rest of the lads. He took his place near The Rat, and the others made a semicircle in front of them. The two leaders had joined forces, so to speak, and the followers fell into line at 'attention'.

Then the newcomer began to talk. It was a good story, that of the Lost Prince, and Marco told it in a way which gave it reality. How could he help it? He knew, as they could not, that it was real. He who had pored over maps of little Samavia since his seventh year, who had studied them with his father, could have found his way to any part of it if he had been dropped in any forest or any mountain of it. He knew every highway and byway, and in the capital city of Melzarr could almost have made his way blindfolded. He knew the palaces and the forts, the churches, the poor streets and the rich ones. His father had once shown him a plan of the royal palace which they had studied together until the boy knew each apartment and corridor in it by heart. But this he did not speak of. He knew it was one of the things to be silent about. But of the mountains and the emerald velvet meadows climbing their sides and only ending where huge bare crags and peaks began, he could speak. He could make pictures of the wide fertile plains where herds of wild horses fed, or raced and sniffed the air; he could describe the fertile valleys where clear rivers ran and flocks of sheep pastured on deep sweet grass. He could speak of them because he could offer a good enough reason for his knowledge of them.

'That torn magazine you found had more than one article about Samavia in it,' he said to The Rat. 'I read them all in a free library. The writer said it was one of the most beautiful countries he had ever travelled in – and the most fertile.'

The group before him knew nothing of fertility or

open country. They only knew London back streets and
courts. They were a rough lot, and as they had stared at
Marco at first sight of him, so they continued to stare at
him as he talked. When he told of the tall Samavians who
had been like giants centuries ago, and who had hunted
the wild horses and captured and trained them to obedience by a sort of strong and gentle magic, their mouths fell
open. This was the sort of thing to allure any boy's
imagination.

'Blimme, if I wouldn't 'ave liked ketchin' one o' them
'orses,' broke in one of the audience, and his exclamation
was followed by a dozen of like nature from the others.

When he told of the deep endless-seeming forests, and
of the herdsmen and shepherds who played on their pipes
and made songs about high deeds and bravery, they
grinned with pleasure without knowing they were grin-
ning. They did not really know that in this neglected,
broken-flagged enclosure, shut in on one side by poverty-
stricken houses, and on the other by a forgotten graveyard, they heard the rustle of green forest boughs where
birds nested, the swish of the summer wind in the river
reeds, and the tinkle and laughter of brooks running.

They heard more or less of it all through the Lost Prince
story, because Prince Ivor had loved lowland woods and
mountain forests and all out-of-door life. When Marco
pictured him tall and strong-limbed and young, winning
all the people when he rode smiling among them, the
boys grinned again with unconscious pleasure.

'Wisht 'e 'adn't got lost!' someone cried out.

When they heard of the unrest and dissatisfaction of
the Samavians, they began to get restless themselves.
When Marco reached the part of the story in which the
mob rushed into the palace and demanded their Prince
from the King, they ejaculated scraps of bad language.
'The old geezer had got him hidden somewhere in some

dungeon, or he'd killed him out an' out – that's what he'd
been up to!' they clamoured. 'Wisht the lot of 'em had
been there then – wisht they 'ad. They'd 'ave give' 'im wot
for, anyway!'

'An' 'im walkin' out o' the place so early in the mornin'
just singin' like that! 'E 'ad 'im follered an' done for!'
they decided with various exclamations of boyish wrath.
Somehow, the fact that the handsome royal lad had strolled into the morning sunshine singing made them more
savage. Their language was extremely bad at this point.

But if it was bad here, it became worse when the old
shepherd found the young huntsman's half-dead body in
the forest. He *had* 'bin "done for" *in the back*! E'd bin
give' no charnst. G-r-r-r!' they groaned in chorus. 'Wisht'
they'd 'bin there when 'e'd bin 'it!' They'd ' 'ave done fur
somebody themselves'. It was a story which had a queer
effect on them. It made them think they saw things; it
fired their blood; it set them wanting to fight for ideals
they knew nothing about – adventurous things, for in-
stance, and high and noble young princes who were full of
the possibility of great and good deeds. Sitting upon the
broken flagstones of the bit of ground behind the deserted
graveyard, they were suddenly dragged into the world of
romance, and noble young princes and great and good
deeds became as real as the sunken gravestones, and far
more interesting.

And then the smuggling across the frontier of the unconscious prince in the bullock cart loaded with sheepskins! They held their breaths. Would the old shepherd
get him past the line! Marco, who was lost in the recital
himself, told it as if he had been present. He felt as if he
had, and as this was the first time he had ever told it to
thrilled listeners, his imagination got him in its grip, and
his heart jumped in his breast as he was sure the old man's
must have done when the guard stopped his cart and
asked him what he was carrying out of the country.

And then the good monks! He had to stop to explain
what a monk was, and when he described the solitude of
the ancient monastery, and its walled gardens full of
flowers and old simples to be used for healing, and the
wise monks walking in the silence and the sun, the boys
stared helplessly, but still as if they were vaguely pleased
by the picture.

And then there was no more to tell – no more. There it
broke off, and something like a low howl of dismay broke
from the semicircle.

'Aw!' they protested, 'it 'adn't ought to stop there!
Ain't there no more? Is that all there is?'

'It's all that was ever known really. And that last part
might only be a sort of story made up by somebody. But I
believe it myself.'

The Rat had listened with burning eyes. He had sat
biting his fingernails, as was a trick of his when he was
excited or angry.

'Tell you what!' he exclaimed suddenly. 'This was
what happened. It was some of the Maranovitch fellows
that tried to kill him. They meant to kill his father and
make their own man king, and they knew the people
wouldn't stand it if young Ivor was alive. They just
stabbed him in the back, the fiends! I dare say they heard
the old shepherd coming, and left him for dead and ran.'

'Right, oh! That was it!' the lads agreed. 'Yer right
there, Rat!'

'When he got well,' The Rat went on feverishly, still
biting his nails, 'he couldn't go back. He was only a boy.
The other fellow had been crowned, and his followers felt
strong because they'd just conquered the country. He
could have done nothing without an army, and he was
too young to raise one. Perhaps he thought he'd wait till
he was old enough to know what to do. I dare say he went
away and had to work for his living as if he'd never been a
prince at all. Then perhaps sometime he married some-

body and had a son, and told him as a secret who he was and all about Samavia.' The Rat began to look vengeful. 'If I'd bin him, I'd have told him not to forget what the Maranovitch had done to me. I'd have told him that if I couldn't get back the throne, he must see what he could do when he grew to be a man. And I'd have made him swear, if he got it back, to take it out of them or their children or their children's children in torture and kill-ing. I'd have made him swear not to leave a Maranovitch alive. And I'd have told him that, if he couldn't do it in his life, he must pass the oath on to his son and his son's son, as long as there was a Fedorovitch on earth. Wouldn't you?' he demanded hotly of Marco.

Marco's blood was also hot, but it was a different kind of blood, and he had talked much to a very sane man.

'No,' he said slowly. 'What would have been the use? It wouldn't have done Samavia any good, and it wouldn't have done him any good to torture and kill people. Better keep them alive and make them do things for the country. If you're a patriot, you think of the country.'

'Torture 'em first and then attend to the country,' snapped The Rat. 'What would you have told your son if you'd been Ivor?'

'I'd have told him to learn everything about Samavia – and all the things kings have to know – and study things about laws and other countries – and about keeping silent – and about governing himself as if he were a general commanding soldiers in battle – so that he would never do anything he did not mean to do or could be ashamed of doing after it was over. And I'd have asked him to tell his son's sons to tell their sons to learn the same things. So, you see, however long the time was, there would always be a king getting ready for Samavia – when Samavia really wanted him. And he would be a real king.'

He stopped himself suddenly and looked at the staring semicircle.

'I didn't make that up myself,' he said. 'I have heard a man who reads and knows things say it. I believe the Lost Prince would have had the same thoughts. If he had, and told them to his son, there has been a line of kings in training for Samavia for five hundred years, and perhaps one is walking about the streets of Vienna, or Budapest, or Paris, or London now, and he'd be ready if the people found out about him and called him.'

'Wisht they would!' someone yelled.

'It would be a queer secret to know all the time when no one else knew it,' The Rat communed with himself as it were; 'that you were a king and you ought to be on a throne wearing a crown. I wonder if it would make a chap look different?'

He laughed his squeaky laugh, and then turned in his sudden way to Marco:

'But he'd be a fool to give up the vengeance. What is your name?'

'Marco Loristan. What's yours? It isn't The Rat really.'

'It's Jem *Rat*cliffe. That's pretty near. Where do you live?'

'No. 7 Philibert Place.'

'This club is a soldier's club,' said The Rat. 'It's called the Squad. I'm the captain. 'Tention, you fellows! Let's show him.'

The semicircle sprang to its feet. There were about twelve lads altogether, and, when they stood upright, Marco saw at once that they were accustomed to obeying the word of command with military precision.

'Form in line!' ordered The Rat.

They did it at once, and held their backs and legs straight and their heads up amazingly well. Each had seized one of the sticks which had been stacked together like guns.

The Rat himself sat up straight on his platform. There

was actually something military in the bearing of his lean body. His voice lost its squeak and its sharpness became commanding.

He put the dozen lads through the drill as if he had been a smart young officer. And the drill itself was prompt and smart enough to have done credit to practised soldiers in barracks. It made Marco stand very straight himself, and watch with surprised interest.

'That's good!' he exclaimed when it was at an end. 'How did you learn that?'

The Rat made a savage gesture.

'If I'd had legs to stand on, I'd have been a soldier!' he said. 'I'd have enlisted in any regiment that would take me. I don't care for anything else.'

Suddenly his face changed, and he shouted a command to his followers.

'Turn your backs!' he ordered.

And they did turn their backs and looked through the railings of the old churchyard. Marco saw that they were obeying an order which was not new to them. The Rat had thrown his arm up over his eyes and covered them. He held it there for several moments, as if he did not want to be seen. Marco turned his back as the rest had done. All at once he understood that, though The Rat was not crying, yet he was feeling something which another boy would possibly have broken down under.

'All right!' he shouted presently, and dropped his ragged-sleeved arm and sat up straight again.

'I want to go to war!' he said hoarsely. 'I want to fight! I want to lead a lot of men into battle! And I haven't got any legs. Sometimes it takes the pluck out of me.'

'You've not grown up yet!' said Marco. 'You might get strong. No one knows what is going to happen. How did you learn to drill the club?'

'I hang about barracks. I watch and listen. I follow

soldiers. If I could get books, I'd read about wars. I can't go to libraries as you can. I can do nothing but scuffle about like a rat.'

'I can take you to libraries,' said Marco. 'There are places where boys can get in. And I can get some papers from my father.'

'Can you?' said The Rat. 'Do you want to join the club?'

'Yes!' Marco answered. 'I'll speak to my father about it.'

He said it because the hungry longing for companionship in his own mind had found a sort of response in the queer hungry look in The Rat's eyes. He wanted to see him again. Strange creature as he was, there was attraction in him. Scuffling about on his low wheeled platform, he had drawn this group of rough lads to him and made himself their commander. They obeyed him; they listened to his stories and harangues about war and soldiering; they let him drill them and give them orders. Marco knew that his father would be interested. The boy wanted to hear what Loristan would say.

'I'm going home now,' he said. 'If you're going to be here tomorrow, I will try to come.'

'We shall be here,' The Rat answered. 'It's our barracks.'

Marco drew himself up smartly and made his salute as if to a superior officer. Then he wheeled about and marched through the brick archway, and the sound of his boyish tread was as regular and decided as if he had been a man keeping time with his regiment.

'He's been drilled himself,' said The Rat. 'He knows as much as I do.'

And he sat up and stared down the passage with new interest.

CHAPTER 5

'Silence is Still the Order'

THEY were even poorer than usual just now, and the supper Marco and his father sat down to was scant enough. Lazarus stood upright behind his master's chair and served him with strictest ceremony. The poor lodgings were always kept with a soldierly cleanliness and order. Lazarus made himself popular by taking the work of caring for his master's rooms entirely out of the hands of the overburdened maids of all work. He had learned to do many things in his young days in barracks. He mended, he patched, he darned, and in the hardest fight the poor must face – the fight with dirt and dinginess – he always held his own. They had nothing but dry bread and coffee this evening, but Lazarus had made the coffee and the bread was good.

As Marco ate, he told his father the story of The Rat and his followers. Loristan listened, as the boy had known he would with the far-off intently-thinking smile in his dark eyes. It was a look which always fascinated Marco because it meant that he was thinking so many things. His spell over the boy lay in the fact that to him he seemed like a wonderful book of which one had only glimpses. It was full of pictures and adventures which were true, and one could not help continually making guesses about them. Yes, the feeling that Marco had was that his father's attraction for him was a sort of spell, and that others felt the same thing. When he stood and talked to people, he held his tall body with singular quiet grace which was like power. He never stirred or moved himself as if he were nervous or uncertain. He could hold his hands (he had beautiful slender and strong hands) quite still; he could stand on his fine arched feet without shuffling them. He could sit without any ungrace or restlessness. His mind knew what his body should do, and gave it orders without speaking, and his fine limbs and muscles and nerves obeyed. So he could stand still and at ease and look at the people he was talking to, and they always looked at him and listened to what he said, and somehow it seemed to Marco as if he were 'giving an audience' as kings give them. Often, people bowed low when they went away from him, and more than once it had happened that some humble person had stepped out of his presence backward, as people do when retiring before a sovereign. And yet his bearing was the quietest and least assuming in the world.

'And they were talking about Samavia? And he knew the story of the Lost Prince?' he said ponderingly. 'Even in that place!'

'He wants to hear about wars – he wants to talk about them,' Marco answered. 'If he could stand and were old enough, he would go and fight for Samavia himself.'

'It is a blood-drenched and sad place now!' said Loristan. 'The people are mad when they are not heartbroken and terrified.'

Suddenly Marco struck the table with a sounding slap of his boy's hand. He did it before he realized any intention in his own mind.

'Why should either one of the Iarovitch or one of the Maranovitch be king!' he cried. 'They were only savage peasants when they first fought for the crown hundreds of years ago. The most savage one got it, and they have been fighting ever since. Only the Fedorovitch were born kings. There is only one man in the world who has the right to the throne – and I don't know whether he is in the world or not. But I believe he is! I do!'

Loristan looked at the hot twelve-year-old face. He saw that the flame which had leaped up in his son had leaped without warning – just as a fierce heart-beat might have shaken him.

'You mean –?' he suggested softly.

'Ivor Fedorovitch. King Ivor he ought to be. And the people would obey him, and the good days would come again.'

'It is five hundred years since Ivor Fedorovitch left the good monks.' Loristan still spoke softly.

'But, Father,' Marco protested, 'even The Rat said what you said – that he was too young to be able to come back while the Maranovitch were in power. And he would have to work and have a home, and perhaps he was as poor as we are. But when he had a son he would call him Ivor and *tell* him – and his son would call *his* son Ivor and tell *him* – and it would go on and on. They could never call their eldest sons anything but Ivor. There would always be a king being trained for Samavia.' In the fire of his feelings he sprang from his chair and stood upright. 'Why! There may be a king of Samavia in some city now and, when he reads about the fighting among his people, his blood gets red-hot. They're his own people – his very own! He ought to go to them – he ought to go and tell them who he is! Don't you think he ought, Father?'

'It would not be as easy as it seems to a boy,' Loristan answered. 'There are many countries which would have something to say – Russia would have her word, and Austria, and Germany; and England never is silent. But, if he were a strong man and knew how to make strong friends in silence, he might sometime be able to declare himself openly.'

'But if he is anywhere, someone – some Samavian – ought to go and look for him. It ought to be a Samavian who is very clever and a patriot –' He stopped at a flash of recognition. 'Father!' he cried out. 'Father! You – you are the one who could find him if anyone in the world

could. But perhaps –' and he stopped a moment again
because new thoughts rushed through his mind. 'Have *you*
ever looked for him?' he asked hesitating.

Perhaps he had asked a stupid question – perhaps his
father had always been looking for him, perhaps that was
his secret and his work.

But Loristan did not look as if he thought him stupid.
Quite the contrary. He kept his handsome eyes fixed on
him as if he were studying him – as if he were deciding to
tell him something.

'Comrade at arms,' he said, with the smile which always
gladdened Marco's heart, 'you have kept your oath of
allegiance like a man. You were not seven years old when
you took it. You are growing older. Silence is still the
order, but you are man enough to be told more.' He
paused and looked down, and then looked up again,
speaking in a low tone. 'I have not looked for him,' he
said, 'because – I believe I know where he is.'

Marco caught his breath.

'Father!' He said only that word. He could say no
more. He knew he must not ask questions. But as they
faced each other in their dingy room at the back of the
shabby house on the side of the roaring road – as Lazarus
stood behind his father's chair and kept his eyes fixed on
the empty coffee cups and the dry bread plate, and everything looked as poor as things always did – there was a
king of Samavia – an Ivor Fedorovitch with the blood of
the Lost Prince in his veins – alive in some town or city
this moment! And Marco's own father knew where he
was!

He glanced at Lazarus, but, though the old soldier's
face looked as expressionless as if it were cut out of wood,
Marco realized that he knew this thing and had always
known it. He had been a comrade at arms all his life. He
continued to stare at the bread plate.

Loristan spoke again and in an even lower voice. 'The

Samavians who are patriots and thinkers,' he said, 'formed themselves into a secret party about eighty years ago. They formed it when they had no reason for hope, but they formed it because one of them discovered that an Ivor Fedorovitch was living. He was head forester on a great estate in the Austrian Alps. The nobleman he served had always thought him a mystery because he had the bearing and speech of a man who had not been born a servant. But he never was familiar or assuming, and never professed superiority over any of his fellows. He was a man of great stature, and was brave and silent. The nobleman who was his master made a sort of companion of him when they hunted together. Once he took him with him when he travelled to Samavia to hunt wild horses. He found that he knew the country well, and that he was familiar with Samavian hunting and customs. Before he returned to Austria, the man obtained permission to go to the mountains alone. He went among the shepherds and made friends among them, asking many questions. One night around a forest fire he heard the songs about the Lost Prince which had not been forgotten even after nearly five hundred years had passed. One very old shepherd tottered to his feet and lifted his face to the myriad stars bestrewn like jewels in the blue sky above the forest trees, and he wept and prayed aloud that the great God would send their king to them. And the stranger huntsman stood upright also and lifted his face to the stars. And, though he said no word, the herdsman nearest to him saw tears on his cheeks – great, heavy tears. The next day, the stranger went to the monastery where the order of monks lived who had taken care of the Lost Prince. When he had left Samavia, the secret society was formed, and the members of it knew that an Ivor Fedorovitch had passed through his ancestors' country as the servant of another man. But the secret society was only a small one, and, though it has been growing ever since, the huntsman died an old man before it was strong enough even to dare to tell Samavia what it knew.'

'Had he a son?' cried Marco. 'Had he a son?'

'Yes. He had a son. His name was Ivor. And he was trained as I told you. There has *always* been a king ready for Samavia – even when he has laboured with his hands and served others. Each one took the oath of allegiance.'

'As I did?' said Marco, breathless with excitement.

'The same,' answered Loristan.

Marco threw up his hand in salute.

'Here grows a man for Samavia! God be thanked!' he quoted. 'And *he* is somewhere? And you know?'

Loristan bent his head in acquiescence.

'For years much secret work has been done, and the Fedorovitch party has grown until it is much greater and more powerful than the other parties dream. The larger countries are tired of the constant war and disorder in Samavia. Their interests are disturbed by them, and they are deciding that they must have peace and laws which can be counted on. There have been Samavian patriots who have spent their lives in trying to bring this about by making friends in the most powerful capitals, and working secretly for the future good of their own land. It has taken a long time; but when King Maran and his family were assassinated and the war broke out, there were great powers which began to say that if some king of good blood and reliable characteristics were given the crown, he should be upheld.'

'*His* blood' – Marco's intensity made his voice drop almost to a whisper – '*his* blood has been trained for five hundred years, Father! If it comes true' – though he laughed a little, he was obliged to wink his eyes hard because suddenly he felt tears rush into them, which no boy likes – 'the shepherds will have to make a new song – it will have to be a shouting one about a prince going away and a king coming back!'

'They are a devout people and observe many an ancient rite and ceremony. They will chant prayers and burn altar-fires on their mountainsides,' Loristan said. 'But the end is not yet – the end is not yet. Sometimes it seems that perhaps it is near – but God knows!'

Then there leaped back upon Marco the story he had to tell, but which he had held back for the last – the story of the man who spoke Samavian and drove in the carriage with the King. He knew now that it might mean some important thing which he could not have before suspected.

'There is something I must tell you,' he said.

He had learned to relate incidents to his father in few but clear words. It had been part of his training. Loristan had said that he might sometime have a story to tell when he had but few moments to tell it in – some story which meant life or death to someone. He told this one quickly and well. He made Loristan see the man with the keen eyes, and he made him hear his voice when he said, 'Tell your father that you are a very well-trained lad.'

'I am glad he said that. He is a man who knows what training is,' said Loristan. 'He is a person who knows what all Europe is doing, and almost all that it will do. He is an ambassador from a powerful and great country. If he saw that you are a well-trained and fine lad, it might – it might even be good for Samavia.'

'Would it matter that *I* was well trained? *Could* it matter to Samavia?' Marco cried out.

Loristan paused for a moment – watching him gravely – looking him over – his big, well-built boy's frame, his shabby clothes, and his eagerly burning eyes.

He smiled one of his slow wonderful smiles.

'Yes. It might even matter to Samavia!' he answered.

CHAPTER 6

The Drill and the Secret Party

LORISTAN did not forbid Marco to pursue his acquaintance with The Rat and his followers.

'You will find out for yourself whether they are friends for you or not,' he said. 'You will know in a few days, and then you can make your own decision. You have known lads in various countries, and you are a good judge of them, I think. You will soon see whether they are going to be *men* or mere rabble. The Rat now – how does he strike you?' And the handsome eyes held their keen look of questioning.

'He'd be a brave soldier if he could stand,' said Marco, thinking him over. 'But he might be cruel.'

'A lad who might make a brave soldier cannot be disdained, but a man who is cruel is a fool. Tell him that from me,' Loristan answered. 'He wastes force – his own and the force of the one he treats cruelly. Only a fool wastes force.'

'May I speak of you sometimes?' asked Marco.

'Yes. You will know how. You will remember the things about which silence is the order.'

'I never forget them,' said Marco. 'I have been trying not to, for such a long time.'

'You have succeeded well, Comrade!' returned Loristan, from his writing-table, to which he had gone and where he was turning over papers.

A strong impulse overpowered the boy. He marched over to the table and stood very straight, making his soldierly young salute, his whole body glowing.

'Father!' he said, 'you don't know how I love you! I wish you were a general and I might die in battle for you.

When I look at you, I long and long to do something for you a boy could not do. I would die of a thousand wounds rather than disobey you – or Samavia!'

He seized Loristan's hand, and knelt on one knee and kissed it. An English or American boy could not have done such a thing from unaffected natural impulse. But he was of warm Southern blood.

'I took my oath of allegiance to you, Father, when I took it to Samavia. It seems as if you were Samavia, too,' he said, and kissed his hand again.

· Loristan had turned towards him with one of the movements which were full of dignity and grace. Marco, looking up at him, felt that there was always a certain remote stateliness in him which made it seem quite natural that anyone should bend the knee and kiss his hand.

A sudden great tenderness glowed in his father's face as he raised the boy and put his hand on his shoulder.

'Comrade,' he said, 'you don't know how much I love you – and what reason there is that we should love each other! You don't know how I have been watching you, and thanking God each year that here grew a man for Samavia. That I know you are – a *man*, though you have lived but twelve years. Twelve years may grow a man – or prove that a man will never grow, though a human thing he may remain for ninety years. This year may be full of strange things for both of us. We cannot know *what* I may have to ask you to do for me – and for Samavia. Perhaps such a thing as no twelve-year-old boy has ever done before.'

'Every night and every morning,' said Marco, 'I shall pray that I may be called to do it, and that I may do it well.'

'You will do it well, Comrade, if you are called. That I could make oath,' Loristan answered him.

*

The Squad had collected in the enclosure behind the
church when Marco appeared at the arched end of the
passage. The boys were drawn up with their rifles, but
they all wore a rather dogged and sullen look. The explanation which darted into Marco's mind was that this
was because The Rat was in a bad humour. He sat
crouched together on his platform biting his nails fiercely,
his elbows on his updrawn knees, his face twisted into a
hideous scowl. He did not look around, or even look up
from the cracked flagstone of the pavement on which his
eyes were fixed.

Marco went forward with military step and stopped
opposite to him with prompt salute.

'Sorry to be late, sir,' he said, as if he had been a private
speaking to his colonel.

'It's 'im, Rat! 'E's come, Rat!' the Squad shouted.
'Look at 'im!'

But The Rat would not look, and did not even move.

'What's the matter?' said Marco, with less ceremony
than a private would have shown. 'There's no use in my
coming here if you don't want me.'

' 'E's got a grouch on 'cos you're late!' called out the
head of the line. 'No doin' nothin' when 'e's got a grouch
on.'

'I shan't try to do anything,' said Marco, his boy-face
setting itself into good stubborn lines. 'That's not what I
came here for. I came to drill. I've been with my father.
He comes first. I can't join the Squad if he doesn't come
first. We're not on active service, and we're not in barracks.'

Then The Rat moved sharply and turned to look at
him.

'I thought you weren't coming at all!' he snapped and
growled at once. 'My father said you wouldn't. He said
you were a young swell for all your patched clothes. He
said your father would think he was a swell, even if he was

only a penny-a-liner on newspapers, and he wouldn't let you have anything to do with a vagabond and a nuisance. Nobody begged you to join. Your father can go to blazes!'

'Don't you speak in that way about my father,' said Marco, quietly, 'because I can't knock you down.'

'I'll get up and let you!' began The Rat, immediately white and raging. 'I can stand up with two sticks. I'll get up and let you!'

'No, you won't,' said Marco. 'If you want to know what my father said, I can tell you. He said I could come as often as I liked – till I found out whether we should be friends or not. He says I shall find that out for myself.'

It was a strange thing The Rat did. It must always be remembered of him that his wretched father, who had each year sunk lower and lower in the underworld, had been a gentleman once, familiar with good manners and in the customs of good breeding. Sometimes when he was drunk, and sometimes when he was partly sober, he talked to The Rat of many things the boy would otherwise never have heard of. That was why the lad was different from the other vagabonds. This, also, was why he suddenly altered the whole situation by doing this strange and unexpected thing. He utterly changed his expression and voice, fixing his sharp eyes shrewdly on Marco's. It was almost as if he were asking him a conundrum. He knew it would have been one to most boys of the class he appeared to belong to. Marco would either know the answer or he wouldn't.

'I beg your pardon,' The Rat said.

That was the conundrum. It was what a gentleman and an officer would have said, if he felt he had been mistaken or rude. He had heard that from his drunken father.

'I beg yours – for being late,' said Marco.

That was the right answer. It was the one another officer and gentleman would have made. It settled the matter at once, and it settled more than was apparent at the moment. It decided that Marco was one of those who knew the things The Rat's father had once known – the things gentlemen do and say and think. Not another word was said. It was all right. Marco slipped into line with the Squad, and The Rat sat erect with his military bearing and begun his drill:

'Squad!
''Tention!
'Number!
'Slope arms!
'Form fours!
'Right!
'Quick march!
'Halt!
'Left turn!
'Order arms!
'Stand at ease!
'Stand easy!'

They did it so well that it was quite wonderful when one considered the limited space at their disposal. They had evidently done it often, and The Rat had been not only a smart, but a severe, officer. This morning they repeated the exercise a number of times, and even varied it with Review Drill, with which they seemed just as familiar.

'Where did you learn it?' The Rat asked, when the arms were stacked again and Marco was sitting by him as he had sat the previous day.

'From an old soldier. And I like to watch it, as you do.'

'If you were a young swell in the Guards, you couldn't be smarter at it,' The Rat said. 'The way you hold yourself! The way you stand! You've got it! Wish I was you! It comes natural to you.'

'I've always liked to watch it and try to do it myself. I did when I was a little fellow,' answered Marco.

'I've been trying to kick it into these chaps for more than a year,' said The Rat. 'A nice job I had of it! It nearly made me sick at first.'

The semicircle in front of him only giggled or laughed outright. The members of it seemed to take very little offence at his cavalier treatment of them. He had evidently something to give them which was entertaining enough to make up for his tyranny and indifference. He thrust his hand into one of the pockets of his ragged coat, and drew out a piece of newspaper.

'My father brought home this, wrapped round a loaf of bread,' he said. 'See what it says there!'

He handed it to Marco, pointing to some words printed in large letters at the head of a column. Marco looked at it and sat very still.

The words he read were: 'The Lost Prince.'

'Silence is still the order,' was the first thought which flashed through his mind. 'Silence is still the order.'

'What does it mean?' he said aloud.

'There isn't much of it. I wish there was more,' The Rat said fretfully. 'Read and see. Of course they say it mayn't be true – but I believe it is. People think someone knows where he is – at least where one of his descendants is. It'd be the same thing. He'd be the real king. If he'd just show himself, it might stop all the fighting. Just read.'

Marco read, and his skin prickled as the blood went racing through his body. But his face did not change. There was a sketch of the story of the Lost Prince to begin with. It had been regarded by most people, the article said, as a sort of legend. Now there was a rumour that it was not a legend at all, but a part of the history of Samavia. It was said that through the centuries there had always been a party secretly loyal to the memory of this lost Fedorovitch and that from father to son, generation after generation had descended the oath of fealty to him and his descendants. Now, romantic as it seemed, it was

an open secret that some persons believed that a descendant had been found and that a certain Secret Party also
held that, if he were called back to the throne of Samavia,
the wars and bloodshed would end.

The Rat had begun to bite his nails fast.

'Do you believe he's found?' he asked feverishly. 'Don't
you? I do!'

'I wonder where he is, if it's true?' exclaimed Marco. He
could say that, and he might seem as eager as he felt.

The Squad all began to jabber at once. 'Yus, where wos
'e? There wos no knowin'. It'd be likely to be in some o'
these furrin places. England'd be too far from Samavia.
'Ow far off wos Samavia? Wos it in Roosha, or where the
Frenchies were, or the Germans? But wherever 'e wos, 'e'd
be the right sort, an' 'e'd be the sort a chap'd turn and
look at in the street.'

The Rat continued to bite his nails.

'He might be anywhere,' he said, his small fierce face
glowing. 'That's what I like to think about. He might be
passing in the street outside there; he might be up in one
of those houses,' jerking his head over his shoulder towards the backs of the enclosing dwellings. 'Perhaps he
knows he's a king, and perhaps he doesn't. He'd know if
what you said yesterday was true – about the King always
being made ready for Samavia.'

'Yes, he'd know,' put in Marco.

'Well, it'd be finer if he did,' went on The Rat. 'However poor and shabby he was, he'd know the secret all the
time. I dare say he'd walk tremendously straight and hold
his head up. If I was him, I'd like to make people suspect
a bit that I wasn't like the common lot o' them.' He put
out his hand and pushed Marco excitedly. 'Let's work out
plots for him! That'd be a splendid game! Let's pretend
we're the Secret Party!'

He was tremendously excited. Out of the ragged pocket
he fished a piece of chalk. Then he leaned forward and

began to draw something quickly on the flagstones closest to his platform. The Squad leaned forward also, quite breathlessly, and Marco leaned forward. The chalk was sketching a roughly outlined map, and he knew what map it was before The Rat spoke.

'That's a map of Samavia,' he said. 'It was in that piece of magazine I told you about – the one where I read about Prince Ivor. I studied it until it fell to pieces. I could draw it myself by that time, so it didn't matter. That's the capital city,' pointing to a spot. 'It's called Melzarr. The palace is there. It's the palace Ivor wandered out of singing the shepherds' song that early morning. It's where the throne is that his descendant would sit upon to be crowned – that he's *going* to sit upon. I believe he is! Let's swear he shall!' He flung down his piece of chalk and sat up. 'Give me two sticks. Help me to get up.'

Two of the Squad sprang to their feet and came to him. Each snatched one of the sticks from the stacked rifles, evidently knowing what he wanted. Marco rose too, and watched with curiosity. He had thought that The Rat could not stand up, but it seemed that he could, in a fashion of his own, and he was going to do it. The boys lifted him by his arms, set him against the stone coping of the iron railings of the churchyard, and put a stick in each of his hands. They stood at his side, but he supported himself.

' 'E could get about if 'e 'ad the money to buy crutches!' said one whose name was Cad, and he said it quite proudly. The queer thing that Marco had noticed was that the ragamuffins were proud of The Rat, and regarded him as their lord and master. '–'E could get about an' stand as well as anyone,' added the other, and he said it in the tone of one who boasts. His name was Ben.

'I'm going to stand now, and so are the rest of you,' said The Rat. 'Squad! 'Tention! You at the head of the line,' to Marco. They were in line in a moment – straight, shoulders back, chins up. And Marco stood at the head.

'We're going to take an oath,' said The Rat. 'It's an oath of allegiance. Allegiance means faithfulness to a thing – a king or a country. Ours means allegiance to the King of Samavia. We don't know where he is, but we swear to be faithful to him, to fight for him, to plot for him, to *die* for him, and to bring him back to his throne!' The way in which he flung up his head when he said the word 'die' was very fine indeed. 'We are the Secret Party. We will work in the dark and find out things – and run risks – and collect an army no one will know anything about until it is strong enough to rise at a secret signal, and overwhelm the Maranovitch and Iarovitch, and seize their forts and citadels. No one even knows we are alive. We are a silent, secret thing that never speaks aloud!'

Silent and secret as they were, however, they spoke aloud at this juncture. It was such a grand idea for a game, and so full of possible larks, that the Squad broke into a cheer.

'Hooray!' they yelled.'Hooray for the oath of 'legiance! 'Ray! 'ray! 'ray!'

'Shut up, you swine!' shouted The Rat. 'Is that the way you keep yourself secret? You'll call the police in, you fools! Look at *him*!' pointing to Marco. 'He's got some sense.'

Marco, in fact, had not made any sound.

'Come here, you Cad and Ben, and put me back on my wheels,' raged the Squad's commander. 'I'll not make up the game at all. It's no use with a lot of fat-head, raw recruits like you.'

The line broke and surrounded him in a moment, pleading and urging.

'Aw, Rat! We forgot. It's the primest game you've ever thought out! Rat! Rat! Don't get a grouch on! We'll keep still, Rat! Primest lark of all 'll be the sneakin' about an' keepin' quiet. Aw, Rat! Keep it up!'

'Keep it up yourselves!' snarled The Rat.

'Not another cove of us could do it but you! Not one! There's no other cove could think it out. You're the only chap that can think out things. You thought out the Squad! That's why you're captain!'

This was true. He was the one who could invent entertainment for them, these street lads who had nothing. Out of that nothing he could create what excited them, and give them something to fill empty, useless, often cold or wet or foggy hours. That made him their captain and their pride.

The Rat began to yield, though grudgingly. He pointed again to Marco, who had not moved, but stood still at attention.

'Look at *him*!' he said. 'He knows enough to stand where he's put until he's ordered to break line. He's a soldier, he is – not a raw recruit that don't know the goose-step.'

But after this outburst, he deigned to go on.

'Here's the oath,' he said. 'We swear to stand any torture and submit in silence to any death rather than betray our secret and our king. We will swim through seas of blood and fight our way through lakes of fire, if we are ordered. Nothing shall bar our way. All we do and say and think is for our country and our king. If any of you have anything to say, speak out before you take the oath.'

He saw Marco move a little, and he made a sign to him.

'You,' he said. 'Have you something to say?'

Marco turned to him and saluted.

'Here stand ten men for Samavia. God be thanked!' he said. He dared say that much, and he felt as if his father himself would have told him that they were the right words.

The Rat thought they were. Somehow he felt that they struck home. He reddened with a sudden emotion.

'Squad!' he said. 'I'll let you give three cheers on that. It's for the last time. We'll begin to be quiet afterwards.'

And to the Squad's exultant relief he led the cheer, and they were allowed to make as much uproar as they liked. They liked to make a great deal, and when it was at an end, it had done them good and made them ready for business.

The Rat opened the drama at once. Never surely had there been heard a conspirator's whisper as hollow as his.

'Secret Ones,' he said, 'it is midnight. We meet in the depths of darkness. We dare not meet by day. When we meet in the daytime, we pretend not to know each other. We are meeting now in a Samavian city where there is a fortress. We shall have to take it when the secret sign is given and we make our rising. We are getting everything ready, so that, when we find the King, the secret sign can be given.'

'What is the name of the city we are in?' whispered Cad.

'It is called Larrina. It is an important seaport. We must take it as soon as we rise. The next time we meet I will bring a dark lantern and draw a map and show it to you.'

It would have been a great advantage to the game if Marco could have drawn for them the map which would have shown every stronghold and every weak place. Being a boy, he knew what excitement would have thrilled each breast, how they would lean forward and pile question on question, pointing to this place and to that. He had learned to draw the map before he was ten, and he had drawn it again and again because there had been times when his father had told him that changes had taken place. But he sat silent and listened, only speaking when he asked a question, as if he knew nothing more about

Samavia than The Rat did. They drew themselves together in the closest of circles; they spoke in unearthly whispers.

'A sentinel ought to be posted at the end of the passage,' Marco whispered.

'Ben, take your gun!' commanded The Rat.

Ben rose stealthily, and, shouldering his weapon, crept on tiptoe to the opening. There he stood on guard.

'My father says there's been a Secret Party in Samavia for a hundred years,' The Rat whispered.

'Who told him?' asked Marco.

'A man who has been in Samavia,' answered The Rat. 'It began among some shepherds and charcoal-burners who bound themselves by an oath to find the Lost Prince and bring him back to the throne. There were too few of them to do anything against the Maranovitch, and when the first lot found they were growing old, they made their sons take the same oath. In each generation the band has grown. No one really knows how large it is now, but they say that there are people in nearly all the countries in Europe who belong to it and are sworn to help it when they are called. They are only waiting. Some are rich people who will give money, and some are poor ones who will slip across the frontier to fight or to help smuggle in arms. They say that for all these years there have been arms made in caves in the mountains, and hidden there year after year. There are men who are called Forgers of the Sword, and they, and their fathers, and grandfathers, and great-grandfathers have always made swords and stored them in caverns no one knows of, hidden caverns underground.'

Marco spoke aloud the thought which had come into his mind as he listened, a thought which brought fear to him. 'If the people in the streets talk about it, they won't be hidden long.'

'It isn't common talk, my father says. Only very few

have guessed, and most of them think it is part of the Lost
Prince legend. The Maranovitch and Iarovitch laugh at
it. They have always been great fools. They're too full of
their own swagger to think anything can interfere with
them.'

'Do you talk much to your father?' Marco asked him.

The Rat showed his sharp white teeth in a grin.

'I know what you're thinking of. You're remembering
that I said he was always drunk. So he is, except when he's
only *half* drunk. and when he's *half* drunk, he's the most
splendid talker in London. I found out almost everything
I know in that way. He didn't know he was teaching me,
but he was. He goes back into being a gentleman when
he's half drunk.'

'I – if you care about the Samavians, you'd better ask
him not to tell people about the Secret Party and the
Forgers of the Sword,' suggested Marco.

The Rat started a little.

'That's true!' he said. 'You're sharper than I am. It
oughtn't to be blabbed about. I'll get him to promise.
There's one queer thing about him,' he added slowly, as
if he were thinking it over, 'I suppose it's part of the
gentleman that's left in him. If he makes a promise, he
never breaks it, drunk or sober.'

'Ask him to make one,' said Marco. The next moment
he changed the subject because it seemed the best thing to
do. 'Go on tell us what our own Secret Party is to do.
We're forgetting,' he whispered.

The Rat took up his game with renewed keenness. It
was a game which attracted him immensely because it
called upon his imagination and held his audience spell-
bound, besides plunging him into war and strategy.

'We're preparing for the rising,' he said. 'It must come
soon. We've waited so long. The caverns are stacked with
arms. The Maranovitch and the Iarovitch are fighting
and using all their soldiers, and now is our time.' He

stopped and thought, his elbows on his knees. He began
to bite his nails again.

'The Secret Signal must be given,' he said. Then he
stopped again, and the Squad held its breath and pressed
nearer with a softly shuffling sound. 'Two of the Secret
Ones must be chosen by lot and sent forth. Must be
chosen *by lot*,' The Rat repeated, looking from one face
to another. 'Each one will take his life in his hand when
he goes forth. He may have to die a thousand deaths, but
he must go. He must steal in silence and disguise from one
country to another. Wherever there is one of the Secret
Party, whether he is in a hovel or on a throne, the messengers must go to him in darkness and stealth and give him
the sign. It will mean, "The hour has come. God save
Samavia!"'

'God save Samavia!' whispered the Squad, excitedly.
And, because they saw Marco raise his hand to his forehead, everyone of them saluted.

They all began to whisper at once.

'Let's draw lots now. Let's draw lots, Rat. Don't let's
'ave no waitin'.'

The Rat began to look about him with dread anxiety.
He seemed to be examining the sky.

'The darkness is not as thick as it was,' he whispered.
'Midnight has passed. The dawn of day will be upon us. If
anyone has a piece of paper or a string, we will draw the
lots before we part.'

Cad had a piece of string, and Marco had a knife which
could be used to cut it into lengths. This The Rat did
himself. Then, after shutting his eyes and mixing them,
he held them in his hand ready for the drawing.

'The Secret One who draws the longest lot is chosen.
The Secret One who draws the shortest is chosen,' he said
solemnly.

The drawing was as solemn as his tone. Each boy
wanted to draw either the shortest lot or the longest one.

The heart of each thumped somewhat as he drew his piece of string.

When the drawing was at an end, each showed his lot. The Rat had drawn the shortest piece of string, and Marco had drawn the longest one.

'Comrade!' said The Rat, taking his hand. 'We will face death and danger together!'

'God save Samavia!' answered Marco.

And the game was at an end for the day. The primest thing, the Squad said, The Rat had ever made up for them. ' 'E wos a wonder, he wos!'

CHAPTER 7

'*The Lamp is Lighted!*'

ON his way home, Marco thought of nothing but the story he must tell his father, the story the stranger who had been to Samavia had told The Rat's father. He felt that it must be a true story. The Forgers of the Sword must be real men, and the hidden caverns stacked through the centuries with arms must be real, too. And if they were real, surely his father was one of those who knew the secret. His thoughts ran fast. The Rat's boyish invention of the rising was only part of a game, but how natural it would be that some time – perhaps before long – there would be a real rising! Surely there would be one if the Secret Party had grown so strong, and if many weapons and secret friends in other countries were ready and waiting. A party which had lasted so long – which passed its oath on from generation to generation – must be of a deadly determination. What might it not have made ready in its caverns and secret meeting-places! He longed to reach home and tell his father, at once, all he had heard.

But when he reached No. 7 Philibert Place, he found Loristan and Lazarus very much absorbed in work. The door of the back sitting-room was locked when he first knocked on it, and locked again as soon he had entered. There were many papers on the table, and they were evidently studying them. Several of them were maps. Some were road maps, some maps of towns and cities, and some of fortifications; but they were all maps of places in Samavia. They were usually kept in a strong box, and when they were taken out to be studied, the door was always kept locked.

Before the evening meal, these were all returned to the box, which was pushed into a corner and had newspapers piled upon it.

'When he arrives,' Marco heard Loristan say to Lazarus, 'we can show him clearly what has been planned. He can see for himself.'

His father spoke scarcely at all during the meal, and, though it was not the habit of Lazarus to speak at such times unless spoken to, this evening it seemed to Marco that he *looked* more silent than he had ever seen him look before. They were plainly both thinking anxiously of serious things. The story of the stranger who had been to Samavia must not be told yet.

Loristan did not say anything until Lazarus had removed the things from the table and made the room as neat as possible. While that was being done, he sat with his forehead resting on his hand, as if absorbed in thought. Then he made a gesture to Marco.

'Come here, Comrade,' he said.

Marco went to him.

'Tonight someone may come to talk with me about grave things,' he said. 'I think he will come, but I cannot be sure. It is important that he should know that, when he comes, he will find me alone. He will come at a late hour, and Lazarus will open the door quietly that no one may hear. It is important that no one should see him. Someone must go and walk on the opposite side of the street until he appears. Then the one who goes to give warning must cross the pavement before him and say in a low voice, "The Lamp is lighted!" and at once turn quietly away.'

Marco's voice almost shook with the thrill of his feeling.

'How shall I know him?' he said at once. Without asking at all, he knew he was the 'someone' who was to go.

'You have seen him before,' Loristan answered. 'He is the man who drove in the carriage with the King.'

'I shall know him,' said Marco. 'When shall I go?'

'Not until it is half past one o'clock. Go to bed and sleep until Lazarus calls you.' Then he added, 'Look well at his face before you speak. He will probably not be dressed as well as he was when you saw him first.'

Marco went to bed as he was told, but it was hard to go to sleep. The rattle and roaring of the road did not usually keep him awake, because he had lived in the poorer quarter of too many big capital cities not to be accustomed to noise. But tonight it seemed to him that, as he lay and looked out at the lamplight, he heard every bus and cab which went past. He could not help thinking of the people who were in them, and on top of them, and of the people who were hurrying along on the pavement. He was wondering what they would think if they knew that things connected with the battles they read of in the daily papers were going on in one of the shabby houses they passed. It must be something connected with the war, if a man who was a great diplomat and the companion of kings came in secret to talk alone with a patriot who was a Samavian. Marco's heart almost beat aloud under his shirt as he lay on the lumpy mattress thinking it over. He must indeed look well at the stranger before he even moved towards him. He must be sure he was the right man. The game he had amused himself with so long – the game of trying to remember pictures and people and places clearly and in detail – had been a wonderful training. If he could draw, he knew he could have made a sketch of the keen-eyed, clever, aquiline face with the well-cut and delicately close mouth, which looked as if it had been shut upon secrets always. If he could draw, he found himself saying again. He *could* draw, though perhaps only roughly. He had often amused himself by making sketches of things he wanted to ask questions about. He had even drawn people's faces in his untrained way, and his father had said that he had a crude gift for catching a likeness. Perhaps he could make a sketch of this face which would show his father that he knew and could recognize it.

He jumped out of bed and went to a table near the window, where paper and pencil were lying. A street lamp exactly opposite threw into the room light enough for him to see by. He half knelt by the table and began to draw. He worked for about twenty minutes steadily, and he tore up two or three unsatisfactory sketches. The poor drawing would not matter if he could catch that subtle look which was not slyness but something more dignified and important. It was not difficult to get the marked, aristocratic outline of the features. A common-looking man with a less pronounced profile would have been less easy to draw. He gave his mind to the recalling of every detail which had photographed itself on his memory. Gradually he saw that the likeness was becoming clearer. It was not long before it was clear enough to be a striking one. Anyone who knew the man would recognize it. He got up, drawing a long and joyful breath.

He did not put on his shoes, but crossed his room as noiselessly as possible, and as noiselessly opened the door. He made no ghost of a sound when he went down the stairs. The woman who kept the lodging-house had gone to bed, and so had the other lodgers and the maid of all work. All the lights were out except the one he saw a glimmer of under the door of his father's room. When he had been a mere baby, he had been taught to make a special sign on the door when he wished to speak to Loristan. He stood still outside the back sitting-room and made it now. It was a low scratching sound – two scratches and a soft tap. Lazarus opened the door and looked troubled.

'It is not yet time, sir,' he said, very low.

'I know,' Marco answered. 'But I must show something to my father.' Lazarus let him in, and Loristan turned round from his writing-table questioningly.

Marco went forward and laid the sketch down before him.

'Look at it,' he said. 'I remember him well enough to draw that. I thought of it all at once – that I could make a sort of picture. Do you think it is like him?' Loristan examined it closely.

'It is very like him,' he answered. 'You have made me feel entirely safe. Thanks, Comrade. It was a good idea.'

There was relief in the grip he gave the boy's hand, and Marco turned away with an exultant feeling. Just as he reached the door, Loristan said to him:

'Make the most of this gift. It *is* a gift. And it is true your mind has had good training. The more you draw, the better. Draw everything you can.'

Neither the street lamps, nor the noises, nor his thoughts kept Marco awake when he went back to bed. But before he settled himself upon his pillow he gave himself certain orders. He had both read, and heard Loristan say, that the mind can control the body when people once find out that it can do so. He had tried experiments himself, and had found out some curious things. One was that if he told himself to remember a certain thing at a certain time, he usually found that he *did* remember it. Something in his brain seemed to remind him. He had often tried the experiment of telling himself to awaken at a particular hour, and had awakened almost exactly at the moment by the clock.

'I will sleep until one o'clock,' he said as he shut his eyes. 'Then I will awaken and feel quite fresh. I shall not be sleepy at all.'

He slept as soundly as a boy can sleep. And at one o'clock he awakened, and found the street lamp still throwing its light through the window. There was a cheap little round clock on the table, and he could see the time. He was quite fresh and not at all sleepy. His experiment had succeeded again.

He got up and dressed. Then he went downstairs as noiselessly as before. He carried his shoes in his hands, as he meant to put them on only when he reached the street. He made his sign at his father's door, and it was Loristan who opened it.

'Shall I go now?' Marco asked.

'Yes. Walk slowly to the other side of the street. Look in every direction. We do not know where he will come from. After you have given him the sign, then come in and go to bed again.'

Marco saluted as a soldier would have done on receiving an order. Then, without a second's delay, he passed noiselessly out of the house.

Loristan turned back into the room and stood silently in the centre of it. The long lines of his handsome body looked particularly erect and stately, and his eyes were glowing as if something deeply moved him.

'There grows a man for Samavia,' he said to Lazarus, who watched him. 'God be thanked!'

Lazarus's voice was low and hoarse, and he saluted quite reverently.

'Your – sir!' he said. 'God save the Prince!'

'Yes,' Loristan answered, after a moment's hesitation – 'when he is found.' And he went back to his table smiling his beautiful smile.

The wonder of silence in the deserted streets of a great city, after midnight has hushed all the roar and tumult to rest, is an almost unbelievable thing. The stillness in the depths of a forest or on a mountain top is not so strange. A few hours ago, the tumult was rushing past; in a few hours more, it will be rushing past again. But now the street is a naked thing; a distant policeman's tramp on the bare pavement has a hollow and almost fearsome sound. It seemed especially so to Marco as he crossed the road. Had it ever been so empty and deadly silent before?

Was it so every night? Perhaps it was, when he was fast asleep on his lumpy mattress with the light from a street lamp streaming into the room. He listened for the step of the policeman on night-watch, because he did not wish to be seen. There was a jutting wall where he could stand in the shadow while the man passed. A policeman would stop to look questioningly at a boy who walked up and down the pavement at half past one in the morning. Marco could wait until he had gone by, and then come out into the light and look up and down the road and the cross streets.

He heard approaching footsteps in a few minutes, and was safely in the shadows before he could be seen. When the policeman passed, he came out and walked slowly down the road, looking on each side, and now and then looking back. At first no one was in sight. Then a late hansom-cab came tinkling along. But the people in it were returning from some festivity, and were laughing and talking, and noticed nothing but their own joking. Then there was silence again, and for a long time, it seemed to Marco, no one was to be seen. It was not really so long as it appeared, because he was anxious. Then a very early vegetable-wagon on the way from the country to Covent Garden market came slowly lumbering by with its driver almost asleep on his piles of potatoes and cabbages. After it had passed there was stillness and emptiness once more, until the policeman showed himself again on his beat, and Marco slipped into the shadow of the wall as he had done before.

When he came out into the light, he had begun to hope that the time would not seem long to his father, whose anxiousness would be greater than his own. Loristan knew all that depended on the coming of this great man. 'It might be something which all Samavia is waiting to know – at least all the Secret Party,' Marco thought. 'The Secret Party is Samavia' – he started at the sound of footsteps. 'Someone is coming!' he said. 'It is a man.'

It was a man who was walking up the road on the same side of the pavement as his own. Marco began to walk towards him quietly but rather rapidly. He thought it might be best to appear as if he were some boy sent on a midnight errand – perhaps to call a doctor. Then, if it was a stranger he passed, no suspicion would be aroused. Was this man as tall as the one who had driven with the King? Yes, he was about the same height, but he was too far away to be recognizable otherwise. He drew nearer, and Marco noticed that he also seemed slightly to hasten his footsteps. Marco went on. A little nearer, and he would be able to make sure. Yes, now he was near enough. Yes, this man was the same height and not unlike in figure, but he was much younger. He was not the one who had been in the carriage with His Majesty. He was not more than thirty years old. He begun swinging his cane and whistling a music-hall song softly as Marco passed him without changing his pace.

It was after the policeman had walked round his beat and disappeared for the third time, that Marco heard footsteps echoing at some distance down a cross street. After listening to make sure that they were approaching, he placed himself at a point where he could watch the length of the thoroughfare. Yes, someone was coming. It was a man's figure again. Marco was able to place himself in the shadow so that the person would not see that he was being watched. The solitary walker reached a recognizable distance in about two minutes' time. He was dressed in an ordinary shop-made suit of clothes which was rather shabby and quite unnoticeable. His common hat was worn so that it rather shaded his face. But even before he had crossed to Marco's side of the road, the boy had clearly recognized him. It was the man who had driven with the King!

Chance was with Marco. The man crossed at exactly the

place which made it easy for the boy to step lightly from behind him, walk a few paces by his side, and then pass directly before him across the pavement, glancing quietly up into his face as he said, in a low voice but distinctly, the words, 'The Lamp is lighted,' and without pausing a second walk on his way down the road. He did not slacken his pace or look back until he was some distance away. Then he glanced over his shoulder, and saw that the figure had crossed the street and was inside the railings. It was all right. His father would not be disappointed. The great man had come.

He walked for about ten minutes, and then went home and to bed. But he was obliged to tell himself to go to sleep several times before his eyes closed for the rest of the night.

CHAPTER 8

An Exciting Game

LORISTAN referred only once during the next day to what had happened.

'You did your errand well. You were not hurried or nervous,' he said. 'The Prince was pleased with your calmness.'

No more was said. Marco knew that the quiet mention of the stranger's title had been made merely as a designation. If it were necessary to mention him again in the future, he could be referred to as 'the Prince'. In various continental countries there were many princes who were not royal or even serene highnesses – who were merely princes as other nobles were dukes or barons. Nothing special was revealed when a man was spoken of as a prince. But though nothing more was said on the subject of the incident, it was plain that much work was being done by Loristan and Lazarus. The sitting-room door was locked, and the maps and documents, usually kept in the iron box, were being used.

Marco went to the Tower of London and spent part of the day in living again the stories which had been enclosed within its massive stone walls. In this way he had become intimate with people who to most boys seemed only the unreal creatures who professed to be alive in school-books. He had learned to know them as men and women because he had stood in the palaces they had been born in and had played in as children, had died in at the end. He had seen the dungeons they had been imprisoned in, the blocks on which they had laid their heads, the battlements on which they had fought to defend their fortressed towers, the thrones they had sat upon, the crowns they had worn, and the jewelled sceptres they had held. He had stood before their portraits and had gazed curiously at their 'Robes of Investiture', sewn with tens of thousands of seed-pearls. To look at a man's face and feel his pictured eyes follow you as you move away from him, to see the splendid garments he once warmed with his living flesh, is to realize that history is not a mere lesson in a school-book, but is a relation of the life stories of men and women who saw strange and splendid days, and sometimes suffered strange and terrible things.

There were only a few people who were being led about sightseeing. The man in the Beefeaters' costume, who was their guide, was good-natured, and fond of talking. He was a big, stout man, rather like pictures of Henry the Eighth himself. He was specially talkative when he stood by the tablet that marks the spot where stood the block on which Lady Jane Grey had laid her young head. One of the sightseers who knew little of English history had asked some questions about the reasons for her execution.

'If her father-in-law, the Duke of Northumberland, had left that young couple alone – her and her husband, Lord Guildford Dudley – they'd have kept their heads on. He was bound to make her a queen, and Mary Tudor was bound to be queen herself. The Duke wasn't clever enough to manage a conspiracy and work up the people. These Samavians we're reading about in the papers would have done it better. And they're half savages.'

'They had a big battle outside Melzarr yesterday,' the sightseer standing next to Marco said to the young woman who was his companion. 'Thousands of 'em killed. I saw it in big letters on the boards as I rode on the top of the bus. They're just slaughtering each other, that's what they're doing.'

The talkative Beefeater heard him.

'They can't even bury their dead fast enough,' he said.

'There'll be some sort of plague breaking out and sweeping into the countries nearest them. It'll end by spreading all over Europe as it did in the Middle Ages. What the civilized countries have got to do is to make them choose a decent king and begin to behave themselves.'

'I'll tell my father that too,' Marco thought. 'It shows that everybody is thinking and talking of Samavia, and that even the common people know it must have a real king. This must be *the time*!' And what he meant was that this must be the time for which the Secret Party had waited and worked so long – the time for the Rising. But his father was out when he went back to Philibert Place, and Lazarus looked more silent than ever as he stood behind his chair and waited on him through his insignificant meal. However plain and scant the food they had to eat, it was always served with as much care and ceremony as if it had been a banquet.

'A man can eat dry bread and drink cold water as if he were a gentleman,' his father had said long ago. 'And it is easy to form careless habits. Even if one is hungry enough to feel ravenous, a man who has been well bred will not allow himself to look so. A dog may, a man may not. Just as a dog may howl when he is angry or in pain and a man may not.'

It was only one of the small parts of the training which had quietly made the boy, even as a child, self-controlled and courteous, had taught him ease and grace of boyish carriage, the habit of holding his body well and his head erect, and had given him a certain look of young distinction which, though it assumed nothing, set him apart from boys of awkward bearing.

'Is there a newspaper here which tells of the battle, Lazarus?' he asked, after he had left the table.

'Yes, sir,' was the answer. 'Your father said that you might read it. It is a black tale!' he added, as he handed him the paper.

It was a black tale. As he read, Marco felt as if he could scarcely bear it. It was as if Samavia swam in blood, and as if the other countries must stand aghast before such furious cruelties.

'Lazarus,' he said, springing to his feet at last, his eyes burning, 'something must stop it! There must be something strong enough. The time has come. The time has come.' And he walked up and down the room because he was too excited to stand still.

How Lazarus watched him! What a strong and glowing feeling there was in his own restrained face!

'Yes, sir. Surely the time has come,' he answered. But that was all he said, and he turned and went out of the shabby back sitting-room at once. It was as if he felt it were wiser to go before he lost power over himself and said more.

Marco made his way to the meeting place of the Squad, to which The Rat had in the past given the name of the Barracks. The Rat was sitting among his followers, and he had been reading the morning paper to them, the one which contained the account of the battle of Melzarr. The Squad had become the Secret Party, and each member of it was thrilled with the spirit of dark plot and adventure. They all whispered when they spoke.

'This is not the Barracks now,' The Rat said. 'It is a subterranean cavern. Under the floor of it thousands of swords and guns are buried, and it is piled to the roof with them. There is only a small place left for us to sit and plot in. We crawl in through a hole, and the hole is hidden by bushes.'

To the rest of the boys this was only an exciting game, but Marco knew that to The Rat it was more. Though The Rat knew none of the things he knew, the whole story seemed to him a real thing. The struggles of Samavia, as he had heard and read of them in the newspapers, had taken possession of him. His passion for soldiering and warfare and his curiously mature brain had led him into following every detail he could lay hold of. He remembered things older people forgot after they had mentioned them. He forgot nothing. He had drawn on the flagstones a map of Samavia which Marco saw was actually correct, and he had made a rough sketch of Melzarr and the battle which had had such disastrous results.

'The Maranovitch had possession of Melzarr,' he explained with feverish eagerness. 'And the Iarovitch attacked them from here,' pointing with his finger. 'That was a mistake. I should have attacked them from a place where they would not have been expecting it. They expected attack on their fortifications, and they were ready to defend them. I believe the enemy could have stolen up in the night and rushed in here,' pointing again. Marco thought he was right. The Rat had argued it all out, and had studied Melzarr as he might have studied a puzzle or an arithmetical problem. He was very clever, and as sharp as his queer face looked.

'I believe you would make a good general if you were grown up,' said Marco. 'I'd like to show your maps to my father and ask him if he doesn't think your stratagem would have been a good one.'

'Does he know much about Samavia?' asked The Rat.

'He has to read the newspapers because he writes things,' Marco answered. 'And everyone is thinking about the war. No one can help it.'

The Rat drew a dingy, folded paper out of his pocket and looked it over with an air of reflection.

'I'll make a clean one,' he said. 'I'd like a grown-up man to look at it and see if it's all right. My father was more than half drunk when I was drawing this, so I couldn't ask him questions. He'll kill himself before long. He had a sort of fit last night.'

'Tell us, Rat, wot you an' Marco 'll 'ave ter do. Let's

'ear wot you've made up,' suggested Cad. He drew closer, and so did the rest of the circle, hugging their knees with their arms.

'This is what we shall have to do,' began The Rat, in the hollow whisper of a Secret Party. '*The hour has come.* To all the Secret Ones in Samavia, and to the friends of the Secret Party in every country, the sign must be carried. It must be carried by someone who could not be suspected. Who would suspect two boys – and one of them a cripple? The best thing of all for us is that I am a cripple. Who would suspect a cripple? When my father is drunk and beats me, he does it because I won't go out and beg in the streets and bring him the money I get. He says that people will nearly always give money to a cripple. I won't be a beggar for him – the swine – but I will be one for Samavia and the Lost Prince. Marco shall pretend to be my brother and take care of me. I say,' speaking to Marco with a sudden change of voice, 'can you sing anything? It doesn't matter how you do it.'

'Yes, I can sing,' Marco replied.

'Then Marco will pretend he is singing to make people give him money. I'll get a pair of crutches and part of the time I will go on crutches and part of the time on my platform. We'll live like beggars and go wherever we want to. I can whiz past a man and give the sign and no one will know. Sometimes Marco can give it when people are dropping money into his cap. We can pass from one country to another and rouse everybody who is of the Secret Party. We'll work our way into Samavia, and we'll be only two boys – and one a cripple – and nobody will think we could be doing anything. We'll beg in great cities and on the highroad.'

'Where'll you get the money to travel?' said Cad.

'The Secret Party will give it to us, and we shan't need much. We could beg enough, for that matter. We'll sleep under the stars, or under bridges, or archways, or in dark

corners of streets. I've done it myself many a time when
my father drove me out of doors. If it's cold weather, it's
bad enough; but if it's fine weather, it's better than sleeping in the kind of place I'm used to. Comrade,' to Marco,
'are you ready?'

He said 'Comrade' as Loristan did, and somehow Marco
did not resent it, because he was ready to labour for
Samavia. It was only a game, but it made them comrades
– and was it really only a game, after all? The Rat's
excited voice and his strange, lined face made it singularly unlike one.

'Yes, Comrade, I am ready,' Marco answered him.

'We shall be in Samavia when the fighting for the Lost
Prince begins.' The Rat carried on his story with fire. 'We
may see a battle. We might do something to help. We
might carry messages under a rain of bullets – a rain of
bullets!' The thought so elated him that he forgot his
whisper and his voice rang out fiercely. 'Boys have been in
battles before. We might find the Lost King – no, the
Found King – and ask him to let us be his servants. He
could send us where he couldn't send bigger people. I
could say to him, "Your Majesty, I am called 'The Rat',
because I can creep through holes and into corners and
dart about. Order me into any danger and I will obey you.
Let me die like a soldier if I can't live like one." '

Suddenly he threw his ragged coat sleeve up across his
eye. He had wrought himself up tremendously with the
picture of the rain of bullets. And he felt as if he saw the
King who had at last been found. The next moment he
uncovered his face.

'That's what we've got to do,' he said. 'Just that, if you
want to know. And a lot more. There's no end to it!'

Marco's thoughts were in a whirl. It ought not to be
nothing but a game. He grew quite hot all over. If the
Secret Party wanted to send messengers no one would
think of suspecting, who could be more harmless-looking

than two vagabond boys picking up their living as best
they could, not seeming to belong to anyone? And one a
cripple. It was true – yes, it was true, as The Rat said, that
his being a cripple made him look safer than anyone else.
Marco actually put his forehead in his hands and pressed
his temples.

'What's the matter?' exclaimed The Rat. 'What are you
thinking about?'

'I'm thinking what a general you would make. I'm
thinking that it might all be real – every word of it. It
mightn't be a game at all,' said Marco.

'No, it mightn't,' The Rat answered. 'If I knew where
the Secret Party was, I'd like to go and tell them about it.
What's that!' he said, suddenly turning his head towards
the street. 'What are they calling out?'

Some newsboy with a particularly shrill voice was
shouting out something at the topmost power of his lungs.

Tense and excited, no member of the circle stirred or
spoke for a few seconds. The Rat listened, Marco listened,
the whole Squad listened, pricking up their ears.

'Startling news from Samavia,' the newsboy was shril-
ling out. 'Amazing story! Descendant of the Lost Prince
found! Descendant of the Lost Prince found!'

'Any chap got a penny?' snapped The Rat, beginning
to shuffle towards the arched passage.

'I have!' answered Marco, following him.

'Come on!' The Rat yelled. 'Let's go and get a paper!'
And he whizzed down the passage with his swiftest rat-
like dart, while the Squad followed him, shouting and
tumbling over each other.

CHAPTER 9

'It is not a Game'

LORISTAN walked slowly up and down the back sitting-room and listened to Marco, who sat by the small fire and talked.

'Go on,' he said, whenever the boy stopped. 'I want to hear it all. He's a strange lad, and it's a splendid game.'

A year later, Marco recalled this evening as a thrilling memory, and as one which would never pass away from him throughout his life. He would always be able to call it all back. The small and dingy back room, the dimness of the one poor gas-burner, which was all they could afford to light, the iron box pushed into the corner with its maps and plans locked safely in it, the erect bearing and beauty of the tall form, which the shabbiness of worn and mended clothes could not hide or dim. His eyes seemed darker and more wonderful than ever in their remote thoughtfulness and interest as he spoke.

'Go on,' he said. 'It is a splendid game. And he has thought it out well. The lad is a born soldier.'

'It is not a game to him,' Marco said. 'And it is not a game to me. The Squad is only playing, but with him it's quite different. He knows he'll never really get what he wants, but he feels as if this was something near it. He said I might show you the map he made. Father, look at it.'

He gave Loristan the clean copy of The Rat's map of Samavia. The city of Melzarr was marked with certain signs. They were to show at what points The Rat – if he had been a Samavian general – would have attacked the capital. As Marco pointed them out, he explained The Rat's reasons for his planning.

Loristan held the paper for some minutes. He fixed his

eyes on it curiously, and his black brows drew themselves together.

'This is very wonderful!' he said at last. 'He is quite right. They might have got in there, and for the very reasons he hit on. How did he learn all this?'

'He thinks of nothing else now,' answered Marco. 'He has always thought of wars and made plans for battles. He's not like the rest of the Squad. His father is nearly always drunk, but he is very well educated, and, when he is only half drunk, he likes to talk. The Rat asks him questions then, and leads him on until he finds out a great deal. Then he begs old newspapers, and he hides himself in corners and listens to what people are saying. He says he lies awake at night thinking it out, and he thinks about it all the day. That was why he got up the Squad.'

Loristan had continued examining the paper.

'Tell him,' he said, when he refolded and handed it back, 'that I studied his map, and he may be proud of it. You may also tell him' – and he smiled quietly as he spoke – 'that in my opinion he is right. The Iarovitch would have held Melzarr today if he had led them.'

Marco was full of exultation.

'I thought you would say he was right. I felt sure you would. That is what makes me want to tell you the rest,' he hurried on. 'If you think he is right about the rest too –' He stopped awkwardly because of a sudden wild thought which rushed upon him. 'I don't know what you will think,' he stammered. 'Perhaps it will seem to you – as if that part of it could – could only be a game.'

He was so fervent in spite of his hesitation that Loristan began to watch him with sympathetic respect, as he always did when the boy was trying to express something he was not sure of.

'Go on,' he said again. 'I am like The Rat and I am like you. It has not seemed quite like a game to me, so far.'

He sat down at the writing-table and Marco drew

nearer and leaned against it, resting on his arms and lowering his voice.

'It is The Rat's plan for giving the signal for a Rising,' he said.

Loristan made a slight movement.

'Does he think there will be a Rising?' he asked.

'He says that must be what the Secret Party has been preparing for all these years. And it must come soon. If the real King is found – but when The Rat bought the newspaper there was nothing in it about where he was. It was only a sort of rumour. Nobody seemed to know anything.' He stopped a few seconds, but he did not utter the words which were in his mind. He did not say: 'But *you* know.'

'And The Rat has a plan for giving the signal?' Loristan said.

Marco forgot his feeling of hesitation. He began to see the plan again as he had seen it when The Rat talked. He made even a clearer picture than The Rat had made of the two vagabond boys – one of them a cripple – making their way from one place to another, free to carry messages or warnings where they chose, because they were so insignificant and poor-looking that no one could think of them as anything but waifs and strays, belonging to nobody and blown about by the wind of poverty and chance. He felt as if he wanted to convince his father that the plan was a possible one. He did not know why he felt so anxious to win approval of the scheme, as if it could actually be done. But this feeling was what inspired him to enter into new details and suggest possibilities.

'Soldiers would listen to a singer if he sang good songs – and they might not be afraid to talk before him. A strolling singer and a cripple would perhaps hear a great many things it might be useful for the Secret Party to know. They might even hear important things. Don't you think so?'

Before he had gone far with his story, the far-away look had fallen upon Loristan's face – the look Marco had known so well all his life. He sat turned a little sidewise from the boy, his elbow resting on the table and his forehead on his hand. He looked down at the worn carpet at his feet, and so he looked as he listened to the end. It was as if some new thought were slowly growing in his mind. He did not even look up or change his position as he answered, 'Yes. I think so.'

But, because of the deep and growing thought in his face, Marco's courage increased. His fear that this part of the planning might seem so bold and reckless that it would appear to belong to a boyish game, gradually faded away. His father was not listening as if to the details of exaggerated fancies. It was as if the thing he was hearing was not impossible. Marco's knowledge of continental countries and of methods of journeying helped him to enter into much detail and give realism to his plans.

'Sometimes we could pretend we knew nothing but English,' he said. 'Then, though The Rat could not understand, I could. I should always understand in each country. I know the cities and the places we should want to go to. I know how boys like us live, and so we should not do anything which would make the police angry or make people notice us. If anyone asked questions, I would let them believe that I had met The Rat by chance, and we had made up our minds to travel together because people gave more money to a boy who sang if he was with a cripple. There was a boy who used to play the guitar in the streets of Rome, and he always had a lame girl with him, and everyone knew it was for that reason. When he played, people looked at the girl and were sorry for her and gave her soldi. You remember.'

'Yes, I remember. And what you say is true,' Loristan answered.

Marco leaned farther forward across the table so that he came closer to him. The tone in which the words were said made his courage leap like a flame. To be allowed to go on with this boldness was to feel that he was being treated almost as if he were a man. If his father had wished to stop him, he could have done it with one quiet glance, without uttering a word. For some wonderful reason he did not wish his son to cease talking. He was willing to hear what he had to say – he was even interested.

'You are growing older,' he had said the night he had revealed the marvellous secret. 'Silence is still the order, but you are man enough to be told more.'

Was he man enough to be thought worthy to help Samavia in any small way – even with boyish fancies which might contain a germ of some thought which older and wiser minds might make useful? Was he being listened to because the plan, made as part of a game, was not an impossible one – if two boys who could be trusted could be found? He caught a deep breath as he went on, drawing still nearer and speaking so low that his tone was almost a whisper.

'If the men of the Secret Party have been working and thinking for so many years – they have prepared everything. They know by this time exactly what must be done by the messengers who are to give the signal. They can tell them where to go and how to know the secret friends who must be warned. If the orders could be written and given to – to someone who has – who has learned to remember things!' He had begun to breathe so quickly that he stopped for a moment.

Loristan looked up. He looked directly into his eyes.

'Someone who has been *trained* to remember things?' he said.

'Someone who has been trained,' Marco went on, catching his breath again. 'Someone who does not forget – who would never forget – never! That one, even if he were only twelve – even if he were only ten – could go and do as he was told.' Loristan put his hand on his shoulder.

'Comrade,' he said, 'you are speaking as if you were ready to go yourself.'

Marco's eyes looked bravely straight into his, but he said not one word.

'Do you know what it would mean, Comrade?' his father went on. 'You are right. It is not a game. And you are not thinking of it as one. But have you thought how it would be if something betrayed you – and you were set up against a wall to be *shot*?'

Marco stood up quite straight. He tried to believe he felt the wall against his back.

'If I were shot, I should be shot for Samavia,' he said. 'And for *you*, Father.'

Even as he was speaking, the front door-bell rang and Lazarus evidently opened it. He spoke to someone, and then they heard his footsteps approaching the back sitting-room.

'Open the door,' said Loristan, and Marco opened it.

'There is a boy who is a cripple here, sir,' the old soldier said. 'He asked to see Master Marco.'

'If it is The Rat,' said Loristan, 'bring him in here. I wish to see him.'

Marco went down the passage to the front door. The Rat was there, but he was not upon his platform. He was leaning upon an old pair of crutches, and Marco thought he looked wild and strange. He was white, and somehow the lines of his face seemed twisted in a new way. Marco wondered if something had frightened him, or if he felt ill.

'Rat,' he began, 'my father –'

'I've come to tell you about *my* father,' The Rat broke in without waiting to hear the rest, and his voice was as strange as his pale face. 'I don't know why I've come, but I – I just wanted to. He's dead!'

'Your father?' Marco stammered. 'He's –'

'He's dead,' The Rat answered shakily. 'I told you he'd kill himself. He had another fit and he died in it. I knew he would, one of these days. I told him so. He knew he would himself. I stayed with him till he was dead – and then I got a bursting headache and I felt sick – and I thought about you.'

Marco made a jump at him because he saw he was suddenly shaking as if he were going to fall. He was just in time, and Lazarus, who had been looking on from the back of the passage, came forward. Together they held him up.

'I'm not going to faint,' he said weakly, 'but I felt as if I was. It was a bad fit, and I had to try and hold him. I was all by myself. The people in the other attic thought he was only drunk, and they wouldn't come in. He's lying on the floor there, dead.'

'Come and see my father,' Marco said. 'He'll tell us what to do. Lazarus, help him.'

'I can get on by myself,' said The Rat. 'Do you see my crutches? I did something for a pawnbroker last night, and he gave them to me for pay.'

But though he tried to speak carelessly, he had plainly been horribly shaken and overwrought. His queer face was yellowish white still, and he was trembling a little.

Marco led the way into the back sitting-room. In the midst of its shabby gloom and under the dim light Loristan was standing in one of his still, attentive attitudes. He was waiting for them.

'Father, this is The Rat,' the boy began. The Rat stopped short and rested on his crutches, staring at the tall, reposeful figure with widened eyes.

'Is that your father?' he said to Marco. And then added, with a jerky half-laugh, 'He's not much like mine, is he?'

CHAPTER 10

The Rat – and Samavia

WHAT The Rat thought when Loristan began to speak to him, Marco wondered. Suddenly he stood in an unknown world, and it was Loristan who made it so because poverty and shabbiness had no power to touch him. He looked at the boy with calm and clear eyes, he asked him practical questions gently, and it was plain that he understood many things without asking questions at all. Marco thought that perhaps he had, at some time in his life, seen drunken men die in strange places. He seemed to know the terribleness of the night through which The Rat had passed. He made him sit down, and ordered Lazarus to bring him some hot coffee and simple food.

'Haven't had a bite since yesterday,' The Rat said, still staring at him. 'How did you know I hadn't?'

'You have not had time,' Loristan answered.

Afterwards he made him lie down on the sofa.

'Look at my clothes,' said The Rat.

'Lie down and sleep,' Loristan replied, putting his hand on his shoulder and gently forcing him towards the sofa. 'You will sleep a long time. You must tell me how to find the place where your father died, and I will see that the proper authorities are notified.'

'What are you doing it for?' The Rat asked, and then he added, 'sir.'

'Because I am a man and you are a boy. And this is a terrible thing,' Loristan answered him.

He went away without saying more, and The Rat lay on the sofa staring at the wall and thinking about it until he fell asleep. As Loristan had told him he would, he slept deeply and long.

When he awakened it was morning, and Lazarus was standing by the side of the sofa looking down at him.

'You will want to make yourself clean,' he said. 'It must be done.'

'Clean!' said The Rat, with his squeaky laugh. 'I couldn't keep clean when I had a room to live in, and now where am I to wash myself?' He sat up and looked about him.

'Give me my crutches,' he said. 'I've got to go. They've let me sleep here all night. They didn't turn me into the street. I don't know why. Marco's father — he's the right sort. He looks like a swell.'

'The Master,' said Lazarus, with a rigid manner, 'the Master is a great gentleman. He would turn no tired creature into the street. He and his son are poor, but they are of those who give. He desires to see and talk to you again. You are to have bread and coffee with him and the young Master. But it is I who tell you that you cannot sit at table with them until you are clean. Come with me,' and he handed him his crutches. His manner was authoritative, but it was the manner of a soldier; his somewhat stiff and erect movements were those of a soldier, also, and The Rat liked them because they made him feel as if he were in barracks. He did not know what was going to happen, but he got up and followed on his crutches.

Lazarus took him to a closet under the stairs where a battered tin bath was already full of hot water, which the old soldier himself had brought in pails. There were soap and coarse, clean towels on a wooden chair, and also there was a much worn but cleanly suit of clothes.

'Put these on when you have bathed,' Lazarus ordered, pointing to them. 'They belong to the young Master and will be large for you, but they will be better than your own.' And then he went out of the closet and shut the door.

It was a new experience for The Rat. So long as he

remembered, he had washed his face and hands – when he had washed them at all – at an iron tap set in the wall of a back street or court in some slum. His father and he had long ago sunk into the world where to wash one's self is not a part of everyday life. They had lived amid dirt and foulness, and when his father had been in a maudlin state, he had sometimes cried and talked of the long-past days when he had shaved every morning and put on a clean shirt.

To stand even in the most battered of tin baths full of clean hot water and to splash and scrub with a big piece of flannel and plenty of soap was a marvellous thing. The Rat's tired body responded to the novelty with a feeling of freshness and comfort.

'I dare say swells do this every day,' he muttered. 'I'd do it myself if I was a swell. Soldiers have to keep themselves so clean they shine.'

When, after making the most of his soap and water, he came out of the closet under the stairs, he was as fresh as Marco himself; and, though his clothes had been built for a more stalwart body, his recognition of their cleanliness filled him with pleasure. He wondered if by any effort he could keep himself clean when he went out into the world again and had to sleep in any hole the police did not order him out of.

He wanted to see Marco again, but he wanted more to see the tall man with the soft dark eyes. There was something about him which made you keep on looking at him. You felt as if you'd take orders from him as you would from your general, if you were a soldier. And yet he had that quiet voice and those fine, easy movements, and he was not a soldier at all, but only a poor man who wrote things for papers which did not pay him well enough to give him and his son a comfortable living. Through all the time of his seclusion with the battered bath and the soap and water, The Rat thought of him, and longed to

have another look at him and hear him speak again. He
did not see any reason why Marco's father should have let
him sleep on his sofa or why he should give him a breakfast before he turned him out to face the world. It was
first-rate of him to do it. The Rat felt that when he was
turned out, after he had had the coffee, he should want to
hang about the neighbourhood just on the chance of
seeing the tall man pass by sometimes. The Rat did not
know what he was going to do. The parish officials would
by this time have taken his dead father, and he would not
see him again. He did not want to see him again. He had
never seemed like a father. They had never cared anything for each other. Perhaps, The Rat thought, he would
be driven to going about on his platform on the pavements and begging, as his father had tried to force him to
do. Could he sell newspapers? What could a crippled lad
do unless he begged or sold papers?

Lazarus was waiting for him in the passage. The Rat
held back a little.

'Perhaps they'd rather not eat their breakfast with me,'
he hesitated. 'I'm not – I'm not the kind they are. I could
swallow the coffee out here and carry the bread away with
me. And you could thank him for me. I'd want him to
know I thanked him.'

Lazarus also had a steady eye. The Rat realized that he
was looking him over as if he were summing him up.

'You may not be the kind they are, but you may be of a
kind the Master sees good in. If he did not see something,
he would not ask you to sit at his table. You are to come
with me.'

The Squad had seen good in The Rat, but no one else
had. Policemen had moved him on whenever they set eyes
on him, the wretched women of the slums had regarded
him as they regarded his darting, thieving namesake;
loafing or busy men had seen in him a young nuisance to
be kicked or pushed out of the way. The Squad had not

called 'good' what they saw in him. They would have yelled with laughter if they had heard anyone else call it so. 'Goodness' was not considered an attraction in their world.

The Rat grinned a little and wondered what was meant, as he followed Lazarus into the back sitting-room.

Loristan was standing on the hearth and Marco was near him. They were waiting for their vagabond guest as if he had been a gentleman.

The Rat hesitated and shuffled at the door for a moment, and then it suddenly occurred to him to stand as straight as he could and salute. When he found himself in the presence of Loristan, he felt as if he ought to do something, but he did not know what.

Loristan's recognition of his gesture and his expression as he moved forward lifted from The Rat's shoulders a load which he himself had not known lay there. Somehow he felt as if something new had happened to him, as if he were not mere 'vermin', after all, as if he need not be on the defensive – even as if he need not feel so much in the dark, and like a thing there was no place in the world for. The straight and far-seeing look of this man's eyes seemed to make a place somewhere for what he looked at. And yet what he said was quite simple.

'This is well,' he said. 'You have rested. We will have some food, and then we will talk together.' He made a slight gesture in the direction of the chair at the right hand of his own place.

The Rat hesitated again. What a swell he was! With that wave of the hand he made you feel as if you were a fellow like himself and he was doing you some honour.

'I'm not –' The Rat broke off and jerked his head towards Marco. 'He knows –' he ended. 'I've never sat at a table like this before.'

'There is not much on it.' Loristan made the slight

gesture towards the right-hand seat again and smiled. 'Let us sit down.'

The Rat obeyed him and the meal began. There were only bread and coffee and a little butter before them. But Lazarus presented the cups and plates on a small japanned tray as if it were a golden salver. When he was not serving, he stood upright behind his master's chair, as though he wore livery of scarlet and gold. To the boy who had gnawed a bone or munched a crust wherever he found them, to watch the two with whom he sat was a new thing. He knew nothing of the everyday decencies of civilized people. The Rat liked to look at them, and he found himself trying to hold his cup as Loristan did, and to sit and move as Marco was sitting and moving — taking his bread or butter, when it was held at his side by Lazarus, as if it were a simple thing to be waited upon. Marco had had things handed to him all his life, and it did not make him feel awkward. The Rat knew that his own father had once lived like this. He himself would have been at ease if chance had treated him fairly. It made him scowl to think of it.

But in a few minutes Loristan began to talk about the copy of the map of Samavia. Then The Rat forgot everything else and was ill at ease no more. He did not know that Loristan was leading him on to explain his theories about the country and the people and the war. He found himself telling all that he had read, or overheard, or *thought* as he lay awake in his garret. He had thought out a great many things in a way not at all like a boy's. His strangely concentrated and over-mature mind had been full of military schemes which Loristan listened to with curiosity and amazement. The Rat had become extraordinarily clever in one direction because he had fixed all his mental powers on one thing. It seemed scarcely natural than an untaught vagabond lad should know so

much and reason so clearly. It was at least extraordinarily
interesting. There had been no skirmish, no attack, no
battle which he had not led and fought in his own imagination, and he had made scores of rough queer plans of
all that had been or should have been done. Lazarus
listened as attentively as his master, and once Marco saw
him exchange a startled glance with Loristan. The Rat
was sketching with his finger on the cloth an attack which
ought to have been made but was not. And Marco knew
at once that the quickly exchanged look meant 'He is
right! If it had been done, there would have been victory
instead of disaster!'

It was a wonderful meal, though it was only of bread
and coffee. The Rat knew he should never be able to
forget it.

Afterwards, Loristan told him of what he had done the
night before. He had seen the parish authorities and all
had been done which a city government provides in the
case of a pauper's death. His father would be buried in
the usual manner. 'We will follow him,' Loristan said in
the end. 'You and I and Marco and Lazarus.'

The Rat's mouth fell open.

'You – and Marco – and Lazarus!' he exclaimed, staring. 'And me! Why should any of us go? I don't want to.
He wouldn't have followed me if I'd been the one.'

Loristan remained silent for a few moments.

'When a life has counted for nothing, the end of it is a
lonely thing,' he said at last. 'If it has forgotten all respect
for itself, pity is all that one has left to give. One would
like to give *something* to anything so lonely.' He said the
last brief sentence after a pause.

'Let us go,' Marco said suddenly; and he caught The
Rat's hand.

The Rat's own movement was sudden. He slipped from
his crutches to a chair, and sat and gazed at the worn carpet as if he were not looking at it at all, but at something

a long way off. After a while he looked up at Loristan.

'Do you know what I thought of, all at once?' he said in a shaky voice. 'I thought of that "Lost Prince" one. He only lived once. Perhaps he didn't live a long time. Nobody knows. But it's five hundred years ago, and, just because he was the kind he was, everyone that remembers him thinks of something fine. It's queer, but it does you good just to hear his name. And if he has been training kings for Samavia all these centuries — they may have been poor and nobody may have known about them, but they've been *kings*. That's what *he* did — just by being alive a few years. When I think of him and then think of — the other — there's such an awful difference that — yes — I'm sorry. For the first time. I'm his son and I can't care about him; but he's too lonely — I want to go.'

So it was that when the forlorn derelict was carried to the graveyard where nameless burdens on the city were given to the earth, a curious funeral procession followed him. There were two tall and soldierly looking men and two boys, one of whom walked on crutches, and behind them were ten other boys who walked two by two. These ten were a queer, ragged lot; but they had respectfully sober faces, held their heads and their shoulders well, and walked with a remarkably regular marching step.

It was the Squad; but they had left their 'rifles' at home.

CHAPTER 11

'Come with Me'

W H E N they came back from the graveyard, The Rat was silent all the way. He was thinking of what had happened and what lay before him. He was, in fact, thinking chiefly that nothing lay before him – nothing. The certainty of that gave his sharp, lined face new lines and sharpness which made it look pinched and hard. He had had nothing before but a corner in a bare garret in which he could find little more than a leaking roof over his head – when he was not turned out into the street. But, if policemen asked him where he lived, he could say he lived in Bone Court with his father. Now he couldn't say it.

He got along very well on his crutches, but he was rather tired when they reached the turn in the street which led in the direction of his old haunts. At any rate, they were haunts he knew, and he belonged to them more than he belonged elsewhere. The Squad stopped at this particular corner because it led to such homes as they possessed. They stopped in a body and looked at The Rat, and The Rat stopped also. He swung himself to Loristan's side, touching his hand to his forehead.

'Thank you, sir,' he said. 'Line and salute, you chaps!' And the Squad stood in line and raised their hands also. 'Thank you, sir. Thank you, Marco. Good-bye.'

'Where are you going?' Loristan asked.

'I don't know yet,' The Rat answered, biting his lips.

He and Loristan looked at each other a few moments in silence. Both of them were thinking very hard. In The Rat's eyes there was a kind of desperate adoration. He did not know what he should do when this man turned and walked away from him. It would be as if the sun itself had dropped out of the heavens – and The Rat had not thought of what the sun meant before.

But Loristan did not turn and walk away. He looked deep into the lad's eyes as if he were searching to find some certainty. Then he said in a low voice, 'You know how poor I am.'

'I – I don't care!' said The Rat. 'You – you're like a king to me. I'd stand up and be shot to bits if you told me to do it.'

'I am so poor that I am not sure that I can give you enough dry bread to eat – always. Marco and Lazarus and I are often hungry. Sometimes you might have nothing to sleep on but the floor. But I can find a *place* for you if I take you with me,' said Loristan. 'Do you know what I mean by a *place*?'

'Yes, I do,' answered The Rat. 'It's what I've never had before – sir.'

What he knew was that it meant some bit of space, out of all the world, where he would have a sort of right to stand, howsoever poor and bare it might be.

'I'm not used to beds or to food enough,' he said. But he did not dare to insist too much on that 'place'. It seemed too great a thing to be true.

Loristan took his arm.

'Come with me,' he said. 'We won't part. I believe you are to be trusted.'

The Rat turned quite white in a sort of anguish of joy. He had never cared for anyone in his life. He had been a sort of young Cain, his hand against every man and every man's hand against him. And during the last twelve hours he had plunged into a tumultuous ocean of boyish hero-worship. This man seemed like a sort of god to him. What he had said and done the day before, in what had been really The Rat's hour of extremity after that appalling night – the way he had looked into his face and under-stood it all, the talk at the table when he had listened to him seriously, actually respecting his plans and rough maps; his silent companionship as they followed the pauper hearse together – these things were enough to make the lad longingly ready to be any sort of servant or slave to him, if he might see and be spoken to by him even once or twice a day.

The Squad wore a look of dismay for a moment, and Loristan saw it.

'I am going to take your captain with me,' he said. 'But he will come back to Barracks. So will Marco.'

'Will yer go on with the game?' asked Cad, as eager spokesman. 'We want to go on being the "Secret Party".'

'Yes, I'll go on,' The Rat answered. 'I won't give it up. There's a lot in the papers today.'

So they were pacified and went on their way, and Loristan and Lazarus and Marco and The Rat went on theirs also.

'Queer thing is,' The Rat thought as they walked together. 'I'm a bit afraid to speak to him unless he speaks to me first. Never felt that way before with anyone.'

He had jeered at policemen and had impudently chaffed 'swells', but he felt a sort of secret awe of this man, and actually liked the feeling.

Loristan talked to him as they went. He was simple enough in his statements of the situation. There was an old sofa in Marco's bedroom. It was narrow and hard, as Marco's bed itself was, but The Rat could sleep upon it. They would share what food they had. There were newspapers and magazines to be read. There were papers and pencils to draw new maps and plans of battles. There was even an old map of Samavia of Marco's which the two boys could study together as an aid to their game. The Rat's eyes began to have points of fire in them.

'If I could see the papers every morning, I could fight the battles on paper by night,' he said, quite panting at the vision of splendour. Were all the kingdoms of the earth to be given to him? Was he going to sleep without a drunken father near him? Was he going to have a chance to wash himself and to sit at a table and hear people say 'Thank you', and 'I beg pardon', as if they were using the most ordinary fashion of speech? His own father, before he had sunk into the depths, had lived and spoken in this way.

'When I have time, we will see who can draw up the best plans,' Loristan said.

'Do you mean that you'll look at mine then – when you have time?' asked The Rat, hesitatingly. 'I wasn't expecting that.'

'Yes,' answered Loristan. 'I'll look at them, and we'll talk them over.'

As they went on, he told him that he and Marco could do many things together.

'My father said you wouldn't let him come back to Barracks when you found out about it,' The Rat said, hesitating again and growing hot because he remembered so many ugly past days. 'But – but I swear I won't do him any harm, sir.'

'When I said I believed you could be trusted, I meant several things,' Loristan answered him. 'That was one of them. You're a new recruit. You and Marco are both under a commanding officer.' He said the words because he knew they would elate him and stir his blood.

CHAPTER 12

'Only Two Boys'

T H E words did elate him, and his blood was stirred by them every time they returned to his mind. He sometimes awakened from his deep sleep on the hard and narrow sofa in Marco's room, and found that he was saying them half aloud to himself. The hardness of the sofa did not prevent his resting as he had never rested before in his life. By contrast with the past he had known, this poor existence was comfort which verged on luxury. He got into the battered tin bath every morning, he sat at the clean table, and could look at Loristan and speak to him and hear his voice. His chief trouble was that he could hardly keep his eyes off him, and he was a little afraid he might be annoyed. But he could not bear to lose a look or a movement.

At the end of the second day, he found his way, at some trouble, to Lazarus's small back room at the top of the house.

'Will you let me come in and talk a bit?' he said.

When he went in, he was obliged to sit on the top of Lazarus's wooden box because there was nothing else for him.

'I want to ask you,' he plunged into his talk at once, 'do you think he minds me looking at him so much? I can't help it – but if he hates it – well – I'll try and keep my eyes on the table.'

'The master is used to being looked at,' Lazarus made answer. 'But it would be well to ask himself. He likes open speech.'

'I want to find out everything he likes and everything he doesn't like,' The Rat said. 'I want – isn't there anything – anything you'd let me do for him? It wouldn't matter what it was. And he needn't know you are not doing it. I know you wouldn't be willing to give up anything particular. But you wait on him night and day. Couldn't you give up something to me?'

Lazarus pierced him with keen eyes. He did not answer for several seconds.

'Now and then,' he said gruffly at last, 'I'll let you brush his boots. But not every day – perhaps once a week.'

'When will you let me have my first turn?' The Rat asked.

Lazarus reflected. His shaggy eyebrows drew themselves down over his eyes as if this were a question of state.

'Next Saturday,' he conceded. 'Not before. I'll tell him when you brush them.'

'You needn't,' said The Rat. 'It's not that I want him to know. I want to know myself that I'm doing something for him. I'll find out things that I can do without interfering with you. I'll think them out.'

'Anything anyone else did for him would be interfering with me,' said Lazarus.

It was The Rat's turn to reflect now, and his face twisted itself into new lines and wrinkles.

'I'll tell you before I do anything,' he said, after he had thought it over. 'You served him first.'

'I have served him ever since he was born,' said Lazarus.

'He's – he's yours,' said The Rat, still thinking deeply.

'I am his,' was Lazarus's stern answer. 'I am his – and the young master's.'

'That's it,' The Rat said. Then a squeak of a half-laugh broke from him. 'I've never been anybody's,' he added.

His sharp eyes caught a passing look on Lazarus's face. Such a queer, disturbed, sudden look. Could he be rather sorry for him? Perhaps the look meant something like that.

'If you stay near him long enough – and it needn't be
long – you will be his too. Everybody is.'

The Rat sat up as straight as he could. 'When it comes
to that,' he blurted out, 'I'm his now, in my way. I was his
two minutes after he looked at me with his queer, handsome eyes. They're queer because they *get* you, and you
want to follow him. I'm going to follow.'

That night Lazarus recounted to his master the story of
the scene. He simply repeated word for word what had
been said, and Loristan listened gravely.

'We have not had time to learn much of him yet,' he
commented. 'But that is a faithful soul I think.'

A few days later, Marco missed The Rat soon after their
breakfast hour. He had gone out without saying anything
to the household. He did not return for several hours, and
when he came back he looked tired. In the afternoon he
fell asleep on his sofa in Marco's room and slept heavily.
No one asked him any questions as he volunteered no
explanation. The next day, he went out again in the same
mysterious manner, and the next and the next. For an
entire week he went out and returned with the tired look;
but he did not explain until one morning, as he lay on his
sofa before getting up, he said to Marco:

'I'm practising walking with my crutches. I don't want
to go about like a rat any more. I mean to be as near like
other people as I can. I walk farther every morning. I
began with two miles. If I practise every day, my crutches
will be like legs.'

'Shall I walk with you?' asked Marco.

'Wouldn't you mind walking with a cripple?'

'Don't call yourself that,' said Marco. 'We can talk together, and try to remember everything we see as we go
along.'

'I want to learn to remember things. I'd like to train
myself in that way too,' The Rat answered. 'I'd give anything to know some of the things your father taught you.

I've got a good memory. I remember a lot of things I don't want to remember. Will you go this morning?'

That morning they went, and Loristan was told the reason for their walk. But though he knew one reason, he did not know all about it. When The Rat was allowed his 'turn' of the boot-brushing, he told more to Lazarus.

'What I want to do,' he said, 'is not only to walk as fast as other people do, but faster. Acrobats train themselves to do anything. It's training that does it. There might come a time when he might need someone to go on an errand quickly, and I'm going to be ready. I'm going to train myself until he needn't think of me as if I were only a cripple who can't do things and has to be taken care of. I want him to know that I am really as strong as Marco, and where Marco can go I can go.'

'He' was what he always said, and Lazarus always understood without explanation.

' "The Master" is your name for him,' he had explained at the beginning. 'And I can't call him just "Mister" Loristan. It sounds like cheek. If he was called "General" or "Colonel" I could stand it – though it wouldn't be quite right. Some day I shall find a name. When I speak to him, I say "Sir".'

The walks were taken every day, and each day were longer. Marco found himself silently watching The Rat with amazement at his determination and endurance. He knew that he must not speak of what he could not fail to see as they walked. He must not tell him that he looked tired and pale and sometimes desperately fatigued. He had inherited from his father the tact which sees what people do not wish to be reminded of. He knew that for some reason of his own The Rat had determined to do this thing at any cost to himself. Sometimes his face grew white and worn and he breathed hard, but he never rested more than a few minutes and never turned back or shortened a walk they had planned.

'Tell me something about Samavia, something to re-member,' he would say, when he looked his worst. 'When I begin to try to remember, I forget – other things.'

So, as they went on their way, they talked, and The Rat committed things to memory. He was quick at it, and grew quicker every day. They invented a game of remem-bering faces they passed. Both would learn them by heart, and on their return home Marco would draw them. They went to the museums and galleries and learned things there, making from memory lists and descriptions which at night they showed to Loristan, when he was not too busy to talk to them.

As the days passed, Marco saw that The Rat was gain-ing strength. This exhilarated him greatly. They often went to Hampstead Heath and walked in the wind and sun. There The Rat would go through curious exercises which he believed would develop his muscles. He began to look less tired during and after his journey. There were even fewer wrinkles on his face, and his sharp eyes looked less fierce. The talks between the two boys were long and curious. Marco soon realized that The Rat wanted to learn – learn– learn.

'Your father can talk to you almost as if you were twenty years older,' he said once. 'He knows you can understand what he's saying. If he were to talk to me, he'd always have to remember that I was only a rat that lived in gutters and seen nothing else.'

They were talking in their room, as they nearly always did after they went to bed. They often sat up clasping their knees, Marco on his poor bed, The Rat on his hard sofa, but neither of them conscious either of the poorness or hardness, because to each one the long unknown sense of companionship was such a satisfying thing. Neither of them had ever talked intimately to another boy, and now they were together day and night. They revealed their thoughts to each other; they told each other things it had never before occurred to either to think of telling anyone. In fact, they found out about themselves, as they talked, things they had not quite known before. Marco had gradually discovered that the admiration The Rat had for his father was an impassioned and curious feeling which possessed him entirely. It seemed to Marco that it was beginning to be like a sort of religion. He evidently thought of him every moment. So when he spoke of Loristan's knowing him to be only a rat of the gutter, Marco felt he himself was fortunate in remembering something he could say.

'My father said yesterday that you had a big brain and a strong will,' he answered from his bed. 'He said that you had a wonderful memory which only needed exercising.'

The Rat shuffled on his sofa and clasped his knees tighter.

'Did he? Did he?' he said.

He rested his chin upon his knees for a few minutes and stared straight before him. Then he turned to the bed.

'Marco,' he said, in a rather hoarse voice, a queer voice; 'are you jealous?'

'Jealous?' said Marco; 'why?'

'I mean, have you ever been jealous? Do you know what it is like?'

'I don't think I do,' answered Marco, staring a little.

'Are you ever jealous of Lazarus because he's always with your father – because he's with him oftener than you are – and knows about his work – and can do things for him you can't?'

Marco loosed his arms from his knees and lay down flat on his pillow.

'No, I'm not. The more people love and serve him, the better,' he said. 'The only thing I care for is – is him. I just care for *him*. Lazarus does too. Don't you?'

The Rat was greatly excited internally. He had been thinking of this thing a great deal. The thought had sometimes terrified him. He might as well have it out now if he could. If he could get at the truth, everything would be easier. But would Marco really tell him?

'Don't you mind?' he said, still hoarse and eager – 'don't you mind how much *I* care for him? Could it ever make you feel savage? Could it ever set you thinking I was nothing but – what I am – and that it was cheek of me to push myself in and fasten on to a gentleman who only took me up for charity? Here's the living truth,' he ended in an outburst; 'if I were you and you were me, that's what I should be thinking. I know it is. I couldn't help it. I should see every low thing there was in you, in your manners and your voice and your looks. I should see nothing but the contrast between you and me and between you and him. I should be so jealous that I should just rage. I should *hate* you – and I should *despise* you!'

He had wrought himself up to such a passion of feeling that he set Marco thinking that what he was hearing meant strange and strong emotions such as he himself had never experienced. The Rat had been thinking over all this in secret for some time, it was evident. Marco lay still a few minutes and then he found something to say, just as he had found something before.

'You might, if you were with other people who thought in the same way,' he said, 'and if you hadn't found out that it is such a mistake to think in that way, that it's even stupid. But, you see, if you were me, you would have lived with my father, and he'd have told you what he knows – what he's been finding out all his life.'

'What's he found out?'

'Oh!' Marco answered, quite casually, 'just that you can't set savage thoughts loose in the world, any more than you can let loose savage beasts with hydrophobia. They spread a sort of rabies, and they always tear and worry you first of all.'

'What do you mean?' The Rat gasped out.

'It's like this,' said Marco, lying flat and cool on his hard pillow and looking at the reflection of the street lamp on the ceiling. 'That day I turned into your Barracks, without knowing that you'd think I was spying, it made you feel savage, and you threw the stone at me. If it had made me feel savage and I'd rushed in and fought, what would have happened to all of us?'

The Rat's spirit of generalship gave the answer.

'I should have called on the Squad to charge with fixed bayonets. They'd have half killed you. You're a strong chap, and you'd have hurt a lot of them.'

A note of terror broke into his voice. 'What a fool I should have been!' he cried out. 'I should never have come here! I should never have known *him*!' Even by the light of the street lamp Marco could see him begin to turn ghastly.

'The Squad could easily have half killed me,' Marco added. 'They could have quite killed me, if they had wanted to do it. And who would have got any good out of it? It would only have been a street-lads' row – with the police and prison at the end of it.'

'But because you'd lived with him,' The Rat pondered, 'you walked in as if you didn't mind, and just asked why we did it, and looked like a stronger chap than any of us – and different – different. I wondered what was the matter with you, you were so cool and steady. I know now. It was because you were like him. He'd taught you. He's like a wizard.'

'He knows things that wizards think they know, but he knows them better,' Marco said. 'He says they're not queer and unnatural. They're just simple laws of nature. You have to be either on one side or the other, like an army. You choose your side. You either build up or you tear down. You either keep in the light where you can see, or you stand in the dark and fight everything that comes near you, because you can't see and you think it's an enemy.'

'And you're *not* jealous?' The Rat's sharp voice was almost hollow. 'You'll swear you're not?'

'I'm not,' said Marco.

The Rat's excitement even increased a shade as he poured forth his confession.

'I was afraid,' he said. 'I've been afraid every day since I came here. It seemed natural that you and Lazarus wouldn't stand me, just as I wouldn't have stood you. It seemed natural that you'd work together to throw me out. Marco – I'll tell you straight out – I'm jealous of you. I'm jealous of Lazarus. It makes me wild when I see you both knowing all about him, and fit and ready to do anything he wants done. I'm not ready and I'm not fit.'

'You'd do anything he wanted done, whether you were fit and ready or not,' said Marco. 'He knows that.'

'Does he? Do you think he does?' cried The Rat. 'I wish he'd try me. I wish he would.'

Marco turned over on his bed and rose up on his elbow so that he faced The Rat on his sofa.

'Let us *wait*,' he said in a whisper. 'Let us *wait*.'

There was a pause, and then The Rat whispered also. 'For what?'

'For him to find out that we're fit to be tried. Don't you see what fools we should be if we spent our time in being jealous, either of us? We're only two boys. Suppose he saw we were only two silly fools. When you are jealous of me or of Lazarus, just go and sit down in a still place and think of *him*. Don't think about yourself or about us. He's so quiet that to think about him makes you quiet yourself. When things go wrong or when I'm lonely, he's taught me to sit down and make myself think of things I like – pictures, books, monuments, splendid places. It pushes the other things out and sets your mind going properly. He doesn't know I nearly always think of him. He's the best thought himself. You try it. You're not really jealous. You only *think* you are. You'll find that out if you always stop yourself in time. Anyone can be such a fool if he lets himself. And he can always stop it if he makes up his mind.'

The Rat caught his breath and threw his arms up over his eyes. 'Oh Lord! Oh Lord!' he said; 'if I'd lived near him always as you have. If I just had.'

'We're both living near him now,' said Marco. 'And here's something to think of,' leaning more forward on his elbow. 'The kings who were being made ready for Samavia have waited all these years; *we* can make ourselves ready and wait so that, if just two boys are wanted to do something – just two boys – we can step out of the ranks when the call comes and say "Here!" Now let's lie down and think of it until we go to sleep.'

CHAPTER 13

Loristan Attends a Drill of the Squad and Marco Meets a Samavian

THE Squad was not forgotten. It found that Loristan himself would have regarded neglect as a breach of military duty.

'You must remember your men,' he said, two or three days after The Rat became a member of his household. 'You must keep up their drill. Marco tells me it was very smart. Don't let them get slack.'

'His men!' The Rat felt what he could not have put into words. He knew he had worked, and that the Squad had worked, in their hidden holes and corners. Only hidden holes and corners had been possible for them. They had tried many refuges before they found the Barracks. No one but resented the existence of a troop of noisy vagabonds. But somehow this man knew that there had evolved from it something more than mere noisy play, that he, The Rat, had *meant* order and discipline.

'His men!' It made him feel as if he had had the Victoria Cross fastened on his coat. He had brain enough to see many things, and he knew that it was in this way that Loristan was finding him his 'place'. He knew now.

When they went to the Barracks, the Squad greeted them with a tumultuous welcome which expressed a great sense of relief. Privately the members had been filled with fears which they had talked over together in deep gloom. Marco's father, they decided, was too big a swell to let the two come back after he had seen the sort the Squad was made up of. He might be poor just now, toffs sometimes lost their money for a bit, but you could see what he was, and fathers like him weren't going to let their sons make friends with 'such as us'. He'd stop the drill and the 'Secret Society' game. That's what he'd do!

But The Rat came swinging in on his secondhand crutches looking as if he had been made a general, and Marco came with him; and the drill the Squad was put through was stricter than any drill they had ever known.

'I wish my father could have seen that,' Marco said to The Rat.

The Rat turned red and white and then red again, but he said not a single word. The mere thought was like a flash of fire passing through him. But no fellow could hope for a thing as big as that. The Secret Party, in its subterranean cavern, surrounded by its piled arms, sat down to read the morning paper.

The war news was bad to read. The Maranovitch held the day for the moment, and while they suffered and wrought cruelties in the capital city, the Iarovitch suffered and wrought cruelties in the country outside. So fierce and dark was the record that Europe stood aghast.

The Rat folded his paper when he had finished, and sat biting his nails. Having done this for a few minutes, he began to speak in his dramatic and hollow Secret Party whisper.

'The hour has come,' he said to his followers. 'The messengers must go forth. They know nothing of what they go for; they only know that they must obey. If they were caught and tortured, they could betray nothing because they know nothing but that, at certain places, they must utter a certain word. They carry no papers. All commands they must learn by heart. When the sign is given, the Secret Party will know what to do – where to meet and where to attack.'

He drew plans of the battle on the flagstones, and he sketched an imaginary route which the two messengers were to follow. But his knowledge of the map of Europe was not worth much, and he turned to Marco.

'You know more about geography than I do. You know more about everything,' he said. 'I only know Italy is at the bottom and Russia is at one side and England's at the other. How would the Secret Messengers go to Samavia? Can you draw the countries they'd have to pass through?'

Because any schoolboy who knew the map could have done the same thing, Marco drew them. He also knew the stations the Secret Two would arrive at and leave by when they entered a city, the streets they would walk through and the very uniforms they would see; but of these things he said nothing. The reality his knowledge gave to the game was a thrilling thing. He wished he could have been free to explain to The Rat the things he knew. Together they could have worked out so many details of travel and possible adventure that it would have been almost as if they had set out on their journey in fact.

As it was, the mere sketching of the route fired The Rat's imagination. He forged ahead with the story of adventure, and filled it with such mysterious purport and design that the Squad at times gasped for breath. In his glowing version the Secret Two entered cities by midnight and sang and begged at palace gates where kings driving outward paused to listen and were given the Sign.

'Though it would not always be kings,' he said. 'Sometimes it would be the poorest people. Sometimes they might seem to be beggars like ourselves, when they were only Secret Ones disguised. A great lord might wear poor clothes and pretend to be a workman, and we should only know him by the signs we had learned by heart. When we were sent to Samavia, we should be obliged to creep in through some back part of the country where no fighting was being done and where no one would attack. Two boys could find a way in if they thought it out.'

He became possessed by the idea of thinking it out on the spot. He drew his rough map of Samavia on the flagstones with his chalk.

'Look here,' he said to Marco, who, with the elated and thrilled Squad, bent over it in a close circle of heads. 'Beltrazo is here and Carnolitz is here – and here is Jiardasia. Beltrazo and Jiardasia are friendly, though they don't take sides. All the fighting is going on in the country about Melzarr. There is no reason why they should prevent single travellers from coming in across the frontiers of friendly neighbours. They're not fighting with the countries outside, they are fighting with themselves.' He paused a moment and thought.

'The article in that magazine said something about a huge forest on the eastern frontier. That's here. We could wander into a forest and stay there until we'd planned all we wanted to do. Even the people who had seen us would forget about us. What we have to do is to make people feel as if we were nothing – nothing.'

They were in the very midst of it, crowded together, leaning over, stretching necks and breathing quickly with excitement, when Marco lifted his head. Some mysterious impulse made him do it in spite of himself.

'There's my father!' he said.

The chalk dropped, everything dropped, even Samavia. The Rat was up and on his crutches as if some magic force had swung him there. How he gave the command, or if he gave it at all, not even he himself knew. But the Squad stood at salute.

Loristan was standing at the opening of the archway as Marco had stood that first day. He raised his right hand in return salute and came forward.

'I was passing the end of the street and remembered the Barracks was here,' he explained. 'I thought I should like to look at your men, Captain.'

He smiled, but it was not a smile which made his words really a joke. He looked down at the chalk map drawn on the flagstones.

'You know that map well,' he said. 'Even I can see that it is Samavia. What is the Secret Party doing?'

'The messengers are trying to find a way in,' answered Marco.

'We can get in there,' said The Rat, pointing with a crutch. 'There's a forest where we could hide and find out things.'

'Reconnoitre,' said Loristan, looking down. 'Yes. Two stray boys could be very safe in a forest. It's a good game.'

That he should be there! That he should, in his own wonderful way, have given them such a thing as this. That he should have cared enough even to look up the Barracks, was what The Rat was thinking. A batch of ragamuffins they were and nothing else, and he standing looking at them with his fine smile. The Rat's heart thumped with startled joy.

'Father,' said Marco, 'will you watch The Rat drill us? I want you to see how well it is done.'

'Captain, will you do me that honour?' Loristan said to The Rat, and to even these words he gave the right tone, neither jesting nor too serious. Because it was so right a tone, The Rat's pulses beat only with exultation. This god of his had looked at his maps, he had talked of his plans, he had come to see the soldiers who were his work! The Rat began his drill as if he had been reviewing an army.

What Loristan saw done was wonderful in its mechanical exactness. The Squad moved like the perfect parts of a perfect machine. That they could so do it in such space, and that they should have accomplished such precision, was an extraordinary testimonial to the military efficiency and curious qualities of this one hunchbacked, vagabond officer.

'That is magnificent!' the spectator said, when it was over. 'It could not be better done. Allow me to congratulate you.'

He shook The Rat's hand as if it had been a man's, and, after he had shaken it, he put his own hand lightly on the boy's shoulder and let it rest there as he talked a few minutes to them all.

The Squad was elated. Sometimes you couldn't understand toffs when they made a shy at being friendly, but you could understand him, and he stirred up your spirits. After the few minutes were over, he went away. Then they sat down again in their circle and talked about him, because they could talk and think about nothing else. They stared at Marco furtively, feeling as if he were a creature of another world because he had lived with this man.

'When you said you wished your father could have seen the drill,' said The Rat, 'you took my breath away. I'd never have had the cheek to think of it. And he came himself! It struck me dumb.'

'If he came,' said Marco, 'it was because he wanted to see it.'

When they had finished talking, it was time for Marco and The Rat to go on their way. Loristan had given The Rat an errand. At a certain hour he was to present himself at a certain shop and receive a package.

'Let him do it alone,' Loristan said to Marco. 'He will be better pleased. His desire is to feel that he is trusted to do things alone.'

So they parted at the corner. Marco turned into one of the better streets, through which he often passed on his way home. It was not a fashionable quarter, but it contained some respectable houses in whose windows here and there were to be seen neat cards bearing the word 'Apartments', which meant that the owner of the house would let to lodgers his drawing-room or sitting-room suite.

As Marco walked up the street, he saw someone come out of the door of one of the houses and walk quickly and lightly down the pavement. It was a young woman wearing an elegant though quiet dress, and a hat which looked as if it had been bought in Paris or Vienna. She had, in fact, a slightly foreign air, and it was this which made Marco look at her long enough to see that she was also a graceful and lovely person. He wondered what her nationality was. Even at some yards' distance he could see that she had long dark eyes and a curved mouth which seemed to be smiling to itself. He thought she might be Spanish or Italian.

He was trying to decide which of the two countries she belonged to, as she drew near to him, but quite suddenly the curved mouth ceased smiling as her foot seemed to catch in a break in the pavement, and she so lost her balance that she would have fallen if he had not leaped forward and caught her.

She was light and slender, and he was a strong lad and managed to steady her. An expression of sharp momentary anguish crossed her face.

'I hope you are not hurt,' Marco said.

She bit her lip and clutched his shoulder hard with her slim hand.

'I have twisted my ankle,' she answered. 'I am afraid I have twisted it badly. Thank you for saving me. I should have had a bad fall.'

Her long, dark eyes were very sweet and grateful. She tried to smile, but there was such distress under the effort that Marco was afraid she must have hurt herself very much.

'Can you stand on your foot at all?' he asked.

'I can stand a little now,' she said, 'but I might not be able to stand in a few minutes. I must get back to the house while I can bear to touch the ground with it. I am so sorry. I am afraid I shall have to ask you to go with me. Fortunately it is only a few yards away.'

'Yes,' Marco answered. 'I saw you come out of the

house. If you will lean on my shoulder, I can soon help you back. I am glad to do it. Shall we try now?'

She had a gentle and soft manner which would have appealed to any boy. Her voice was musical and her enunciation exquisite. Whether she was Spanish or Italian, it was easy to imagine her a person who did not always live in London lodgings, even of the better class.

'If you please,' she answered him. 'It is very kind of you. You are very strong, I see. But I am glad to have only a few steps to go.'

She rested on his shoulder as well as on her umbrella, but it was plain that every movement gave her intense pain. She caught her lip with her teeth, and Marco thought she turned white. He could not help liking her. She was so lovely and gracious and brave. He could not bear to see the suffering in her face.

'I am so sorry!' he said, as he helped her, and his boy's voice had something of the wonderful sympathetic tone of Loristan's. The beautiful lady herself remarked it, and thought how unlike it was to the ordinary boy-voice.

'I have a latch-key,' she said, when they stood on the low step.

She found it in her purse and opened the door. Marco helped her into the entrance-hall. She sat down at once in a chair near the hat-stand. The place was quite plain and old-fashioned inside.

'Shall I ring the front door-bell to call someone?' Marco inquired.

'I am afraid that the servants are out,' she answered. 'They had a holiday. Will you kindly close the door? I shall be obliged to ask you to help me into the sitting-room at the end of the hall. I shall find all I want there – if you will kindly hand me a few things. Someone may come in presently – perhaps one of the other lodgers – and, even if I am alone for an hour or so, it will not really matter.'

'Perhaps I can find the landlady,' Marco suggested. The beautiful person smiled.

'She has gone to her sister's wedding. That is why I was going out to spend the day myself. I arranged the plan to accommodate her. How good you are! I shall be quite comfortable directly. I can get to my easy-chair in the sitting-room now I have rested a little.'

Marco helped her to her feet, and her sharp exclamation of pain made him wince internally. Perhaps it was a worse sprain than she knew.

The house was of the early-Victorian London order. A 'front lobby' with a dining-room on the right hand, and a 'back lobby', after the foot of the stairs was passed, out of which opened the basement kitchen staircase and a sitting-room looking out on a gloomy flagged back yard enclosed by high walls. The sitting-room was rather gloomy itself, but there were a few luxurious things among the ordinary furnishings. There was an easy-chair with a small table near it, and on the table were a silver lamp and some rather elegant trifles. Marco helped his charge to the easy-chair and put a cushion from the sofa under her foot. He did it very gently, and, as he rose after doing it, he saw that the long, soft dark eyes were looking at him in a curious way.

'I must go away now,' he said, 'but I do not like to leave you. May I go for a doctor?'

'How dear you are!' she exclaimed. 'But I do not want one, thank you. I know exactly what to do for a sprained ankle. And perhaps mine is not really a sprain. I am going to take off my shoe and see.'

'May I help you?' Marco asked, and he kneeled down again and carefully unfastened her shoe and withdrew it from her foot. It was a slender and delicate foot in a silk stocking, and she bent and gently touched it and rubbed it.

'No,' she said, when she raised herself, 'I do not think it

is a sprain. Now that the shoe is off and the foot rests on the cushion, it is much more comfortable. Thank you, thank you. If you had not been passing I might have had a dangerous fall.'

'I am very glad to have been able to help you,' Marco answered, with an air of relief. 'Now I must go, if you think you will be all right.'

'Don't go yet,' she said, holding out her hand. 'I should like to know you a little better, if I may. I am so grateful. I should like to talk to you. You have such beautiful manners for a boy,' she ended, with a pretty, kind laugh, 'and I believe I know where you got them from.'

'You are very kind to me,' Marco answered, wondering if he did not redden a little. 'But I must go because my father will –'

'Your father would let you stay and talk to me,' she said, with even a prettier kindliness than before. 'It is from him you have inherited your beautiful manner. He was once a friend of mine. I hope he is my friend still, though perhaps he has forgotten me.'

All that Marco had ever learned and all that he had ever trained himself to remember, rushed back upon him now. Here was a beautiful lady of whom he knew nothing at all but that she had twisted her foot in the street and he had helped her back into her house. If silence was still the order, it was not for him to know things or ask questions or answer them.

'I do not think my father ever forgets anyone,' he answered.

'No, I am sure he does not,' she said softly. 'Has he been to Samavia during the last three years?'

Marco paused a moment.

'Perhaps I am not the boy you think I am,' he said. 'My father has never been to Samavia.'

'He has not? But – you are Marco Loristan?'

'Yes. That is my name.'

Suddenly she leaned forward and her long lovely eyes filled with fire.

'Then you are a Samavian, and you know of the disasters overwhelming us. You know all the hideousness and barbarity of what is being done. Your father's son must know all!'

'Everyone knows it,' said Marco.

'But it is your country – your own! Your blood must burn in your veins!'

Marco stood quite still and looked at her. His eyes told whether his blood burned or not, but he did not speak. His look was answer enough, since he did not wish to say anything.

'What does your father think? I am a Samavian myself, and I think night and day. What does he think of the rumour about the descendant of the Lost Prince? Does he believe it?' eagerly.

Marco was thinking rapidly. Her beautiful face was glowing with emotion, her beautiful voice trembled. That she should be Samavian, and love Samavia, and pour her feeling forth even to a boy, was deeply moving to him. But howsoever one was moved, one must remember that silence was still the order.

'It might be only a newspaper story,' he said. 'He says one cannot trust such things. If you know him, you know he is very calm.'

'Has he taught you to be calm too?' she said pathetically. 'You are only a boy. Boys are not calm. Neither are women when their hearts are wrung. Oh, my Samavia! Oh, my poor little country! My brave, tortured country!' and with a sudden sob she covered her face with her hands.

A great lump mounted to Marco's throat. Boys could not cry, but he knew what she meant when she said her heart was wrung.

When she lifted her head, the tears in her eyes made them softer than ever.

'If I were a million Samavians instead of one woman, I should know what to do!' she cried. 'If your father were a million Samavians, he would know, too. He would find Ivor's descendant, if he is on the earth, and he would end all this horror!'

'Who would not end it if they could?' cried Marco, quite fiercely.

'But men like your father, men who are Samavians, must think night and day about it as I do,' she insisted. 'You see, I cannot help pouring my thoughts out even to a boy – because he is a Samavian. Only Samavians care. Samavia seems so little and unimportant to other people. Men like your father must think, and plan, and feel that they must – must find a way. Even a woman feels it. Even a boy must. He cannot be sitting quietly at home, knowing that Samavian hearts are being shot through and Samavian blood poured forth. He cannot think and say *nothing*!'

Marco started in spite of himself. He felt as if his father had been struck in the face. How dare she say such words! Big as he was, suddenly he looked bigger, and the lady saw that he did.

'He is my father,' he said slowly.

She was a clever, beautiful person, and saw that she had made a great mistake.

'You must forgive me,' she exclaimed. 'I used the wrong words because I was excited. I meant that I knew he was giving his heart and strength, his whole being, to Samavia, even though he must stay in London.'

She started and turned her head to listen to the sound of someone using the latch-key and opening the front door. Then someone came in with the heavy step of a man.

'It is one of the lodgers,' she said. 'I think it is the one who lives in the third-floor sitting-room.'

'Then you won't be alone when I go,' said Marco. 'I am

glad someone has come. May I tell my father your name?'

'Tell me that you are not angry with me for expressing myself so awkwardly,' she said.

'You couldn't have meant it. I know that,' Marco answered boyishly. 'You couldn't.'

'No, I couldn't,' she repeated, with the same emphasis on the words.

She took a card from a silver case on the table and gave it to him.

'Your father will remember my name,' she said, 'I hope he will let me see him and tell him how you took care of me.'

She shook his hand warmly and let him go. But just as he reached the door she spoke again.

'Oh, may I ask you to do one thing more before you leave me?' she said suddenly. 'I hope you won't mind. Will you run upstairs into the drawing-room and bring me the purple book from the small table? I shall not mind being alone if I have something to read.'

'A purple book? On a small table?' said Marco.

'Between the two long windows,' she smiled back at him.

The drawing-room of such houses as these is always to be reached by one short flight of stairs.

Marco ran up lightly.

CHAPTER 14

Marco does not Answer

By the time he turned the corner of the stairs, the lady had risen from her seat in the back room and walked into the dining-room at the front. A heavily built, dark-bearded man was standing inside the door as if waiting for her.

'I could do nothing with him,' she said at once, in her soft voice, speaking quite prettily and gently, as if what she said was the most natural thing in the world. 'I managed the little trick of the sprained foot really well, and got him into the house. He is an amiable boy with perfect manners, and I thought it might be easy to surprise him into saying more than he knew he was saying. You can generally do that with young things. But he either knows nothing or has been trained to hold his tongue. He's not stupid, and he's of a high spirit. I made a pathetic little scene about Samavia, because I saw he could be worked up. It did work him up. I tried him with the Lost Prince rumour; but, if there is truth in it, he does not or will not know. I tried to make him lose his temper and betray something in defending his father, but I made a mistake. I saw that. It's a pity. Boys can sometimes be made to tell anything.' She spoke very quickly under her breath. The man spoke quickly too.

'Where is he?' he asked.

'I sent him up to the drawing-room to look for a book. He will look for a few minutes. Listen. He's an innocent boy. He sees me only as a gentle angel. Nothing will *shake* him so much as to hear me tell him the truth suddenly. It will be such a shock to him that perhaps you can do something with him then. He may lose his hold on himself.'

'You're right,' said the bearded man. 'And when he finds out he is not free to go, it may alarm him and we may get something worth while.'

'If we could find out what is true, or what Loristan thinks is true, we should have a clue to work from,' she said.

'We have not much time,' the man whispered. 'We are ordered to Bosnia at once. Before midnight we must be on the way.'

'Let us go into the other room. He is coming.'

When Marco entered the room, the heavily built man with the pointed dark beard was standing by the easy-chair.

'I am sorry I could not find the book,' he apologized. 'I looked on all the tables.'

'I shall be obliged to go and search for it myself,' said the Lovely Person.

She rose from her chair and stood up smiling. And at her first movement Marco saw that she was not disabled in the least.

'Your foot!' he exclaimed. 'It's better?'

'It wasn't hurt,' she answered, in her softly pretty voice and with her softly pretty smile. 'I only made you think so.'

It was part of her plan to spare him nothing of shock in her sudden transformation. Marco felt his breath leave him for a moment.

'I made you believe I was hurt because I wanted you to come into the house with me,' she added. 'I wished to find out certain things I am sure you know.'

'They were things about Samavia,' said the man. 'Your father knows them, and you must know something of them at least. It is necessary that we should hear what you can tell us. We shall not allow you to leave the house until you have answered certain questions I shall ask you.'

Then Marco began to understand. He had heard his father speak of political spies. He knew it was their work to search out secrets, to disguise themselves and live among innocent people as if they were merely ordinary neighbours.

They must be spies who were paid to follow his father because he was a Samavian and a patriot. He did not know that they had taken the house two months before, had discovered Loristan and had learned to know his outgoings and incomings. They meant, if possible, to learn other things. If the boy could be startled and terrified into unconscious revelations, it might prove well worth their while to have played this bit of melodrama before they locked the front door behind them and hastily crossed the Channel leaving their landlord to discover for himself that the house had been vacated.

In Marco's mind strange things were happening. They were spies! But that was not all. The Lovely Person had been right when she said that he would receive a shock. His strong young chest swelled. In all his life, he had never come face to face with black treachery before. He could not grasp it. This gentle and friendly being with the grateful soft voice and grateful soft eyes had betrayed – *betrayed* him! It seemed impossible to believe it, and yet the smile on her curved mouth told him that it was true. When he had sprung to help her, she had been playing a trick! When he had been sorry for her pain and had winced at the sound of her low exclamation, she had been deliberately laying a trap to harm him. For a few seconds he was stunned – perhaps, if he had not been his father's son, he might have been stunned only. But he was more. When the first few seconds had passed, there arose slowly within him a sense of something like high, remote disdain. It grew in his deep boy's eyes as he gazed directly into the pupils of the long soft dark ones. His body felt as if it were growing taller.

'You are very clever,' he said slowly. Then, after a

second's pause, he added, 'I was too young to know that there was anyone so – clever – in the world.'

The Lovely Person laughed, but she did not laugh easily. She spoke to her companion.

'A *grand seigneur*!' she said. 'As one looks at him, one half believes it is true.'

The man with the beard was looking very angry. His eyes were savage and his dark skin reddened. Marco thought that he looked at him as if he hated him, and was made fierce by the mere sight of him.

'Two days before you left Moscow,' he said, 'three men came to see your father. They looked like peasants. They talked to him for more than an hour. They brought with them a roll of parchment. Is that not true?'

'I know nothing,' said Marco.

'Before you went to Moscow, you were in Budapest. You went there from Vienna. You were there for three months, and your father saw many people. Some of them came in the middle of the night.'

'I know nothing,' said Marco.

'You have spent your life in travelling from one country to another,' persisted the man. 'You know the European languages as if you were a courier, or the *portier* in a Viennese hotel. Do you not?' insultingly.

Marco did not answer.

The Lovely Person began to speak to the man rapidly in Russian.

'A spy and an adventurer Stefan Loristan has always been and always will be,' she said. 'We know what he is. The police in every capital in Europe know him as a sharper and a vagabond, as well as a spy. And yet, with all his cleverness, he does not seem to have money. What did he do with the bribe the Maranovitch gave him for betraying what he knew of the old fortress? The boy doesn't even suspect him. Perhaps it's true that he knows nothing. Or perhaps it is true that he has been so ill-treated and

flogged from his babyhood that he dare not speak. There
is a cowed look in his eyes in spite of his childish swagger.
He's been both starved and beaten.'

The outburst was well done. She did not look at Marco
as she poured forth her words. She spoke with the abrupt-
ness and impetuosity of a person whose feelings had got
the better of her. If Marco was sensitive about his father,
she felt sure that his youth would make his face reveal
something if his tongue did not – if he understood Russian, which was one of the things it would be useful to
find out.

Marco's face disappointed her. No change took place in
it, and the blood did not rise to the surface of his skin. He
listened with an uninterested air, blank and cold and
polite. Let them say what they chose.

The man twisted his pointed beard and shrugged his
shoulders.

'We have a good little wine-cellar downstairs,' he said.
'You are going down into it, and you will probably stay
there for some time if you do not make up your mind to
answer my questions. You think that nothing can happen
to you in a house in a London street where policemen
walk up and down. But you are mistaken. If you yelled
now, even if anyone chanced to hear you, they would only
think you were a lad getting a thrashing he deserved. You
can yell as much as you like in the black little wine-cellar,
and no one will hear at all. We only took this house for
three months, and we shall leave it tonight without men-
tioning the fact to anyone. If we choose to leave you in
the wine-cellar, you will wait there until somebody begins
to notice that no one goes in and out, and chances to
mention it to the landlord – which few people would take
the trouble to do. Did you come here from Moscow?'

'I know nothing,' said Marco.

'You might remain in the good little black cellar an
unpleasantly long time before you were found,' the man

went on, quite coolly. 'Do you remember the peasants who came to see your father two nights before you left?'.

'I know nothing,' said Marco.

'By the time it was discovered that the house was empty and people came in to make sure, you might be too weak to call out and attract their attention. Did you go to Budapest from Vienna, and were you there for three months?' asked the inquisitor.

'I know nothing,' said Marco.

'You are too good for the little black cellar,' put in the Lovely Person. 'I like you. Don't go into it!'

'I know nothing,' Marco answered, but the eyes which were like Loristan's gave her just such a look as Loristan would have given her, and she felt it. It made her uncomfortable.

'I don't believe you were ever ill-treated or beaten,' she said. 'I tell you, the little black cellar will be a hard thing. Don't go there!'

And this time Marco said nothing, but looked at her still as if he were some great young noble who was very proud.

He knew that every word the bearded man had spoken was true. To cry out would be of no use. If they went away and left him behind them, there was no knowing how many days would pass before the people of the neighbourhood would begin to suspect that the place had been deserted. And in the meantime, neither his father nor Lazarus nor The Rat would have the faintest reason for guessing where he was. And he would be sitting alone in the dark in the wine-cellar. He did not know in the least what to do about this thing. He only knew that silence was still the order.

'It is a jet-black little hole,' the man said. 'You might crack your throat in it, and no one would hear. Did men come to talk with your father in the middle of the night when you were in Vienna?'

'I know nothing,' said Marco.

'He won't tell,' said the Lovely Person. 'I am sorry for this boy.'

'He may tell after he has sat in the good little black wine-cellar for a few hours,' said the man with the pointed beard. 'Come with me!'

He put his powerful hand on Marco's shoulder and pushed him before him. Marco made no struggle. He remembered what his father had said about the game not being a game. It wasn't a game now, but somehow he had a strong haughty feeling of not being afraid.

He was taken through the hallway, towards the rear, and down the flagged steps which led to the basement. Then he was marched through a narrow, ill-lighted passage to a door which stood a trifle ajar. His companion pushed it farther open and showed part of a wine-cellar which was so dark that it was only the shelves nearest the door that Marco could faintly see. His captor pushed him in and shut the door. It was as black a hole as he had described. Marco stood still in the midst of darkness like black velvet. His guard turned the key.

'The peasants who came to your father in Moscow spoke Samavian and were big men. Do you remember them?' he asked from outside.

'I know nothing,' answered Marco.

'You are a young fool,' the voice replied. 'Your father will be greatly troubled when you do not come home. I will come back to see you in a few hours, if it is possible. I will tell you, however, that I have had disturbing news which might make it necessary for us to leave in a hurry. I might not have time to come down here again.'

Marco stood with his back against a bit of wall and remained silent.

There was stillness for a few minutes, and then the sound of footsteps marching away.

When the last distant echo died all was silent, and

Marco drew a long breath. Unbelievable as it may appear, it was in one sense almost a breath of relief. In the rush of strange feeling which had swept over him when he found himself facing the astounding situation upstairs, it had not been easy to realize what his thoughts really were; there were so many of them and they came so fast. How could he quite believe the evidence of his eyes and ears? A few minutes, only a few minutes, had changed his grateful acquaintance into a subtle and cunning creature whose love for Samavia had been part of a plot to harm it and his father.

What did she and her companion want to do – what could they do if they knew the things they were trying to force him to tell?

Marco braced his back against the wall stoutly.

'What will it be best to think about first?'

One of the most fascinating things he and his father talked about together was the power of the thoughts which human beings allowed to pass through their minds – the strange strength of them. When they talked of this, Marco felt as if he were listening to some marvellous Eastern story of magic which was true. In Loristan's travels, he had visited the far Oriental countries, and he had seen and learned many things which seemed marvels. He had known, and reasoned through days with men who believed that when they desired a thing, clear and exalted thought would bring it to them.

What he himself believed, he had taught Marco quite simply from his childhood. It was this: he himself – Marco, with the strong boy-body, the thick mat of black hair, and the patched clothes – was the magician. He held and waved his wand himself – and his wand was his own Thought. When special privation or anxiety beset them, it was their rule to say, 'What will it be best to think about first?' which was Marco's reason for saying it to himself now as he stood in the darkness which was like black velvet.

He waited a few minutes for the right thing to come to him.

'I am not afraid,' Marco said aloud. 'I shall not be afraid. In some way I shall get out.'

This was the image he wanted most to keep steadily in his mind – that nothing could make him afraid, and that in some way he could get out of the wine-cellar.

He thought of this for some minutes, and said the words over several times. He felt more like himself when he had done it.

'When my eyes are accustomed to the darkness, I shall see if there is any little glimmer of light anywhere,' he said next.

He waited with patience, and it seemed for some time that he saw no glimmer at all. He put out his hands on either side of him, and found that, on the side of the wall against which he stood, there seemed to be no shelves. Perhaps the cellar had been used for other purposes than the storing of wine, and, if that was true, there might be somewhere some opening for ventilation. The air was not bad, but then the door had not been shut tightly when the man opened it.

'I am not afraid,' he repeated, 'I shall not be afraid. In some way I shall get out.'

He would not allow himself to stop and think about his father waiting for his return. He knew that would only arouse his emotions and weaken his courage. He began to feel his way carefully along the wall. It reached farther than he had thought it would. The cellar was not so very small. He crept round it gradually, and then he made his way across it, keeping his hands extended before him and setting down each foot cautiously. Then he sat down on the stone floor and thought again, and what he thought was that there was a way out of this place for him, and he should somehow find it, and, before too long a time had passed, be walking in the street again.

It was while he was thinking in this way that he felt a startling thing. It seemed almost as if something touched him. It made him jump, though the touch was so light and soft that it was scarcely a touch at all, in fact he could not be sure that he had not imagined it. He stood up and leaned against the wall again. Perhaps the suddenness of his movement placed him at some angle he had not reached before, or perhaps his eyes had become more completely accustomed to the darkness, for, as he turned his head to listen, he made a discovery: above the door there was a place where the velvet blackness was not so dense. There was something like a slit in the wall, though, as it did not open upon daylight but upon the dark passage, it was not light it admitted so much as a lesser shade of darkness. But even that was better than nothing, and Marco drew another long breath.

'That is only the beginning. I shall find a way out,' he said. 'I *shall*.'

He remembered reading a story of a man who, being shut by accident in a safety vault, passed through such terrors before his release that he believed he had spent two days and nights in the place when he had been there only a few hours.

'His thoughts did that. I must remember. I will sit down again and begin thinking of all the pictures in the cabinet rooms of the Art History Museum in Vienna. It will take some time, and then there are the others,' he said.

It was a good plan. While he could keep his mind upon the game, he could think of nothing else, as it required close attention – and perhaps, as the day went on, his captors would begin to feel that it was not safe to run the risk of doing a thing as desperate as this would be. They might think better of it before they left the house at least.

He had walked in imagination through three of the cabinet rooms and was turning mentally into a fourth, when he found himself starting again quite violently. This time it was not at a touch but at a sound. Surely it was a sound. And it was in the cellar with him. But it was the tiniest possible noise, a ghost of a squeak and a suggestion of a movement. It came from the opposite side of the cellar, the side where the shelves were. He looked across in the darkness, and in the darkness saw a light which there could be no mistake about. It *was* a light, two lights indeed, two round phosphorescent greenish balls. They were two eyes staring at him. And then he heard another sound. Not a squeak this time, but something so homely and comfortable that he actually burst out laughing. It was a cat purring, a nice warm cat! And she was curled up on one of the lower shelves purring to some new-born kittens. He knew there were kittens because it was plain now what the tiny squeak had been, and it was made plainer by the fact that he heard another much more distinct one and then another. They had all been asleep when he had come into the cellar. If the mother had been awake, she had probably been very much afraid. Afterwards she had perhaps come down from her shelf to investigate, and had passed close to him. The feeling of relief which came upon him at this simple discovery was wonderful. It was so natural and comfortable an everyday thing that it seemed to make spies and criminals unreal, and only natural things possible. With a mother cat purring away among her kittens, even a dark wine-cellar was not so black. He got up and kneeled by the shelf. The greenish eyes did not shine in an unfriendly way. He could feel that the owner of them was a nice big cat, and he counted four round little balls of kittens. It was a curious delight to stroke the soft fur and talk to the mother cat. She answered with purring, as if she liked the

sense of friendly human nearness. Marco laughed to himself.

'It's queer what a difference it makes!' he said. 'It is
almost like finding a window.'

The presence of these harmless living things was companionship. He sat down close to the low shelf and listened to the motherly purring, now and then speaking
and putting out his hand to touch the warm fur. The
phosphorescent light in the green eyes was a comfort in
itself.

'We shall get out of this – both of us,' he said. 'We shall
not be here very long, Puss-cat.'

He was not troubled by the fear of being really hungry
for some time. He was so used to eating scantily from
necessity, and to passing long hours without food during
his journeys, that he had proved to himself that fasting is
not, after all, such a desperate ordeal as most people
imagine. If you begin by expecting to feel famished and
by counting the hours between your meals, you will begin
to be ravenous. But he knew better.

The time passed slowly; but he had known it would
pass slowly, and he had made up his mind not to watch it
nor ask himself questions about it. He was not a restless
boy, but, like his father, could stand or sit or lie still. Now
and then he could hear distant rumblings of carts and
vans passing in the street. There was a certain degree of
companionship in these also. He kept his place near the
cat and his hand where he could occasionally touch her.
He could lift his eyes now and then to the place where the
dim glimmer of something like light showed itself.

Perhaps the stillness, perhaps the darkness, perhaps the
purring of the mother cat, probably all three, caused his
thoughts to begin to travel through his mind slowly and
more slowly. At last they ceased and he fell asleep. The
mother cat purred for some time, and then fell asleep
herself.

CHAPTER 15

A Sound in a Dream

MARCO slept peacefully for several hours. There was nothing to awaken him during that time. But at the end of it, his sleep was penetrated by a definite sound. He had dreamed of hearing a voice at a distance, and, as he tried in his dream to hear what it said, a brief metallic ringing sound awakened him outright. It was over by the time he was fully conscious, and at once he realized that the voice of his dream had been a real one, and was speaking still. It was the Lovely Person's voice, and she was speaking rapidly, as if she were in the greatest haste. She was speaking through the door.

'You will have to search for it,' was all he heard. 'I have not a moment!' And, as he listened to her hurriedly departing feet, there came to him with their hastening echoes the words, 'You are too good for the cellar. I like you!'

He sprang to the door and tried it, but it was still locked. The feet ran up the cellar steps and through the upper hall, and the front door closed with a bang. The two people had gone away, as they had threatened. The voice had been excited as well as hurried. Something had happened to frighten them, and they had left the house in great haste.

Marco turned and stood with his back against the door. The cat had awakened and she was gazing at him with her green eyes. She began to purr encouragingly. She had really helped Marco to think. He was thinking with all his might and trying to remember.

'What did she come for? She came for something,' he said to himself. 'What did she say? I only heard part of it, because I was asleep. The voice in the dream was part of it. The part I heard was, "You will have to search for it. I have not a moment." And as she ran down the passage, she called back, "You are too good for the cellar. I like you." ' He said the words over and over again and tried to recall exactly how they had sounded, and also to recall the voice which had seemed to be part of a dream but had been a real thing.

What did she come for? It was certain that she was in too great a hurry to be able, without a reason, to spare the time to come. What was the reason? She had said she liked him. If she liked him, she had come to do something which was not unfriendly. The only good thing she could do for him was something which would help him to get out of the cellar. She had said twice that he was too good for the cellar. If he had been awake, he would have heard all she said and have understood what she wanted him to do or meant to do for him. The first words he had heard – what had they been? They had been less clear to him than her last because he had heard them only as he was awakening. But he thought that they had been, 'You will have to search for it.' Search for it. For what? He thought and thought. What must he search for?

He sat down on the floor of the cellar and held his head in his hands, pressing his eyes so hard that curious lights floated before them.

And in a few minutes, he recalled something which seemed so much a part of his sleep that he had not been sure that he had not dreamed it. The ringing sound! He sprang up on his feet with a little gasping shout. The ringing sound! It had been the ring of metal, striking as it fell. Anything made of metal might have sounded like that. She had thrown something made of metal into the cellar. She had thrown it through the slit in the bricks near the door. She had thrown to him the only thing which could set him free. She had thrown him the *key* of the cellar!

For a few minutes the feelings which surged through him were so full of excitement that they set his brain in a whirl. He knew what his father would say – that would not do. If he was to think, he must hold himself still and not let even joy overcome him. The key was in the black little cellar, and he must find it in the dark. Even the woman who liked him enough to give him a chance of freedom knew that she must not open the door and let him out. There must be a delay. He would have to find the key himself, and it would be sure to take time. The chances were that they would be at a safe enough distance before he could get out.

'I will kneel down and crawl on my hands and knees,' he said. 'I will crawl back and forth and go over every inch of the floor with my hands until I find it. If I go over every inch, I shall find it.'

So he kneeled down and began to crawl, and the cat watched him and purred.

'We shall get out, Puss-cat,' he said to her. 'I told you we should.'

He crawled from the door to the wall at the side of the shelves, and then back again. The key might be quite a small one, and it was necessary that he should pass his hands over every inch, as he had said. The difficulty was to be sure, in the darkness that he did not miss an inch. Sometimes he was not sure enough, and then he went over the ground again. He crawled backward and forward, and he crawled forward and backward. He crawled cross-wise and lengthwise, he crawled diagonally, and he crawled round and round. But he did not find the key. If he had had only a little light, but he had none. He was so absorbed in his search that he did not know he had been engaged in it for several hours, and that it was the middle of the night. But at last he realized that he must stop for a rest, because his knees were beginning to feel bruised, and the skin of his hands was sore as a result of the rubbing on the flags. The cat and her kittens had gone to sleep and awakened again two or three times.

'But it is somewhere!' he said obstinately. 'It is inside the cellar. I heard something fall which was made of metal. That was the ringing sound which awakened me.'

When he stood up, he found his body ached and he was very tired. He stretched himself and exercised his arms and legs.

'I wonder how long I have been crawling about,' he thought. 'But the key is in the cellar. It is in the cellar.'

He sat down near the cat and her family, and, laying his arm on the shelf above her, rested his head on it. He began to think of another experiment.

'I am so tired, I believe I shall go to sleep again. Thought which Knows All! Show me this little thing. Lead me to it when I awake.'

And he did fall asleep, sound and fast.

He slept all the rest of the night. When he awakened, it was daylight in the streets, and the milk-carts were beginning to jingle about, and the early postmen were knocking big double-knocks at front doors. The cat may have heard the milk-carts; she was hungry and wanted to go in search of food. Just as Marco lifted his head from his arm and sat up, she jumped down from her shelf and went to the door. She had expected to find it ajar as it had been before. When she found it shut, she scratched at it and was disturbed to find this of no use. Because she knew Marco was in the cellar, she felt she had a friend who would assist her, and she mewed appealingly.

This reminded Marco of the key.

'I will when I have found it,' he said. 'It is inside the cellar.'

The cat mewed again, this time very anxiously indeed.

The kittens heard her and began to squirm and squeak piteously.

'Lead me to this little thing,' said Marco, as if speaking to Something in the darkness about him, and he got up.

He put his hand out towards the kittens, and it touched something lying not far from them. It must have been lying near his elbow all night while he slept.

It was the key! It had fallen upon the shelf, and not on the floor at all.

Marco picked it up and then stood still for a moment. He made the sign of the cross.

Then he found his way to the door and fumbled until he found the keyhole and got the key into it. Then he turned it and pushed the door open – and the cat ran out into the passage before him.

CHAPTER 16

The Rat to the Rescue

MARCO walked through the passage and into the kitchen part of the basement. The doors were all locked, and they were solid doors. He ran up the flagged steps and found the door at the top shut and bolted also, and that too was a solid door. His jailers had plainly made sure that it should take time enough for him to make his way out into the world, even after he got out of the wine-cellar. The cat had run away to some part of the place where mice were plentiful. Marco was by this time rather gnawingly hungry himself. If he could get into the kitchen, he might find some fragments of food left in a cupboard; but there was no moving the locked door. He tried the outlet into the area, but that was immovable. Then he saw near it a smaller door. It was evidently the entrance to the coal-cellar under the pavement. This was proved by the fact that trodden coal-dust marked the flagstones, and near it stood a scuttle with coal in it.

This coal-scuttle was the thing which might help him! Above the area door was a small window which was supposed to light the entry. He could not reach it, and if he reached it, he could not open it. He could throw pieces of coal at the glass and break it, and then he could shout for help when people passed by. They might not notice or understand where the shouts came from at first, but, if he kept them up, someone's attention would be attracted in the end.

He picked a large-sized solid piece of coal out of the heap in the scuttle, and threw it with all his force against the grimy glass. It smashed through and left a big hole. He threw another, and the entire pane was splintered and fell outside into the area. Then he saw it was broad daylight, and guessed that he had been shut up a good many hours. There was plenty of coal in the scuttle, and he had a strong arm and a good aim. He smashed pane after pane, until only the framework remained. When he shouted, there would be nothing between his voice and the street. No one could see him, but if he could do something which would make people slacken their pace and listen, then he could call out that he was in the basement of the house with the broken window.

'Hallo!' he shouted. 'Hallo! Hallo! Hallo! Hallo!'

But vehicles were passing in the street, and the passersby were absorbed in their own business. If they heard a sound, they did not stop to inquire into it.

'Hallo! Hallo! I am locked in!' yelled Marco, at the topmost power of his lungs. 'Hallo! Hallo!'

After half an hour's shouting, he began to think that he was wasting his strength.

'They only think it is a boy shouting,' he said. 'Someone will notice in time. At night, when the streets are quiet, I might make a policeman hear. But my father does not know where I am. He will be trying to find me – so will Lazarus – so will The Rat. One of them might pass through this very street, as I did. What can I do!'

A new idea flashed light upon him.

'I will begin to sing a Samavian song, and I will sing it very loud. People nearly always stop a moment to listen to music and find out where it comes from. And if any of my own people came near, they would stop at once – and now and then I will shout for help.'

Once when they had stopped to rest on Hampstead Heath, he had sung a valiant Samavian song for The Rat. The Rat had wanted to hear how he would sing when they went on their secret journey. He wanted him to sing for the Squad some day, to make the thing seem real. The Rat had been greatly excited, and had begged for the

song often. It was a stirring martial thing with a sort of a
trumpet call of a chorus. Thousands of Samavians had
sung it together on their way to the battlefield, hundreds
of years ago.

He drew back a step or so, and, putting his hands on his
hips, began to sing, throwing his voice upward that it
might pass through the broken window. He had a splendid and vibrant young voice, though he knew nothing of
its fine quality. Just now he wanted only to make it loud.

In the street outside very few people were passing. An
irritable old gentleman who was taking an invalid walk
quite jumped with annoyance when the song suddenly
trumpeted forth. Boys had no right to yell in that manner. He hurried his step to get away from the sound. Two
or three other people glanced over their shoulders, but
had no time to loiter. A few others listened with pleasure
as they drew near and passed on.

'There's a boy with a fine voice,' said one.

'What's he singing?' said his companion. 'It sounds
foreign.'

'Don't know,' was the reply as they went by. But at last
a young man who was a music-teacher, going to give a
lesson, hesitated and looked about him. The song was
very loud and spirited just at this moment. The music-
teacher could not understand where it came from, and
paused to find out. The fact that he stopped attracted the
attention of the next comer, who also paused.

'Who's singing?' he asked. 'Where is he singing?'

'I can't make out,' the music-teacher laughed. 'Sounds
as if it came out of the ground.'

And, because it was queer that a song should seem to be
coming out of the ground, a costermonger stopped, and
then a little boy, and then a working-woman, and then a
lady.

There was quite a little group when another person

turned the corner of the street. He was a shabby boy on crutches, and he had a frantic look on his face.

And Marco actually heard, as the boy drew near to the group, the tap – tap – tap of crutches.

'It might be,' he thought. 'It might be!'

And he sang the trumpet-call of the chorus as if it were meant to reach the skies, and he sang it again and again. And at the end of it he shouted, 'Hallo! Hallo! Hallo! Hallo!'

The Rat swung himself into the group and looked as if he had gone crazy. He hurled himself against the people.

'Where is he! Where is he!' he cried, and he poured out some breathless words; it was almost as if he sobbed them out.

'We've been looking for him all night!' he shouted. 'Where is he! Marco! Marco! No one else sings it but him. Marco! Marco!' And out of the area, as it seemed, came a shout of answer.

'Rat! Rat! I'm here in the cellar – locked in. I'm here!' and a big piece of coal came hurtling through the broken window and fell crashing on the area flags. The Rat got down the steps into the area as if he had not been on crutches but on legs, and banged on the door, shouting back:

'Marco! Marco! Here I am! Who locked you in? How can I get the door open?'

Marco was close against the door inside. It was The Rat! It was The Rat! And he would be in the street again in a few minutes.

'Call a policeman!' he shouted through the keyhole. 'The people locked me in on purpose and took away the keys.'

Then the group of lookers-on began to get excited and press against the area railings and ask questions. They could not understand what had happened to cause the boy with the crutches to look as if he were crazy with terror and relief at the same time. And the little boy ran on to fetch a policeman, and found one in the next street, and persuaded him that it was his business to come and get a door open in an empty house where a boy who was a street singer had got locked up in a cellar.

CHAPTER 17

'It is a very Bad Sign'

THE policeman was not so much excited as out of temper. He did not know what Marco knew or what The Rat knew. Some common lad had got himself locked up in a house, and someone would have to go to the landlord and get a key from him. He had no intention of breaking into a private house with his truncheon, as The Rat expected him to do.

'He got himself in through some of his larks, and he'll have to wait till he's got out without smashing locks,' he growled, shaking the area door. 'How did you get in there?' he shouted.

It was not easy for Marco to explain through a keyhole that he had come in to help a lady who had met with an accident. The policeman thought this mere boy's talk. As to the rest of the story, Marco knew that it could not be related at all without saying things which could not be explained to anyone but his father. He quickly made up his mind that he must let it be believed that he had been locked in by some queer accident. It must be supposed that the people had not remembered, in their haste, that he had not yet left the house.

When the young clerk from the house agency came with the keys, he was much disturbed and bewildered after he got inside.

'They've made a bolt of it,' he said. 'That happens now and then, but there's something queer about this. Why did they lock these doors in the basement and the one on the stairs? What did they say to you?' he asked Marco, staring at him suspiciously.

'They said they were obliged to go suddenly,' Marco answered.

'What were you doing in the basement?'

'The man took me down.'

'And left you there and bolted? He must have been in a hurry.'

'The lady said they had not a moment's time.'

'Her ankle must have got well in short order,' said the young man.

'I knew nothing about them,' answered Marco. 'I have never seen them before.'

'The police were after them,' the young man said. 'That's what I should say. They paid three months rent in advance, and they have only been here two. Some of these foreign spies lurking about London; that's what they were.'

The Rat had not waited until the keys arrived. He had swung himself at his swiftest pace back through the streets. People turned and stared at his wild pale face for he almost shot past them.

He had left himself barely breath enough to speak with when he reached the house and banged on the door with his crutch to save time.

Both Loristan and Lazarus came to answer.

The Rat leaned against the door gasping.

'He's found! He's all right!' he panted. 'Someone had locked him in a house and left him. They've sent for the keys. I'm going back. Brandon Terrace, No. 10.'

Loristan and Lazarus exchanged glances. Both of them were at the moment as pale as The Rat.

'Help him into the house,' said Loristan to Lazarus. 'He must stay here and rest. We will go.' The Rat knew it was an order. He did not like it, but he obeyed.

'This is a bad sign, Master,' said Lazarus, as they went out together.

'It is a very bad one,' answered Loristan.

'God of the Right, defend us!' Lazarus groaned.

'Amen!' said Loristan. 'Amen!'

The group had become a small crowd by the time they reached Brandon Terrace. Marco had not found it easy to leave the place because he was being questioned by the policeman and the agent's clerk.

The entrance of Loristan produced its usual effect. The agent's clerk lifted his hat, and the policeman stood straight and made salute. Loristan laid his hand on Marco's shoulder and held it there as he spoke.

'My boy knew nothing of these people,' he said. 'That I can guarantee. He has seen neither of them before. He has been shut up in this place for nearly twenty-four hours and has had no food. I must take him home. This is my address.' He handed the young man a card.

Then they went home together, and all the way to Philibert Place Loristan's firm hand held closely to his boy's shoulder as if he could not endure to let him go. But on the way they said very little.

'Father,' Marco said, rather hoarsely, when they first got away from the house in the terrace. 'I can't talk well in the street. For one thing, I am so glad to be with you again. It seemed as if – it might turn out badly.'

'Beloved one,' Loristan said the words in their own Samavian, 'until you are fed and at rest, you shall not talk at all.'

Afterwards, when he was himself again and was allowed to tell his strange story, Marco handed to Loristan the card which the lady had given him: 'She said you would remember the name.' Loristan looked at the lettering with an ironic half-smile.

'I never heard it before,' he replied. 'She would not send me a name I knew. Probably I have never seen either of them. But I know the work they do. They are spies of the Maranovitch, and suspect that I know something of the Lost Prince. They believed they could terrify you into saying things which would be a clue. Men and

women of their class will use desperate means to gain their
end.'

The look in his father's eyes as he spoke, and the pressure of the hand he stretched out to touch him, made
Marco's heart thrill. He had won a new love and trust
from his father. When they talked together that night,
they were closer to each other than they had ever been
before.

They sat in the firelight. Marco upon the worn hearth-
rug, and they talked about Samavia – about the war and
its heartrending struggles, and about how they might end.

'Do you think that some time we might be exiles no
longer?' the boy said wistfully. 'Do you think we might go
there together – and see it – you and I, father?'

There was a silence for a while. Loristan looked into
the sinking bed of red coal.

'For years – for years I have made for my soul that
image,' he said slowly.

CHAPTER 18

'Cities and Faces'

THE hours of Marco's unexplained absence had been terrible to Loristan and Lazarus. They had reason for fears which it was not possible for them to express. As the night drew on, the fears took stronger form. They forgot the existence of The Rat, who sat biting his nails in the bedroom, afraid to go out lest he might lose the chance of being given some errand to do, but also afraid to show himself lest he should seem in the way.

'I'll stay upstairs,' he had said to Lazarus. 'If you just whistle, I'll come.'

The anguish he passed through as the day went by and Lazarus went out and came in and he himself received no orders, could not have been expressed in any ordinary words. He writhed in his chair, he bit his nails to the quick, he wrought himself into a frenzy of misery and terror by recalling one by one all the crimes his knowledge of London police-courts supplied him with. He was doing nothing, yet he dare not leave his post. It was his post after all, though they had not given it to him. He must do something.

In the middle of the night Loristan opened the door of the back sitting-room, because he knew he must at least go upstairs and throw himself on his bed even if he could not sleep.

He started back as the door opened. The Rat was sitting huddled on the floor near it with his back against the wall. He had a piece of paper in his hand and his twisted face was a weird thing to see.

'Why are you here?' Loristan asked.

'I've been here three hours, sir. I knew you'd have come

out sometime and I thought you'd let me speak to you. Will you – will you?'

'Come into the room,' said Loristan. 'I will listen to anything you want to say. What have you been drawing on that paper?' as The Rat got up in the wonderful way he had taught himself. The paper was covered with lines which showed it to be another of his plans.

'Please look at it,' he begged. 'I daren't go out lest you might want to send me somewhere. I daren't sit doing nothing. I began remembering and thinking things out. I put down all the streets and squares he *might* have walked through on his way home. I've not missed one. If you'll let me start out and walk through every one of them and talk to the policemen on the beat and look at the houses – and think things out and work at them – I'll not miss an inch – I'll miss a brick or a flagstone – I'll –' His voice had a hard sound but it shook, and he himself shook.

'You are a good comrade,' he said. 'It is well for us that you are here. You have thought of a good thing.'

'May I go now?' said The Rat.

'This moment, if you are ready,' was the answer. The Rat swung himself to the door.

Loristan said to him a thing which was like the sudden lighting of a great light in the very centre of his being.

'You are one of us. Now that I know you are doing this I may even sleep. You are one of us.' And it was because he was following this plan that The Rat had turned into Brandon Terrace and heard the Samavian song ringing out from the locked basement of No. 10.

'Yes, he is one of us,' Loristan said, when he told this part of the story to Marco as they sat by the fire. 'I had not been sure before. I wanted to be very sure. Last night I saw into the depths of him and *knew*. He may be trusted.'

From that day The Rat held a new place. He was taken into the intimacy which had before enclosed only three.

Loristan talked to him as he talked to Marco, drawing him within the circle which held so much that was comprehended without speech. The Rat knew that he was being trained and observed. His idol had said that he was 'one of them' and he was watching and putting him to tests so that he might find out how much he was one of them.

'Sir,' he said one night when they were alone together, because The Rat had been copying a road-map. His voice was very low – 'do you think that – sometime – you could trust me as you trust Marco? Could it ever be like that – ever?'

'The time has come,' and Loristan's voice was almost as low as his own, though strong and deep feeling underlay its quiet – 'the time has come when I can trust you with Marco – to be his companion – to care for him, to stand by his side at any moment. And Marco is – Marco is my son.' That was enough to uplift The Rat to the skies. But there was more to follow.

'It may not be long before it may be his part to do work in which he will need a comrade who can be trusted – as a rock can be trusted.'

'A rock! A rock!' the boy broke out. 'Let me show you, sir. Send me with him for a servant. The crutches are nothing. You've seen that they're as good as legs, haven't you? I've trained myself.'

'I know, I know, dear lad.' Marco had told him all of it. He gave a smile which seemed as if it held a sort of fine secret. 'You shall go as his aide-de-camp. It shall be part of the game.'

He had always encouraged 'the game', and during the last weeks he had even found time to help them in their plannings for the mysterious journey of the Secret Two. He had been so interested that once or twice he had called on Lazarus as an old soldier and Samavian to give his opinions of certain routes – and of the customs and habits of people in towns and villages by the way. Here they would find simple pastoral folk who danced, sang after their day's work, and who would tell all they knew; here they would find those who served or feared the Maranovitch and who would not talk at all. In one place they would meet with hospitality, in another with unfriendly suspicion of all strangers. Through talk and stories The Rat began to know the country almost as Marco knew it. Marco's part was to recall and sketch faces. Loristan one night gave him a number of photographs of people to commit to memory. Under each face was written the name of a place.

'Learn these faces,' he said, 'until you would know each one of them at once wherever you met it. Fix them upon your mind, so that it will be impossible for you to forget them. You must be able to sketch any one of them and recall the city or town or neighbourhood connected with it.'

Even this was still called 'the game', but Marco began to know in his secret heart that it was so much more, that his hand sometimes trembled with excitement as he made his sketches over and over again. To make each one many times was the best way to embed it in his memory. The Rat knew, too, though he had no reason for knowing, but mere instinct. He used to lie awake in the night and think it over and remember what Loristan had said of the time coming when Marco might need a comrade in his work. What was his work to be? It was to be something like 'the game'. And they were being prepared for it. And though Marco often lay awake on his bed when The Rat lay awake on his sofa, neither boy spoke to the other of the thing his mind dwelt on. And Marco worked as he had never worked before. The game was very exciting when he could prove his prowess. The four gathered together at night in the back sitting-room. Lazarus was obliged to be with them because a second judge was needed. Loristan would mention the name of a place, perhaps a street in

Paris or a hotel in Vienna, and Marco would at once make a rapid sketch of the face under whose photograph the name of the locality had been written. There was a great hotel near the Place de la Concorde in Paris, of which Marco felt he should never hear the name during all his life without there starting up before his mental vision a tall woman with fierce black eyes and a delicate high-bridged nose across which the strong eyebrows almost met. In Vienna there was a palace which would always bring back at once a pale cold-faced man with a heavy blond lock which fell over his forehead. A certain street in Munich meant a stout genial old aristocrat with a sly smile; a village in Bavaria, a peasant with a vacant and simple countenance. A curled and smoothed man who looked like a hairdresser brought up a place in an Austrian mountain town. He knew them all as he knew his own face and No. 7 Philibert Place.

But still night after night the game was played.

Then came a night when, out of a deep sleep, he was awakened by Lazarus touching him. He had so long been secretly ready to answer any call that he sat up straight in bed at the first touch.

'Dress quickly and come downstairs,' Lazarus said. 'The Prince is here and wishes to speak with you.'

Marco made no answer but got out of bed and began to slip on his clothes.

Lazarus touched The Rat.

The Rat was as ready as Marco and sat upright as he had done.

'Come down with the young Master,' he commanded. 'It is necessary that you should be seen and spoken to.' And having given the order he went away.

No one heard the shoeless feet of the two boys as they stole down the stairs.

An elderly man in ordinary clothes, but with an unmistakable face, was sitting quietly talking to Loristan, who with a gesture called both forward.

'The Prince has been much interested in what I have told him of your game,' he said in his lowest voice. 'He wishes to see you make your sketches, Marco.'

Marco looked very straight into the Prince's eyes which were fixed intently on him as he made his bow.

'His Highness does me honour,' he said, as his father might have said it. He went to the table at once and took from a drawer his pencils and pieces of cardboard.

'I should know he was your son and a Samavian,' the Prince remarked.

Then his keen and deep-set eyes turned themselves on the boy with the crutches.

'This,' said Loristan, 'is the one who calls himself The Rat. He is one of us.'

The Rat saluted.

'Please tell him, sir,' he whispered, 'that the crutches don't matter.'

'He has trained himself to an extraordinary activity,' Loristan said. 'He can do anything.'

The keen eyes were still taking The Rat in.

'They are an advantage,' the Prince said at last.

Lazarus had nailed together a light, rough easel which Marco used in making his sketches when the game was played. Lazarus was standing in state at the door, and he came forward, brought the easel from its corner, and arranged the necessary drawing material upon it.

Marco stood near it and waited the pleasure of his father and his visitor. The Rat noticed, as he had noticed before, that the big boy could stand still in perfect ease and silence. It was not necessary for him to say things or to ask questions – to look at people as if he felt restless if they did not speak to or notice him. He did not seem to require notice, and The Rat felt vaguely that, young as he was, this very freedom from any anxiety to be looked at or

addressed made him somehow look like a great gentleman.

Loristan and the Prince advanced to where he stood.

'L'Hotel de Marigny,' Loristan said.

Marco began to sketch rapidly. He began the portrait
of the handsome woman with the delicate high-bridged
nose and the black brows which almost met. As he did it,
the Prince drew nearer and watched the work over his
shoulder. It did not take very long and, when it was finished, the inspector turned, and after giving Loristan a
long and strange look, nodded twice.

'It is a remarkable thing,' he said. 'In that rough sketch
she is not to be mistaken.'

Loristan bent his head.

Then he mentioned the name of another street in
another place – and Marco sketched again. This time it
was the peasant with the simple face. The Prince bowed
again. Then Loristan gave another name, and after that
another and another; and Marco did his work until it was
at an end.

'You would know these faces wherever you saw them?'
said the Prince. 'If you passed one in Bond Street or in the
Marylebone Road, you would recognize it at once?'

'As I know yours, sir,' Marco answered.

Then followed a number of questions. Loristan asked
them as he had often asked them before. They were questions as to the height and build of the originals of the
pictures, of the colour of their hair and eyes, and the
order of their complexions. Marco answered them all. He
knew all but the names of these people, and it was plainly
not necessary that he should know them, as his father had
never uttered them.

After this questioning was at an end the Prince
pointed to The Rat, who had leaned on his crutches
against the wall, his eyes fiercely eager like a ferret's.

'And he?' the Prince said. 'What can he do?'

'Let me try,' said The Rat. 'Marco knows.'

Marco looked at his father.

'May I help him to show you?' he asked.

'Yes,' Loristan answered, and then, as he turned to the Prince, he said again in a low voice: '*He is one of us.*'

Then Marco began a new form of the game. He held up one of the pictured faces before The Rat, and The Rat named at once the city and place connected with it, he detailed the colour of the eyes and hair, the height, the build, all the personal details as Marco himself had detailed them. To these he added descriptions of the cities, and points concerning the police system, the palaces, the people. His face twisted itself, his eyes burned, his voice shook, but he was amazing in his readiness of reply and his exactness of memory.

'I can't draw,' he said at the end. 'But I can remember. I didn't want anyone to be bothered with thinking I was trying to learn it. So only Marco knew.'

This he said to Loristan with appeal in his voice.

'It was he who invented "the game",' said Loristan. 'I showed you his strange maps and plans.'

'It is a good game,' the Prince answered in the manner of a man extraordinarily interested and impressed. 'They know it well. They can be trusted.'

'No such thing has ever been done before,' Loristan said. 'It is as new as it is daring and simple.'

'Therein lies the safety,' the Prince answered.

'Perhaps only in boyhood,' said Loristan, 'could one have dared to imagine it.'

'The Prince thanks you,' he said after a few more words spoken aside to his visitor. 'We both thank you. You may go back to your beds.'

And the boys went.

CHAPTER 19

'That is One!'

A WEEK had not passed before Marco brought to The Rat in their bedroom an envelope containing a number of slips of paper on each of which was written something.

'This is another part of the game,' he said gravely. 'Let us sit down together by the table and study it.'

They sat down and examined what was written on the slips. At the head of each was the name of one of the places with which Marco had connected a face he had sketched. Below were clear and concise directions as to how it was to be reached and the words to be said when each individual was encountered.

'This person is to be found at his stall in the market,' was written on the vacant-faced peasant. 'You will first attract his attention by asking the price of something. When he is looking at you, touch your left thumb lightly with the forefinger of your right hand. Then utter in a low distinct tone the words "The Lamp is lighted". That is all you are to do.'

Sometimes the directions were not quite so simple, but they were all instructions of the same order. The originals of the sketches were to be sought out – always with precaution which should conceal that they were being sought at all, and always in such a manner as would cause an encounter to appear to be mere chance. Then certain words were to be uttered, but always without attracting the attention of any bystander or passer-by.

The boys worked at their task through the entire day. They concentrated all their powers upon it. They wrote and re-wrote – they repeated to each other what they committed to memory as if it were a lesson. Marco worked with the greater ease and more rapidly, because exercise of this order had been his practice and entertainment from his babyhood. The Rat, however, almost kept pace with him, as he had been born with a phenomenal memory and his eagerness and desire were a fury.

But throughout the entire day neither of them once referred to what they were doing as anything but 'the game'.

At night, it is true, each found himself lying awake and thinking. It was The Rat who broke the silence from his sofa.

'It is what the messengers of the Secret Party would be ordered to do when they were sent out to give the Sign for the Rising,' he said. 'I made that up the first day I invented the party, didn't I?'

'Yes,' answered Marco.

After a third day's concentration they knew by heart everything given them to learn. That night Loristan put them through an examination.

'Can you write these things?' he asked, after each had repeated them and emerged safely from all cross-questioning.

Each boy wrote them correctly from memory.

'Write yours in French – in German – in Russian – in Samavian,' Loristan said to Marco.

He was pale that night and there was a shadow on his face. His eyes held a great longing as they rested on Marco. It was a yearning which had a sort of dread in it.

Lazarus also did not seem quite himself. He was red instead of pale, and his movements were uncertain and restless. He cleared his throat nervously at intervals and more than once left his chair as if to look for something.

It was almost midnight when Loristan, standing near Marco, put his arm round his shoulders.

'The Game—' he began, and then was silent a few moments while Marco felt his arm tighten its hold. Both Marco and The Rat felt a hard quick beat in their breasts, and, because of this and because the pause seemed long, Marco spoke.

'The Game – yes, Father?' he said.

'The Game is about to give you work to do – both of you,' Loristan answered.

Lazarus cleared his throat and walked to the easel in the corner of the room. But he only changed the position of a piece of drawing-paper on it and then came back.

'In two days you are to go to Paris – as you,' to The Rat, 'planned in the game.'

'As I planned?' The Rat barely breathed the words.

'Yes,' answered Loristan. 'The instructions you have learned you will carry out. There is no more to be done than to manage to approach certain persons closely enough to be able to utter certain words to them.'

'Only two young strollers whom no man could suspect,' put in Lazarus in an astonishingly rough and shaky voice. 'They could pass near the Emperor himself without danger. The young Master' – his voice became so hoarse that he was obliged to clear it loudly – 'the young Master must carry himself less finely. It would be well to shuffle a little and slouch as if he were of the common people.'

'Yes,' said The Rat hastily. 'He must do that. I can teach him. He holds his head and his shoulders like a gentleman. He must look like a street lad.'

'I will look like one,' said Marco, with determination.

'I will trust you to remind him,' Loristan said to The Rat, and he said it with gravity. 'That will be your charge.'

As he lay upon his pillow that night, it seemed to Marco as if a load had lifted itself from his heart. It was the load of uncertainty and longing. He had so long borne the pain of feeling that he was too young to be allowed to serve in any way. But now the hour had come and he, Marco, was to be its messenger. No one would know what he did. What he achieved could only be attained if he remained obscure and unknown. His father had given him a gift so splendid that he trembled with awe and joy as he thought of it. The Game had become real. He and The Rat were to carry with them The Sign.

As he had awakened out of his sleep when Lazarus touched him, so he awakened in the middle of the night again. But he was not aroused by a touch. When he opened his eyes he knew it was a look which had penetrated his sleep – a look in the eyes of his father who was standing by his side. The only light was that of the lamp in the street, but he could see Loristan's face clearly enough to know that the intensity of his gaze had awakened him. The Rat was sleeping profoundly. Loristan spoke in Samavian and under his breath.

'Beloved one,' he said. 'You are very young. Because I am your father – just at this hour I can feel nothing else. I have trained you for this through all the years of your life. I am proud of your young maturity and strength, but you are a child! Can I do this thing!'

For the moment, his face and his voice were scarcely like his own.

He kneeled by the bedside, and, as he did so, Marco half sitting up caught his hand and held it hard against his breast.

'Father, I know!' he cried under his breath also. 'It is true. I am a child but am I not a man also? You yourself said it. I always knew that you were teaching me to be one – for some reason. It was my secret that I knew it. I learned well because I never forgot it. And I learned. Did I not?'

He was so eager that he looked more like a boy than ever. But his young strength and courage were splendid to see.

Loristan answered slowly. 'You did your part – and now if I – drew back – you would feel that *I had failed you*.'

'You!' Marco breathed it proudly. 'You *could* not fail even the weakest thing in the world.'

There was a moment's silence in which the two pairs of eyes dwelt on each other with meaning, and then Loristan rose to his feet.

'The end will be all that our hearts most wish,' he said. 'Tomorrow you may begin the new part of "the Game". You may go to Paris.'

When the train which was to meet the boat that crossed from Dover to Calais steamed out of the noisy Charing Cross Station, it carried in a third-class carriage two shabby boys. One of them would have been a handsome lad if he had not carried himself slouchingly and walked with a street lad's careless shuffling gait. The other was a cripple who moved slowly, and apparently with difficulty, on crutches. There was nothing about them to attract attention. They sat in a corner of the carriage and neither talked much nor seemed to be particularly interested in the journey or each other. When they went on board the steamer, they were soon lost among the passengers.

'What can such a poor-looking pair of lads be going to Paris for?' someone asked his companion.

'Not for pleasure, certainly; perhaps to get work,' was the casual answer.

In the evening they reached Paris, and Marco led the way to a small café in a side-street where they got some cheap food. In the same side-street they found a bed they could share for the night in a tiny room over a baker's shop.

The Rat was too much excited to go to bed early. He begged Marco to guide him about the brilliant streets. They went slowly along the broad Avenue des Champs–

Elysées under the lights glittering among the horse-chestnut trees. The Rat's sharp eyes took it all in – the light of the cafés, the many carriages rolling by, the people who loitered and laughed or sat at little tables drinking wine and listening to music, the broad stream of life which flowed on to the Arc de Triomphe and back again.

'It's brighter and clearer than London,' he said to Marco. 'The people look as if they were having more fun than they do in England.'

The Place de la Concorde, spreading its stately spaces, held him as though by a fascination. He wanted to stand still and stare at it, first from one point of view and then from another. It was bigger and more wonderful than he had been able to picture it when Marco had described it to him and told him of the part it had played in the days of the French Revolution when the guillotine had stood in it and the tumbrils had emptied themselves at the foot of its steps.

'I can see it all happening,' he said at last, and he pulled Marco away.

Before they returned home, they found their way to a large house which stood in a courtyard. In the iron work of the handsome gates which shut it in was wrought a gilded coronet. The gates were closed and the house was not brightly lighted.

They walked past it and round it without speaking, but, when they neared the entrance for the second time, The Rat said in a low tone:

'She is five feet seven, has black hair, a nose with a high bridge, her eyebrows are black and almost meet across it, she has a pale olive skin and holds her head proudly.'

'That is the one,' Marco answered.

They were a week in Paris and each day passed this big house. There were certain hours when great ladies were more likely to go out and come in than they were at others. Marco knew this, and they managed to be within

sight of the house or to pass it at these hours. For two days
they saw no sign of the person they wished to see, but one
morning the gates were thrown open and they saw flowers
and palms being taken in.

'She has been away and is coming back,' said Marco.
The next day they passed three times – once at the hour
when fashionable women drive out to do their shopping,
once at the time when afternoon visiting is the more likely
to begin, and once when the streets were brilliant with
lights and the carriages had begun to roll by to dinner-
parties and theatres.

Then, as they stood at a little distance from the iron
gates, a carriage drove through them and stopped before
the big door which was thrown open by two footmen in
livery.

'She is coming out,' said The Rat.

They would be able to see her plainly when she came,
because the lights over the entrance were so bright.

Marco slipped from under his coat sleeve a carefully
made sketch. He looked at it and The Rat looked at it.

A handsome woman appeared upon the threshold. She
paused and gave some order to the footman who stood on
the right. Then she came out in the full light and got into
the carriage which drove out of the courtyard and quite
near the place where the two boys waited.

When it was gone, Marco drew a long breath as he tore
the sketch into very small pieces. He did not throw them
away then but put them into his pocket.

The Rat drew a long breath also.

'Yes,' he said positively.

'Yes,' said Marco.

When they were safely shut up in their room over the
baker's shop, they discussed the chances of their being
able to pass her in such a way as would seem accidental.
Two common boys could not enter the courtyard. There
was a back entrance for trades-people and messengers.

When she drove, she would always enter her carriage from the same place. Unless she sometimes walked, they could not approach her. What should be done? The thing was difficult. After they had talked some time, The Rat sat and gnawed his nails.

'Tomorrow afternoon,' he broke out at last, 'we'll watch and see if her carriage drives in for her – then, when she comes to the door, I'll go in and begin to beg. The servant will think I'm a foreigner and don't know what I'm doing. You can come after me to tell me to come away, because you know better than I do that I shall be ordered out. She may be a good-natured woman and listen to us – and you might get near her.'

'We might try it,' Marco answered. 'It might work. We will try it.'

The Rat never failed to treat him as his leader. He had begged Loristan to let him come with Marco as his servant, and his servant he had been more than willing to be. When Loristan had said he should be his aide-de-camp, he had felt his trust lifted to a military dignity which uplifted him with it. As his aide-de-camp he must serve him, watch him, obey his slightest wish, make everything easy for him. Sometimes, Marco was troubled by the way in which he insisted on serving him, this queer, once dictatorial and cantankerous lad who had begun by throwing stones at him.

'You must not wait on me,' he said to him. 'I must wait upon myself.'

The Rat flushed.

'He told me that he would let me come with you as your aide-de-camp,' he said. 'It – it's part of the game. It makes things easier if we keep up the game.'

It would have attracted attention if they had spent too much time in the vicinity of the big house. So it happened that the next afternoon the great lady drove out at an hour when they were not watching for her. They were on their way to try if they could carry out their plan, when, as they walked together along the Rue Royale, The Rat suddenly touched Marco's elbow.

'The carriage stands before the shop with lace in the windows,' he whispered hurriedly.

Marco saw and recognized it at once. The owner had evidently gone into the shop to buy something. This was a better chance than they had hoped for, and when they approached the carriage itself, they saw that there was another point in their favour. Inside were three beautiful little Pekingese spaniels that looked exactly alike. They were all trying to look out of the window and were pushing against each other. They were so perfect and so pretty that few people passed by without looking at them. What better excuse could two boys have for lingering about a place?

Through the shop-window Marco caught a glimpse of the great lady.

'She does not look much interested. She won't stay long,' he whispered, and added aloud, 'that little one is the master. See how she pushes the others aside! He is stronger than the other two, though he is so small.'

'He can snap, too,' said The Rat.

'She is coming now,' warned Marco, and then laughed aloud as if at the Pekingese, which, catching sight of their mistress at the shop door, began to leap and yelp for joy.

Their mistress herself smiled, and was smiling as Marco drew near her.

'May we look at them, Madame?' he said in French, and, as she made an amiable gesture of acquiescence and moved towards the carriage with him, he spoke a few words, very low, but very distinctly, in Russian.

'The Lamp is lighted,' he said.

The Rat was looking at her keenly, but he did not see her face change at all. What he noticed most throughout their journey was that each person to whom they gave the

Sign had complete control over his or her countenance, and never betrayed by any change of expression that the words meant anything unusual.

The great lady merely went on smiling, and spoke only of the dogs, allowing Marco and himself to look at them through the window of the carriage as the footman opened the door for her to enter.

'They are beautiful little creatures,' Marco said, lifting his cap, and, as the footman turned away, he uttered his few Russian words once more and moved off without even glancing at the lady again.

'That is *one*!' he said to The Rat that night before they went to sleep, and with a match he burned the scraps of the sketch he had torn and put into his pocket.

CHAPTER 20

Marco Goes to the Opera

THEIR next journey was to Munich, but the night before they left Paris an unexpected thing happened.

To reach the narrow staircase which led to their bedroom it was necessary to pass through the baker's shop. The baker's wife was a friendly woman who liked the two boy lodgers who were so quiet and gave no trouble. More than once she had given them a hot roll or a freshly baked tartlet with fruit in the centre. When Marco came in this evening, she greeted him with a nod and handed him a small parcel as he passed through.

'This was left for you this afternoon,' she said. 'I see you are making purchases for your journey. My man and I are very sorry you are going.'

'Thank you, Madame. We also are sorry,' Marco answered, taking the parcel. 'They are not large purchases you see,' smiling.

But neither he nor The Rat had bought anything at all, though the ordinary-looking little package was plainly addressed to him and bore the name of one of the big cheap shops. It felt as if it contained something soft.

When he had reached their bedroom, The Rat was gazing out of the window watching every living thing which passed in the street below. He who had never seen anything but London was absorbed by the spell of Paris and was learning it by heart.

'Something has been sent to us. Look at this,' said Marco.

The Rat was at his side at once. 'What is it? Where did it come from?'

They opened the little package and at first sight saw

only several pairs of woollen socks. As Marco took up the sock in the middle of the parcel, he felt that there was something inside it. He put his hand in and drew out a number of five-franc notes – not new ones, because new ones would have betrayed themselves by crackling. These were old enough to be soft. But there were enough of them to amount to a substantial sum.

Each of them believed the package had been sent by the great lady, but it had been done so carefully that not the slightest clue was furnished.

To The Rat, part of the deep excitement of 'the Game' was the working out of the plans and methods of each person concerned. He could not have slept without working out some scheme which might have been used in this case. It thrilled him to contemplate the difficulties the great lady might have found herself obliged to overcome.

'Perhaps,' he said after thinking it over for some time, 'she went to a big common shop dressed as if she were an ordinary woman and bought the socks and pretended she was going to carry them home herself. She would do that so she could take them into some corner and slip the money in. Then, as she wanted to have them sent from the shop, perhaps she bought some other things and asked the people to deliver the packages to different places. The socks were sent to us and the other things to someone else. She would go to a shop where no one knew her and no one would expect to see her and she would wear clothes which looked neither rich nor too poor.'

He created the whole episode with all its details and explained them to Marco. It fascinated him for the entire evening and he felt relieved after it and slept well.

Even before they had left London, certain newspapers had swept out of existence the story of the descendant of the Lost Prince. This had been done by derision and light handling – by treating it as a romantic legend.

At first, The Rat had resented this bitterly, but one day at a meal, when he had been producing arguments to prove that the story must be a true one, Loristan somehow checked him by his own silence.

'If there is such a man,' he said after a pause, 'it is well for him that his existence should not be believed in – for some time at least.'

The Rat came to a dead stop. He felt hot for a moment and then felt cold. He saw a new idea all at once. He had been making a mistake in tactics.

No more was said but, when they were alone afterwards, he poured himself forth to Marco.

'I was a fool!' he cried out. 'Why couldn't I see it for myself! Shall I tell you what I believe has been done? There is someone who has influence in England and who is a friend to Samavia. They've got the newspapers to make fun of the story so that it won't be believed. If it was believed, both the Iarovitch and the Maranovitch would be on the lookout, and the Secret Party would lose their chances. There's someone watching and working here who is a friend to Samavia.'

'But there is someone in Samavia who has begun to suspect that it might be true,' Marco answered. 'If there were not, I should not have been shut up in the cellar. Someone thought my father knew something. The spies had orders to find out what it was.'

'Yes. Yes. That's true, too!' The Rat answered anxiously. 'We shall have to be very careful.'

In the lining of the sleeve of Marco's coat there was a slit into which he could slip any small thing he wished to conceal and also wished to be able to reach without trouble. In this he had carried the sketch of the lady which he had torn up in Paris. When they walked in the streets of Munich, the morning after their arrival, he carried still another sketch. It was the one picturing the genial-looking old aristocrat with the sly smile.

One of the things they had learned about this one was his passion for music. He spent much time in Munich because he loved its musical atmosphere and the earnestness of its opera-goers.

'The military bands play in the Feldherrn-halle at midday. When something very good is being played, sometimes people stop their carriages so that they can listen. We will go there' said Marco.

'It's a chance,' said The Rat. 'We mustn't lose anything like a chance.'

The day was brilliant and sunny, the people passing through the streets looked comfortable and homely, the mixture of old streets and modern ones was picturesque and cheerful. The Rat swinging through the crowd on his crutches was full of interest and exhilaration. He had begun to grow, and the change in his face and expression which had begun in London had become more noticeable. He had been given his 'place' and a work to do which entitled him to hold it.

No one could have suspected them of carrying a strange and vital secret with them as they strolled along together. They seemed only two ordinary boys who looked in at shop-windows and talked over their contents. Sometimes it would have been easy for The Rat to forget that there was anything graver in the world than the new places and new wonders he was seeing, as if he were a wandering minstrel in a story.

But in Samavia bloody battles were being fought, and bloody plans were being wrought out, and in anguished anxiety the Secret Party and the Forgers of the Sword waited breathless for the Sign for which they had waited so long. And inside the lining of Marco's coat was hidden the sketched face, as the two unnoticed lads made their way to the Feldherrn-halle to hear the band play and see who might chance to be among the audience.

Because the day was sunny, and also because the band

was playing a specially fine programme, the crowd in the square was larger than usual. Several vehicles had stopped, and among them were one or two which were not merely hired cabs but were the carriages of private persons.

One of them had evidently arrived early, as it was drawn up in a good position when the boys reached the corner. It was a big open carriage and a grand one, luxuriously upholstered in green. The footman and coachman wore green and silver liveries and seemed to know that people were looking at them and their master. He was a stout, genial-looking old aristocrat with a sly smile. In the carriage with him were a young officer and a little boy, and they also listened attentively. Standing near the carriage door were several people who were plainly friends or acquaintances, as they occasionally spoke to him. Marco touched The Rat's coat sleeve as the two boys approached.

'It would not be easy to get near him,' he said. 'Let us go and stand as close to the carriage as we can get without pushing. Perhaps we may hear someone say something about where he is going after the music is over.'

Yes, there was no mistaking him. He was the right man. Each of them knew by heart the creases on his stout face and the sweep of his grey moustache. But there was nothing noticeable in a boy looking for a moment at a piece of paper, and Marco sauntered a few steps to a bit of space left bare by the crowd and took a last glance at his sketch. His rule was to make sure at the final moment.

'The Chancellor is music mad,' a looker-on near the boys said to another. 'At the opera every night unless serious affairs keep him away! There you may see him nodding his old head and bursting his gloves with applauding when a good thing is done.'

There was a group about the carriage to the last, when the music came to an end and it drove away. There had been no opportunity of passing close to it even had the presence of the young officer and the boy not presented an insurmountable obstacle.

Marco and The Rat went on their way and passed by the Hof-Theatre and read the bills. *Tristan and Isolde* was to be presented at night and a great singer would sing Isolde.

'He will go to hear that,' both boys said at once. 'He will be sure to go.'

It was decided between them that Marco should go on his quest alone when night came. One boy who hung about the entrance of the opera would be observed less than two.

'People notice crutches more than they notice legs,' The Rat said, 'I'd better keep out of the way unless you need me. My time hasn't come yet. Even if it doesn't come at all I've – I've been on duty. I've gone with you and I've been ready – that's what an aide-de-camp does.'

Marco went to the opera. Even if he had not known his way to the square near the place where the Hof-Theatre stood he could easily have found it by following the groups of people in the streets who all seemed to be walking in one direction. There were students in their odd caps walking three or four abreast, there were young couples and older ones, and here and there whole families; there were soldiers of all ages, officers and privates.

For some time Marco waited in the square and watched the carriages roll up and pass under the huge pillared portico to deposit their contents at the entrance and at once drive away in orderly sequence. He must make sure that the grand carriage with the green and silver liveries rolled up with the rest. If it came, he would buy a cheap ticket and go inside.

It was rather late when it arrived. The green and silver footman leaped to the ground and opened the carriage door almost before it stopped. The Chancellor got out

looking less genial than usual because he was afraid that
he might lose some of the overture. A rosy-cheeked girl in
a white frock was with him and she was evidently trying
to soothe him.

'I do not think we are really late, father,' she said.
'Don't feel cross, dear. It will spoil the music for you.'

This was not a time in which a man's attention could
be attracted quietly. Marco ran to get the ticket which
would give him a place among the rows of young soldiers,
artists, male and female students, and musicians who were
willing to stand four or five deep throughout the perfor-
mance of even the longest opera. He knew that, unless
they were in one of the few boxes which belonged only to
the court, the Chancellor and his rosy-cheeked daughter
would be in the best seats in the front curve of the balcony. He soon saw them. They had secured the central
places directly below the large royal box where two quiet
princesses and their attendants were already seated.

When he found he was not too late to hear the overture
the Chancellor's face became more genial than ever. He
settled himself down to an evening of enjoyment and
evidently forgot everything else in the world. Marco did
not lose sight of him. When the audience went out between the acts to promenade in the corridors, he might go
also and there might be a chance to pass near to him in
the crowd. He watched him closely.

The pretty daughter who sat beside him was attentive
but not so enthralled. After the first act two glittering
young officers appeared and made elegant and low bows,
drawing their heels together as they kissed her hand.
They looked sorry when they were obliged to return to
their seats again.

After the second act the Chancellor sat for a few minutes as if he were in a dream. The people in the seats near
him began to rise from their chairs and file out into the
corridors. The young officers were to be seen rising also.

The rosy daughter leaned forward and touched her father's arm gently.

'She wants him to take her out,' Marco thought. 'He will take her because he is good-natured.'

He saw him recall himself from his dream with a smile and then he rose and, after helping to arrange a silvery blue scarf round the girl's shoulders, gave her his arm just as Marco skipped out of his fourth-row standing place.

It was a rather warm night and the corridors were full. By the time Marco had reached the balcony floor, the pair had issued from the little door and were temporarily lost in the moving numbers.

Marco quietly made his way among the crowd trying to look as if he belonged to somebody. Once or twice his strong body and his dense black eyes and lashes made people glance at him, but he was not the only boy who had been brought to the opera so he felt safe enough to stop at the foot of the stairs and watch those who went up and those who passed by.

Suddenly he heard a low laugh and a moment later a hand lightly touched him.

'You *did* get out, then?' a soft voice said.

When he turned he felt his muscles stiffen. He ceased to slouch and did not smile as he looked at the speaker. What he felt was a wave of fierce and haughty anger. It swept over him before he had time to control it.

A lovely person who seemed swathed in several shades of soft violet drapery was smiling at him with long, lovely eyes.

It was the woman who had trapped him in No. 10 Brandon Terrace.

CHAPTER 21

'Help!'

'DID it take you long to find it?' asked the Lovely Person with a smile. 'Of course I knew you would find it in the end. But we had to give ourselves time. How long did it take?'

Marco removed himself from beneath the touch of her hand. It was quietly done, but there was a disdain in his young face which made her wince though she pretended to shrug her shoulders amusedly.

'You refuse to answer?' she laughed.

'I refuse.'

At that very moment he saw at the curve of the corridor the Chancellor and his daughter approaching slowly. They were on their way back to their box. Was he going to lose them? Was he?

The delicate hand was laid on his shoulder again, but this time he felt that it grasped him firmly.

'Naughty boy!' the soft voice said. 'I am going to take you home with me. If you struggle I shall tell these people that you are my bad boy who is here without permission. What will you answer? My escort is coming down the staircase and will help me. Do you see?' And in fact there appeared in the crowd at the head of the staircase the figure of the man he remembered.

He did see. A dampness broke out on the palms of his hands. If she did this bold thing, what could he say to those she told her lie to? How could he bring proof or explain who he was – and what story dare he tell? His protestations and struggles would merely amuse the lookers-on, who would see in them only the impotent rage of an insubordinate youngster.

There swept over him a wave of remembrance which brought back, as if he were living through it again, the moment when he had stood in the darkness of the wine-cellar with his back against the door and had heard the man walk away and leave him alone. He felt again as he had done then – but now he was in another land and far away from his father. He could do nothing to help himself unless Something showed him a way.

He made no sound, and the woman who held him saw only a flame leap under his dense black lashes.

But something within him called out. It was as if he heard it. It was that strong self – the self that was Marco, and it called – it called as if it shouted.

'Help!' it called – to that Unknown Stranger Thing which had made words and which he and his father so often talked of and in whose power they so believed. 'Help!'

The Chancellor was drawing nearer. Perhaps? Should he – ?

'You are too proud to kick and shout,' the voice went on. 'And people would only laugh. Do you see?'

The stairs were crowded and the man who was at the head of them could only move slowly. But he had seen the boy.

Marco turned so that he could face his captor squarely as if he were going to say something in answer to her. But he was not. Even as he made the movement of turning, the help he had called for came and he knew what he should do. And he could do two things at once – save himself and give his Sign – because, the Sign once given, the Chancellor would understand.

'He will be here in a moment. He has recognized you,' the woman said.

As he glanced up the stairs, the delicate grip of her hand unconsciously slackened.

Marco whirled away from her. The bell rang which was

to warn the audience that they must return to their seats and he saw the Chancellor hasten his pace.

A moment later, the old aristocrat found himself amazedly looking down at the pale face of a breathless lad who spoke to him in German and in such a manner that he could not but pause and listen.

'Sir,' he was saying, 'the woman in violet at the foot of the stairs is a spy. She trapped me once and she threatens to do it again. Sir, may I beg of you to protect me?'

He said it low and fast. No one else could hear his words.

'What! What!' the Chancellor exclaimed and made a movement.

And then, drawing a step nearer and quite as low and rapidly but with perfect distinctness, Marco uttered four words:

'The Lamp is lighted.'

The Help cry had been answered instantly. Marco saw it at once in the old man's eyes, notwithstanding that he turned to look at the woman at the foot of the staircase as if she only concerned him.

'What! What!' he said again, and made a movement towards her, pulling his large moustache with a fierce hand.

Then Marco recognized that a curious thing happened. The Lovely Person saw the movement and the grey moustache, and that instant her smile died away and she turned quite white – so white, that under the brilliant electric light she was almost green and scarcely looked lovely at all. She made a sign to the man on the staircase and slipped through the crowd like an eel. She was a slim, flexible creature and never was a disappearance more wonderful in its rapidity. Between stout matrons and their thin or stout escorts and families she made her way and lost herself – but always making towards the exit. In two minutes there was no sight of her violet draperies to be seen. She was gone and so, evidently, was her male companion.

It was plain to Marco that to follow the profession of a spy was not by any means a safe thing. The Chancellor had recognized her – she had recognized the Chancellor who turned looking ferociously angry and spoke to one of the young officers.

'She and the man with her are two of the most danger-ous spies in Europe. She is a Roumanian and he is a Russian. What they wanted of this innocent lad I don't pretend to know. What did she threaten?' to Marco.

Marco was feeling rather cold and sick and had lost his healthy colour for the moment.

'She said she meant to take me home with her and would pretend I was her son who had come here without permission,' he answered. 'She believes I know something I do not.' He made a hesitating but grateful bow. 'The third act, sir – I must not keep you. Thank you! Thank you!'

The Chancellor moved towards the entrance door of the balcony seats, but he did it with his hand on Marco's shoulder.

'See that he gets home safely,' he said to the younger of the two officers. 'Send a messenger with him. He's young to be attacked by creatures of that kind.'

Polite young officers naturally obey the commands of chancellors and dignitaries. This one found without trouble a young private who marched with Marco through the deserted streets to his lodgings. He was a stolid young Bavarian peasant and seemed to have no curiosity or even any interest in the reason for the com-mand given him. He scarcely gave a glance to the school-boy he was to escort, he neither knew nor wondered why.

The Rat had fallen asleep over his papers and lay with his head on his folded arms on the table. But he was awakened by Marco's coming into the room and sat up blinking his eyes in the effort to get them open.

'Did you see him? Did you get near enough?' he drowsed.

'Yes,' Marco answered. 'I got near enough.'

The Rat sat upright suddenly.

'It's not been easy,' he exclaimed. 'I'm sure something happened – something went wrong.'

'Something nearly went wrong – *very* nearly,' answered Marco. But as he spoke he took the sketch of the Chancellor out of the slit in his sleeve and tore it and burned it with a match. 'But I did get near enough. And that's *two*.'

They talked long, before they went to sleep that night. The Rat grew pale as he listened to the story of the woman in violet.

'I ought to have gone with you!' he said. 'I see now. An aide-de-camp must always be in attendance. It would have been harder for her to manage two than one. I must always be near to watch, even if I am not close by you. If you had not come back – if you had not come back!' He struck his clenched hands together fiercely. 'What should I have done!'

When Marco turned towards him from the table near which he was standing, he looked like his father.

'You would have gone on with the Game just as far as you could,' he said. 'You could not leave it. You remember the places, and the faces, and the Sign. There is some money; and when it was all gone, you could have begged, as we used to pretend we should. We have not had to do it yet, and it was best to save it for country places and villages. But you could have done it if you were obliged to. The Game would have to go on.'

The Rat caught at his thin chest as if he had been struck breathless.

'Without you?' he gasped. 'Without you?'

'Yes,' said Marco. 'And we must think of it, and plan in case anything like that should happen.'

He stopped himself quite suddenly, and sat down, looking straight before him, as if at some far away thing he saw.

'Nothing will happen,' he said. 'Nothing can.'

'What are you thinking of?' The Rat gulped, because his breath had not quite come back. 'Why will nothing happen?'

'Because –' the boy spoke in an almost matter-of-fact tone – in quite an exalted tone at all events, 'you see I can always make a strong call, as I did tonight.'

'Did you shout?' The Rat asked. 'I didn't know you shouted.'

'I didn't. I said nothing aloud. But I – the myself that is in me,' Marco touched himself on his breast, 'called out, "Help! Help!" with all its strength. And help came.'

The Rat regarded him dubiously.

'What did it call to?' he asked.

'To the Power – to the Strength-place – to the Thought that does things.'

A reluctant suspicion betrayed itself in The Rat's eyes.

'Do you mean you prayed?' he inquired, with a slight touch of disfavour.

Marco's eyes remained fixed upon him in vague thoughtfulness for a moment or so of pause.

'I don't know,' he said at last. 'Perhaps it's the same thing – when you need something so much that you cry out loud for it. But it's not words, it's a strong thing without a name. I called like that when I was shut up in the wine-cellar.'

The Rat moved restlessly.

'The help came that time,' he admitted. 'How did it come tonight?'

'In that thought which flashed into my mind almost the next second. It came like lightning. All at once I knew that if I ran to the Chancellor and said the woman was a spy, it would startle him into listening to me; and that then I could give him the Sign; and that when I gave him the Sign, he would know I was speaking the truth and would protect me.'

They heard a clumping step upon the staircase, and, when it reached the landing, it stopped at their door. Then there was a solid knock.

When Marco opened the door, the young soldier who had escorted him from the Hof-Theatre was standing outside. He looked as uninterested and stolid as before, as he handed in a small flat package.

'You must have dropped it near your seat at the Opera,' he said. 'I was to give it into your own hands. It is your purse.'

After he had clumped down the staircase again, Marco and The Rat drew a quick breath at one and the same time.

'I had no seat and I had no purse,' Marco said. 'Let us open it.'

There was a flat, limp leather note-holder inside. In it was a paper, at the head of which were photographs of the Lovely Person and her companion. Beneath were a few lines which stated that they were the well-known spies, Eugenia Karovna and Paul Varel, and that the bearer must be protected against them. It was signed by the Chief of Police. On a separate sheet was written the command: 'Carry this with you as protection.'

'That is help,' The Rat said. 'It would protect us, even in another country. The Chancellor sent it – but you made the strong call – and it's here!'

There was no street lamp to shine into their windows when they went at last to bed. When the blind was drawn up, they were nearer the sky than they had been in the Marylebone Road. The last thing each of them saw, as he went to sleep, was the stars.

CHAPTER 22

A Night Vigil

ON a hill in the midst of a great Austrian plain, around which high Alps wait watching through the ages, stands a venerable fortress, almost more beautiful than anything one has ever seen. Perhaps, if it were not for the great plain flowing broadly about it with its widespread beauties of meadow-land, and wood, and dim-toned buildings gathered about farms, and its dream of a small ancient city at its feet, it might seem something less a marvel of medieval picturesqueness. But out of the plain rises the low hill, and surrounding it at a stately distance stands guard the giant majesty of Alps, with shoulders in the clouds and god-like heads above them, looking on – sometimes themselves clouds of snow-whiteness, sometimes bare crags which pierce the blue, and whose silence seems to know the secret of the everlasting. And on the hill which this circle holds in its embrace, as though it enclosed a treasure, stands the old fortress built as a citadel for the prince archbishops, who were kings in their domain in the long past centuries when the splendour and power of ecclesiastical princes was among the greatest upon earth.

And as you approach the town and as you walk through its streets, whether you climb or descend – or cross bridges, or gaze at churches, or step out on your balcony at night to look at the mountains and the moon – always it seems that from some point you can see it gazing down at you – the citadel of Hohen-Salzburg.

It was to Salzburg they went next, because at Salzburg was to be found the man who looked like a hairdresser and who worked in a barber's shop. To him also must be carried the Sign.

'There may be people who come to him to be shaved —
soldiers, or men who know things,' The Rat worked it
out, 'and he can speak to them when he is standing close
to them. It will be easy to get near him. You can go and
have your hair cut.'

The journey from Munich was not a long one, and
during the latter part of it they had the wooden-seated
third-class carriage to themselves. To Marco the mountains were long-known wonders. Surely they had been the
first of the world! Surely they had been standing there
waiting when it was said 'Let there be Light'. The Light
had known it would find them there. They were so silent,
and yet it seemed as if they said some amazing thing —
something which would take your breath from you if you
could hear it. And they never changed. The clouds
changed, they wreathed them, and hid them, and trailed
down them, and poured out storm torrents on them, and
thundered against them, and darted forked lightnings
round them. But the mountains stood there afterwards as
if such things had not been. Winds roared and tore at
them, centuries passed over them — centuries of millions
of lives, of changing of kingdoms and empires, of battles
and world-wide fame which grew and died and passed
away; and temples crumbled, and kings' tombs were forgotten, and cities were buried and others built over them
after hundreds of years — and perhaps a few stones fell
from a mountainside, or a fissure was worn, which the
people below could not even see. And that was all. There
they stood, and perhaps their secret was that they had
been there for ever and ever and ever. That was what the
mountains said to Marco, which was why he did not want
to talk much, but sat and gazed out of the carriage window.

As they arrived early in the day, they had plenty of
time to wander about the marvellous little old city. But
through the wide streets and through the narrow ones,

under the archways into the market gardens, across the bridge and into the square where the Glockenspeil played its old tinkling tune, everywhere the Citadel looked down.

They found the hairdresser's shop in one of the narrow streets. There were no grand shops there, and this particular shop was a modest one. They walked past it once, and then went back. It was a shop so humble that there was nothing remarkable in two common boys going into it to have their hair cut. An old man came forward to receive them. He undertook to attend to The Rat himself, but, having arranged him in a chair, he turned about and called to someone in the back room.

'Heinrich,' he said.

In the slit in Marco's sleeve was the sketch of the man with smooth curled hair, who looked like a hairdresser. They had found a corner in which to take their final look at it before they turned back to come in. Heinrich, who came forth from the small back room, had smooth curled hair. He looked extremely like a hairdresser. He had features like those in the sketch – his nose and mouth and chin and figure were like what Marco had drawn and committed to memory. But –

He gave Marco a chair and tied the professional white covering around his neck. Marco leaned back and closed his eyes a moment.

'That is *not* the man!' he was saying to himself. 'He is *not* the man.'

How he knew he was not, he could not have explained, but he felt sure. It was a strong conviction. But for the sudden feeling, nothing would have been easier than to give the Sign. And if he could not give it now, where was the one to whom it must be spoken, and what would be the result if that one could not be found? And if there were two who were so much alike, how could he be sure?

Each owner of each of the pictured faces was a link in a

powerful secret chain; and if a link were missed, the chain would be broken. Each time Heinrich came within the line of his vision, he recorded every feature afresh and compared it with the remembered sketch. Each time the resemblance became more close, but each time some persistent inner conviction repeated, 'No; the Sign is not for him!'

It was disturbing, also, to find that The Rat was all at once as restless as he had previously been silent and preoccupied. He moved in his chair, to the great discomfort of the old hairdresser. He kept turning his head to talk. He asked Marco to translate questions he wished him to ask the two men. They were questions about the Citadel – about the Mönchsberg – the Residenz – the Glockenspiel – the mountains. He added one query to another and could not sit still.

'The young gentleman will get an ear snipped,' said the old man to Marco. 'And it will not be my fault.'

'What shall I do?' Marco was thinking. 'He is not the man.'

He did not give the Sign. He must go away and think it out, though where his thoughts would lead him he did not know. This was a more difficult problem than he had ever dreamed of facing. There was no one to ask advice of. Only himself and The Rat, who was nervously wriggling and twisting in his chair.

'You must sit still,' he said to him. 'The hairdresser is afraid you will make him cut you by accident.'

'But I want to know who lives at the Residenz?' said The Rat. 'These men can tell us things if you ask them.'

'It is done now,' said the old hairdresser with a relieved air. 'Perhaps the cutting of his hair makes the young gentleman nervous. It is sometimes so.'

The Rat stood close to Marco's chair and asked questions until Heinrich also had done his work. Marco could not understand his companion's mood. He realized that,

if he had wished to give the Sign, he had been allowed no
opportunity. He could not have given it. The restless
questioning had so directed the old man's attention to his
son and Marco that nothing could have been said to
Heinrich without his observing it.

'I could not have spoken if he had been the man,'
Marco said to himself.

Their very exit from the shop seemed a little hurried.
When they were in the street, The Rat made a clutch at
Marco's arm.

'You didn't give it?' he whispered breathlessly. 'I kept
talking and talking to prevent you.'

Marco tried not to feel breathless, and he tried to speak
in a low and level voice with no hint of exclamation in it.

'Why did you say that?' he asked.

The Rat drew closer to him.

'That was not the man!' he whispered. 'It doesn't
matter how much he looks like him, he isn't the right
one.'

He was pale and swinging along swiftly as if he were in
a hurry.

'There's a place not far away where we can get a look at
the mountains. Let's go there and sit down,' said Marco. 'I
knew it was not the right one, too.'

They got away from the streets and the people and
reached the quiet place where they could see the mountains. There they sat down by the wayside. The Rat took
off his cap and wiped his forehead, but it was not only the
quick walking which had made it damp.

'The queerness of it gave me a kind of fright,' he said.
'When he came out and he was near enough for me to see
him, a sudden strong feeling came over me. It seemed as if
I knew he wasn't the man. Then I said to myself – "but he
looks like him" – and I began to get nervous. And then I
was sure again – and then I wanted to try to stop you
from giving him the Sign.'

Marco was very quiet. He was looking at the farthest and highest peaks and wondering about many things.

'It was the expression of his face that was different,' he said. 'And his eyes. They are rather smaller than the right man's are. The light in the shop was poor, and it was not until the last time he bent over me that I found out what I had not seen before. His eyes are grey – the other ones are brown.'

'Did you see that!' The Rat exclaimed. 'Then we're sure! We're safe!'

'We're not safe till we've found the right man,' Marco said. 'Where is he? Where is he?'

He said the words dreamily and quietly, as if he were lost in thought – but also rather as if he expected an answer. And he still looked at the far-off peaks. The Rat, after watching him a moment or so, began to look at them also. They were like a loadstone to him too. There was something stilling about them, and when your eyes had rested upon them a few moments they did not want to move away.

'There must be a ledge up there somewhere,' he said at last. 'Let's go up and look for it and sit there and think and think – about finding the right man.'

There seemed nothing fantastic in this to Marco. To go into some quiet place and sit and think about the thing he wanted to remember or to find out was an old way of his. To be quiet was always the best thing, his father had taught him. It was like listening to something which could speak without words.

'There is a little train which goes up the Gaisberg,' he said. 'When you are at the top, a world of mountains spreads around you. Lazarus went once and told me. And we can lie out on the grass all night. Let us go, Aide-de-camp.'

So they went, each one thinking the same thoughts. Marco was the calmer of the two, because his belief that

there was always help to be found was an accustomed one.
He believed quite simply that it was the working of a law,
not the breaking of one, which gave answer and led him
in his quests. The Rat, who had known nothing of laws
other than those administered by police-courts, was at
once awed and fascinated by the suggestion of crossing
some borderland of the Unknown.

'You wouldn't get everything for nothing, as far as I can
make out,' he had said to Marco. 'You'd have to sweep all
the rubbish out of your mind – sweep it as if you did it
with a broom – and then keep on thinking straight and
believing you were going to get things – and working for
them – and they'd come.'

Then he had laughed a short ugly laugh because he
recalled something.

'There was something in the Bible that my father used
to jeer about – something about a man getting what he
prayed for if he believed it,' he said.

'Oh, yes, it's there,' said Marco. 'That if a man pray
believing he shall receive what he asks it shall be given
him. All the books say something like it. It's been said so
often it makes you believe it.'

'He didn't believe it, and I didn't,' said The Rat.

'Nobody does – really,' answered Marco, as he had done
once before. 'It's because we don't know.'

They went up the Gaisberg in the little train, which
pushed and dragged and panted slowly upward with
them. It took them with it stubbornly and gradually
higher and higher until it had left Salzburg and the
Citadel below and had reached the world of mountains
which rose and spread and lifted great heads behind each
other and beside each other and beyond each other.

There were only a few sightseers in the small carriages,
and they were going to look at the view from the summit.
They were not in search of a ledge.

The Rat and Marco were. When the little train stop-

ped at the top, they got out with the rest. They wandered
about with them over the short grass on the treeless summit and looked out from this viewpoint and the other.
The Rat grew more and more silent, and his silence was
not merely a matter of speechlessness but of expression. He
looked silent and as if he were no longer aware of the
earth. They left the sightseers at last and wandered away
by themselves. They found a ledge where they could sit or
lie and where even the world of mountains seemed below
them. They had brought some simple food with them,
and they laid it behind a jutting bit of rock. When the
sightseers boarded the labouring little train again and
were dragged back down the mountain, their night of
vigil would begin.

That was what it was to be. A night of stillness on the
heights, where they could wait and watch and hold themselves ready to hear any thought which spoke to them.

The Rat was so thrilled that he would not have been
surprised if he had heard a voice from the place of the
stars. But Marco only believed that in this great stillness
and beauty, if he held himself quiet enough, he should
find himself at last thinking of something that would lead
him to the place which held what it was best that he
should find. The people returned to the train and it set
out upon its way down the steepness.

They heard it labouring, and then they were alone, and
it was a loneness such as an eagle might feel when it held
itself poised high in the curve of blue. And they sat and
watched. They saw the sun go down, and shade by shade,
deepen and make radiant and then draw away with it the
last touches of colour – rose-gold, rose-purple, and rose-
grey. One mountain top after another held its blush a few
moments and lost it. It took long to gather them all but at
length they were gone and the marvel of night fell.

The breath of the forests below was sweet about them,
and soundlessness enclosed them which was of unearthly

peace. The stars began to show themselves, and presently the two who waited found their faces turned upwards to the sky and they both were speaking in whispers.

'The stars look large here,' The Rat said.

'Yes,' answered Marco, 'it seems like the top of the world.'

'There is a light on the side of the mountain yonder which is not a star,' The Rat whispered.

'It is a light in a hut where the guides take the climbers to rest and to spend the night,' answered Marco.

'It is so still,' The Rat whispered again after a silence, and Marco whispered back:

'It is so still.'

They had eaten their meal of black bread and cheese after the setting of the sun, and now they lay down on their backs and looked up until the first few stars had multiplied themselves into myriads. They began a little low talk, but the soundlessness was stronger than themselves.

They were only two boys, and they had begun their journey on the earliest train and had been walking about all day and thinking of great and anxious things.

'It is so still,' The Rat whispered again at last.

'It is so still,' whispered Marco.

And the mountains rising behind each other and beside each other and beyond each other in the night, and also the myriads of stars which had so multiplied themselves, looking down knew that they were asleep – as sleep the human things which do not watch for ever.

'Someone is smoking,' Marco found himself saying in a dream. After which he awakened and found that the smoke was not part of a dream at all. It came from the pipe of a young man who had an alpenstock and who looked as if he had climbed to see the sunrise. He wore

the clothes of a climber and a green hat with a tuft at the
back. He looked down at the two boys, surprised.

'Good day,' he said. 'Did you sleep here so that you
could see the sun get up?'

'Yes,' answered Marco.

'Were you cold?'

'We slept too soundly to know. And we brought our
thick coats.'

'I slept half-way down the mountain,' said the smoker.
'I am a guide in these days, but I have not been one long
enough to miss a sunrise it is no work to reach. My father
and brother think I am mad about such things. They
would rather stay in their beds. Oh! he is awake, is he?'
turning towards The Rat, who had risen on one elbow
and was staring at him. 'What is the matter? You look as
if you were afraid of me.'

Marco did not wait for The Rat to recover his breath
and speak.

'I know why he looks at you so,' he answered for him.
'He is startled. Yesterday we went to a hairdresser's shop
down below there, and we saw a man who was almost
exactly like you – only –' he added, looking up, 'his eyes
were grey and yours are brown.'

'He was my twin brother,' said the guide, puffing at his
pipe cheerfully. 'My father thought he could make hair-
dressers of us both, and I tried it for four years. But I
always wanted to be climbing the mountains and there
were not holidays enough. So I cut my hair, and washed
the pomade out of it, and broke away. I don't look like a
hairdresser now, do I?'

He did not. Not at all. But Marco knew him. He was
the man. There was no one on the mountain top but
themselves, and the sun was just showing a rim of gold
above the farthest and highest giants' shoulders. One
need not be afraid to do anything, since there was no one
to see or hear. Marco slipped the sketch out of the slit in

his sleeve. He looked at it and he looked at the guide, and then he showed it to him.

'That is not your brother. It is you!' he said.

The man's face changed a little – more than any other face had changed when its owner had been spoken to. On a mountain top as the sun rises one is not afraid.

'The Lamp is lighted,' said Marco. 'The Lamp is lighted.'

'God be thanked!' burst forth the man. And he took off his hat and bared his head. Then the rim behind the mountain's shoulder leaped forth into a golden torrent of splendour.

And The Rat stood up, resting his weight on his crutches in utter silence, and stared and stared.

'That is three!' said Marco.

CHAPTER 23

The Silver Horn

DURING the next week, which they spent in journeying towards Vienna, they gave the Sign to three different persons at places which were on the way. In a village across the frontier in Bavaria they found a giant of an old man sitting on a bench under a tree before his mountain Gasthaus or inn; and when the four words were uttered, he stood up and bared his head as the guide had done. When Marco gave the Sign in some quiet place to a man who was alone, he noticed that they all did this and said their 'God be thanked' devotedly, as if it were part of some religious ceremony. In a small town a few miles away he had to search some hours before he found a stalwart young shoemaker with bright red hair and a horseshoe-shaped scar on his forehead. He was not in his workshop when the boys first passed it, because, as they found out later, he had been climbing the day before, and had been detained in the descent because his companion had hurt himself.

When Marco went in and asked him to measure him for a pair of shoes, he was quite friendly and told them all about it.

'There are some good fellows who should not climb,' he said. 'When they find themselves standing on a bit of rock jutting out over emptiness, their heads begin to whirl round – and then, if they don't turn head over heels a few thousand feet, it is because some comrade is near enough to drag them back. There can be no ceremony then and they sometimes get hurt – as my friend did yesterday.'

'Did you never get hurt yourself?' The Rat asked.

'When I was eight years old I did that,' said the young

shoemaker, touching the scar on his forehead. 'But it was not much. My father was a guide and took me with him. He wanted me to begin early. There is nothing like it – climbing. I shall be at it again. This won't do for me. I tried shoemaking because I was in love with a girl who wanted me to stay at home. She married another man. I am glad of it. Once a guide, always a guide.' He knelt down to measure Marco's foot, and Marco bent a little forward.

'The Lamp is lighted,' he said.

There was no one in the shop, but the door was open and people were passing in the narrow street; so the shoemaker did not lift his red head. He went on measuring.

'God be thanked!' he said, in a low voice. 'Do you want these shoes really, or did you only want me to take your measure?'

'I cannot wait until they are made,' Marco answered. 'I must go on.'

'Yes, you must go on,' answered the shoemaker. 'But I'll tell you what I'll do – I'll make them and keep them. Some great day might come when I shall show them to people and swagger about them.' He glanced round cautiously, and then added, still bending over his measuring: 'They will be called the shoes of the Bearer of the Sign. And I shall say, "He was only a lad. This was the size of his foot." ' Then he stood up with a great smile.

'There'll be climbing enough to be done now,' he said, 'and I look to see you again somewhere.'

Strange were the places they went to and curiously unlike each other were the people to whom they carried their message. The most singular of all was an old woman who lived in so remote a place that the road to it wound round and round the mountain, for miles. It was not a bad road and it was an amazing one to travel, dragged in a small cart by a mule, when one could be dragged, and clambering slowly with rests between when one could not, as the road mounted and wound, higher and higher.

'How can anyone live higher than this?' said The Rat as they sat on the thick moss by the wayside after the mule and cart had left them. 'Look at the bare crags looming up above there. Let us look at her again. Her picture looked as if she were a hundred years old.'

Marco took out his hidden sketch. It seemed surely one of the strangest things in the world that a creature as old as this one seemed could reach such a place, or, having reached it, could ever descend to the world again to give aid to any person or thing.

Her old face was crossed and recrossed with a thousand wrinkles. Her profile was splendid yet, and she had been a beauty in her day. Her eyes were like an eagle's – and not an old eagle's. And she had a long neck which held her head high.

'How could she get here?' exclaimed The Rat.

'Those who sent us know, though we don't,' said Marco. 'Will you sit here and rest while I go on farther?'

'No!' The Rat answered stubbornly. 'I didn't train myself to stay behind. But we shall come to bare-rock climbing soon and then I shall be obliged to stop,' and he said the last bitterly. He knew that, if Marco had come alone, he would have ridden in no cart but would have trudged upward and onward sturdily to the end of his journey.

But they did not reach the crags, as they had thought must be inevitable. Suddenly, half-way up to the sky, as it seemed, they came to a bend in the road and found themselves mounting into a new green world, with velvet slopes and soft meadows and thick woodland, and cows feeding in pastures, and an ancient huddled village which might have rested there through all time.

There it stood. And the monsters in the blue above it themselves looked down upon it as if it were an incredible thing – this ancient, steep-roofed, hanging-balconied, crumbling cluster of human nests, which seemed a thousand miles from the world. Marco and The Rat stood and stared at it. Then they sat down and stared at it.

'How did it get here?' The Rat cried.

Marco shook his head. He certainly could see no explanation of its being there.

An old peasant driving a cow came down a steep path. He looked with a dull curiosity at The Rat and his crutches; but when Marco advanced and spoke to him in German, he did not seem to understand, but shook his head saying something in a sort of dialect Marco did not know.

'If they all speak like that, we shall have to make signs when we want to ask anything.' The Rat said. 'What will she speak?'

'She will know the German for the Sign or we should not have been sent here,' answered Marco. 'Come on.'

They made their way to the village, which huddled itself together evidently with the object of keeping warm when through the winter months the snows strove to bury it and the winds roared down from the mountain crags and tried to tear it from among its rocks. The doors and windows were few and small, and glimpses of the inside of the houses showed earthen floors and dark rooms. It was plain that it was counted a more comfortable thing to live without light than to let in the cold.

It was easy enough to reconnoitre. The few people they saw were evidently not surprised that strangers who discovered their unexpected existence should be curious and want to look at them and their houses.

The boys wandered about as if they were casual explorers, who having reached the place by chance were interested in all they saw. They went into the little Gasthaus and got some black bread and sausage and some milk. The mountaineer owner was a brawny fellow who

understood some German. He told them that few strangers knew of the village, but that bold hunters and
climbers came for sport. In the forests on the mountainsides were bears and, in the high places, chamois. Now
and again, some great gentlemen came with parties of the
daring kind – very great gentlemen indeed, he said, shaking his head with pride. There was one who had castles
in other mountains, but liked best to come here.

Marco began to wonder if several strange things might
not be true if great gentlemen sometimes climbed to the
mysterious place. But he had not been sent to give the
Sign to a great gentleman. He had been sent to give it to
an old woman with eyes like an eagle which was young.

He had a sketch in his sleeve, with that of her face, of
her steep-roofed, black-beamed, balconied house. If they
walked about a little, they would be sure to come upon it
in this tiny place. Then he could go in and ask her for a
drink of water.

They roamed about for an hour after they left the
Gasthaus. They went into the little church and looked at
the graveyard and wondered if it was not buried out of
all sight in the winter. After they had done this, they sauntered out and walked through the clusters of houses,
examining each one as they drew near it and passed.

'I see it!' The Rat exclaimed at last. 'It is that very old-
looking one standing a little way from the rest. It is not as
tumbled down as most of them. And there are some red
flowers on the balcony.'

'Yes! That's it!' said Marco.

They walked up to the low black door and, as he
stopped on the threshold, Marco took off his cap. He did
this because, sitting in the doorway on a low wooden
chair, the old, old woman with the eagle eyes was sitting
knitting.

There was no one else in the room and no one anywhere within sight. When the woman looked up at him,

holding her head high on her long neck, Marco knew he need not ask for water or for anything else.

'The Lamp is lighted,' he said, in his low but strong and clear young voice.

She dropped her knitting upon her knees and gazed at him a moment in silence. She knew German it was clear, for it was in German she answered him.

'God be thanked!' she said. 'Come in, young Bearer of the Sign, and bring your friend in with you. I live alone and not a soul is within hearing.'

She was a wonderful old woman. Neither Marco nor The Rat would forget the hours they spent in her strange dark house. She made them spend the night with her.

'It is quite safe,' she said. 'I live alone since my man fell into the crevasse and was killed because his rope broke when he was trying to save his comrade. So I have two rooms to spare, and sometimes climbers are glad to sleep in them. Mine is a good warm house, and I am well known in the village. You are very young,' she added shaking her head. 'You are very young. You must have good blood in your veins to be trusted with this.'

'I have my father's blood,' answered Marco.

'You are like someone I once saw,' the old woman said, and her eager eyes set themselves hard upon him. 'Tell me your name.'

There was no reason why he should not tell it to her.

'It is Marco Loristan,' he said.

'What! It is that!' she cried out, not loud but low.

To Marco's amazement she got up from her chair and stood before him, showing what a tall old woman she really was. There was a startled look in her face. And suddenly she actually made a sort of curtsey to him – bending her knee as peasants do when they pass a shrine.

'Is that it!' she said again. 'And yet they dare let you go on a journey like this! That speaks for your courage and for theirs.'

But Marco did not know what she meant. Her strange obeisance made him feel awkward. He stood up because his training had told him that when a woman stands a man also rises.

'The name speaks for the courage,' he said, 'because it is my father's.'

She watched him almost anxiously.

'You do not even know!' she breathed – and it was an exclamation and not a question.

'I know what I have been told to do,' he answered. 'I do not ask anything else.'

'Who is that?' she asked, pointing to The Rat.

'He is the friend my father sent with me,' said Marco smiling. 'He called him my Aide-de-camp. It was a sort of joke because we had played soldiers together.'

It seemed as if she were obliged to collect her thoughts. She stood with her hand at her mouth, looking down at the earth floor.

'God guard you!' she said at last. 'You are very – very young!'

'But all his years,' The Rat broke in, 'he has been training for just this thing. He did not know it was training, but it was. A soldier who had been trained for thirteen years would know his work.'

He was so eager that he forgot she could not understand English. Marco translated what he said into German and added: 'What he says is true.'

She nodded her head, still with questioning and anxious eyes.

'Yes. Yes,' she muttered. 'But you are very young.' Then she asked in a hesitating way:

'Will you not sit down until I do?'

'No,' answered Marco. 'I would not sit while my mother or grandmother stood.'

'Then I must sit – and forget,' she said.

She passed her hand over her face as though she were

sweeping away the sudden puzzled trouble in her expression. Then she sat down, as if she had obliged herself to become again the old peasant she had been when they entered.

'All the way up the mountain you wondered why an old woman should be given the Sign,' she said. 'You asked each other how she could be of use.'

Neither Marco nor The Rat said anything.

'When I was young and fresh,' she went on, 'I went to a castle over the frontier to be foster-mother to a child who was born a great noble – one who was near the throne. He loved me and I loved him. He was a strong child and he grew up a great hunter and climber. When he was not ten years old, my man taught him to climb. He always loved these mountains better than his own. He comes to see me as if he were only a young mountaineer. He sleeps in the room there,' with a gesture over her shoulder into the darkness. 'He has great power, and, if he chooses to do a thing, he will do it – just as he will attack the biggest bear or climb the most dangerous peak. He is one who can bring things about. It is very safe to talk in this room.'

Then all was quite clear. Marco and The Rat understood.

No more was said about the Sign. It had been given and that was enough. The old woman told them that they must sleep in one of her bedrooms. The next morning one of her neighbours was going down to the valley with a cart and he would help them on their way. The Rat knew that she was thinking of his crutches and he became restless.

'Tell her,' he said to Marco, 'how I have trained myself until I can do what anyone else can. And tell her I am growing stronger every day. Tell her. She thinks I'm no use.'

Marco explained and the old woman listened attentively. When The Rat got up and swung himself about up and down the steep path near her house she seemed relieved.

'If he has taught himself to be like that just for love of your father, he will go to the end,' she said. 'It is more than one could believe, that a pair of crutches could do such things.'

The Rat was pacified and could afterwards give himself up to watching her as closely as he wished to. He was soon 'working out' certain things in his mind. What he watched was her way of watching Marco. It was as if she was fascinated and could not keep her eyes from him. She told them stories about the mountains and the strangers who came to climb or hunt. She told them about the storms, which sometimes seemed about to put an end to the little world among the crags. She described the winter when the snow buried them and the strong ones were forced to dig out the weak, and some lived for days under the masses of soft whiteness, glad to keep their cows or goats in their rooms that they might share the warmth of their bodies.

While she talked, she watched Marco as if she were always asking herself some question about him. The Rat was sure that she liked him and greatly admired his strong body and good looks. It was not necessary for him to carry himself slouching in her presence, and he looked glowing and noble. There was a sort of reverence in her manner when she spoke to him. She reminded him of Lazarus more than once. When she gave them their evening meal, she insisted on waiting on him with a certain respectful ceremony. She would not sit at table with him, and The Rat began to realize that she felt that he himself should be standing to serve him.

'She thinks I ought to stand behind your chair as Lazarus stands behind your father's,' he said to Marco. 'Perhaps an aide ought to do it. Shall I? I believe it would please her.'

'A Bearer of the Sign is not a royal person,' answered Marco. 'My father would not like it – and I should not. We are only two boys.'

It was very wonderful when, after their supper was over, they all three sat together before the fire.

The red glow of the bed of wood-coal and the orange yellow of the flame from the big logs filled the room with warm light, which made a mellow background for the figure of the old woman as she sat in her low chair and told them more and more enthralling stories.

Her eyes glowed and her long neck held her head splendidly high as she described great feats of courage and endurance in aiding those in peril, and, when she glowed most in the telling, they always knew that the hero of the adventure had been her foster-child who was the baby born a great noble and near the throne. To her, he was the most splendid of human beings, and yet he never forgot the long-past days when she had held him on her knee and told him tales of chamois and bear-hunting, and the mountain-tops in mid-winter.

'Yes! Yes!' she said. ' "Good Mother",' he calls me. And I bake him a cake on the hearth, as I did when he was ten years old and my man was teaching him to climb. And when he chooses that a thing shall be done – done it is! He is a great lord.'

The flames had died down and only the big bed of red coal made the room glow, and they were thinking of going to bed when the old woman started very suddenly, turning her head as if to listen.

Marco and The Rat heard nothing, but they saw that she did, and they sat so still that each held his breath.

Then they did hear something – a clear silver sound, piercing the pure mountain air.

The old woman sprang upright with the fire of delight in her eyes.

'It is his silver horn!' she cried out striking her hands

together. 'It is his own call to me when he is coming. He
has been hunting somewhere and wants to sleep in his
good bed there. Help me to put on more faggots,' to The
Rat, 'so that he will see the flame on them through the
open door as he comes.'

'Shall we be in the way?' said Marco. 'We can go at
once.'

She was going towards the door to open it, and she
stopped for a moment and turned.

'No, no!' she said. 'He must see your face. He will want
to see it. I want him to see – how young you are.'

She threw the door wide open and they heard the silver
horn send out its gay call again. The brushwood and
faggots The Rat had thrown on the coals crackled and
sparkled and roared into flames, which threw out in relief
the figure which stood on the threshold and looked so
tall.

And in but a few minutes her great lord came to her.
And in his green hunting-suit with its green hat and
eagle's feather he was as splendid as she had said he was.
He was big and royal-looking and laughing, and he bent
and kissed her as if he had been her own son.

'Yes, Good Mother,' they heard him say. 'I want my
warm bed and one of your good suppers. I sent the others
to the Gasthaus.'

He came into the redly-glowing room and his head
almost touched the blackened rafters. Then he saw the
two boys.

'Who are these?' he asked.

She lifted his hand and kissed it.

'They are the Bearers of the Sign,' she said rather softly.
' "The Lamp is lighted." '

Then his whole look changed. His laughing face became quite grave and for a moment looked even anxious.
Marco knew it was because he was startled to find them

only boys. He made a step forward to look at them more closely.

Marco stood out in the fire-glow that he might see him well. He saluted with respect.

'My name is Marco Loristan, Highness,' he said. 'And my father sent me.'

The change which came upon his face then was even greater than at first. Marco even felt that there was a flash of alarm in it. But almost at once that passed.

'Loristan is a great man and a great patriot,' he said. 'If he sent you, it is because he knows you are the one safe messenger. He has worked too long for Samavia not to know what he does.'

Marco saluted again. He knew what it was right to say next.

'If we have your Highness's permission to retire,' he said, 'we will leave you and go to bed. We go down the mountain at sunrise.'

'Where next?' asked the hunter, looking at him with curious intentness.

'To Vienna, Highness,' Marco answered.

His questioner held out his hand, still with the intent interest in his eyes.

'Good night, fine lad,' he said. 'Samavia has need to vaunt itself on its Sign-bearer. God go with you.'

He stood and watched him as he went towards the room in which he and his aide-de-camp were to sleep. The Rat followed him closely. At the little back door the old, old woman stood, having opened it for them. As Marco passed and bade her good night, he saw that she again made the strange obeisance, bending the knee as he went by.

CHAPTER 24

'How Shall we Find Him?'

In Vienna they came upon a pageant. In celebration of a century-past victory the Emperor drove in state to attend at the cathedral and do honour to the ancient banners and laurel-wreathed statue of the long-dead soldier-prince. The broad pavements were crowded with a cheering populace watching the martial splendour as it passed by with marching feet, prancing horses, and glitter of scabbard and chain.

The Rat was enormously thrilled by the imperial palace. Its immense spaces, the squares and gardens, reigned over by statues of emperors and warriors and queens, seemed to sweep out of his world all atmosphere but that of splendid cities down whose broad avenues emperors rode with waving banners, and golden trumpets blaring forth. It seemed as if it must always be like this – that lances and cavalry and emperors would never cease to ride by. 'I should like to stay here a long time,' he said almost as if he were in a dream. 'I should like to see it all.'

He leaned on his crutches in the crowd and watched the glitter of the passing pageant. Now and then he glanced at Marco, who watched also with a steady eye which, The Rat saw, nothing would escape. How absorbed he always was in the Game! Often it seemed that he was not a boy at all. And the Game was a game no more, but a thing of deadly earnest, which touched kings and thrones. And they – two lads pushed about by the crowd as they stood and stared at the soldiers – carried with them that which was even now lighting the Lamp. The blood in The Rat's veins ran quickly and made him feel hot as he remembered certain thoughts which had forced themselves into his mind during the past weeks. As his brain had the trick of 'working things out', it had been following a wonderful even if rather fantastic and fever-ish fancy. A mere trifle had set it at work, but, its labour once begun, things which might have once seemed to be trifles appeared so no longer. When Marco was asleep, The Rat lay awake looking backward and recalling every detail of their lives since they had known each other. Sometimes it seemed to him that almost everything he remembered had pointed to but one thing. And then again he would all at once feel that he was a fool and had better keep his head steady. Marco, he knew, had no wild fancies. He had learned too much and his mind was too well balanced. He did not try to 'work out things'. He only thought of what he was under orders to do.

'But,' said The Rat more than once in these midnight hours, 'if it ever comes to a draw whether he is to be saved or I am, he is the one that must come to no harm. Killing can't take long — and his father sent me with him.'

He managed to work himself closer to Marco's side. 'Isn't it splendid?' he said. 'I wish I was an emperor myself. I'd have these fellows out like this every day.' He said it only because he wanted to say something, to speak, as a reason for getting closer to him. He wanted to be near enough to touch him and feel that they were really to-gether and that the whole thing was not a sort of mag-nificent dream from which he might awaken to find himself lying on his heap of rags in his corner of the room in Bone Court.

The crowd swayed forward in its eagerness to see the principal feature of the pageant — the Emperor in his carriage. The Rat swayed forward with the rest to look as it passed.

A white-haired personage in splendid uniform decor-ated with jewelled orders and with a cascade of emerald-green plumes nodding in his military helmet gravely saluted the shouting people on either side. By him sat a man uniformed, decorated, and emerald-plumed also, but many years younger.

Marco's arm touched The Rat's almost at the same moment that his own touched Marco. Under the nodding plumes each saw the rather tired and cynical pale face, a sketch of which was hidden in the slit of Marco's sleeve.

'Is the one who sits with the Emperor an archduke?' Marco asked the man nearest to him in the crowd. The man answered amiably enough. No, he was not, but he was a prince, and a great favourite of the Emperor's, and a great personage, whose palaces contained pictures celebrated throughout Europe.

'He pretends it is only pictures he cares for,' he went on, shrugging his shoulders and speaking to his wife, who had begun to listen, 'but he is a clever one who amuses himself with things he professes not to concern himself about — big things. It's his way to look bored, and interested in nothing, but it's said he's a wizard for knowing dangerous secrets.'

'Does he live at the Hofburg with the Emperor?' asked the woman, craning her neck to look after the imperial carriage.

'No, but he's often there. The Emperor is lonely and bored too, no doubt, and this one has ways of making him forget his troubles.'

The two boys followed the celebration to its end. They managed to get near enough to see the entrance to the church where the service was held and to get a view of the ceremonies at the laurel-wreathed statue. They saw the man with the pale face several times, but it was not possible to get within yards of him. It happened once, however, that he looked through a temporary break in the crowding people and saw a dark, strong-featured and remarkably intent boy's face, whose vivid scrutiny of him caught his eye. Marco met his gaze squarely.

'Look at me! Look at me!' the boy was saying to him mentally. 'I have a message for you. A message!'

The tired eyes in the pale face rested on him with growing interest and curiosity, but the crowding people moved and the temporary break closed up, so that the two could see each other no more. Marco and The Rat were pushed backward by those taller and stronger than themselves until they were on the outskirts of the crowd.

'Let us go to the Hofburg,' said Marco. 'They will come back there, and we shall see him again even if we can't get near.'

They made their way through the less crowded streets, and waited as near to the great palace as they could get. They were there when the imperial carriages returned, but, though they saw their man again, they were at some distance from him and he did not see them.

Then followed four singular days, full of tantalizing incidents. Nothing seemed easier than to hear talk of, and see the Emperor's favourite, but nothing was more impossible than to get near him. Tonight he would be sure to be at this great house or that, at this ball or that banquet. There was no difficulty in discovering that he would be sure to go to the opera, or the theatre, or to drive to Schönbrunn with his imperial master. Marco and The Rat heard casual speech of him again and again, and from one part of the city to the other they followed and waited for him. But it was like chasing a will-o'-the-wisp. He was too brilliant and important a person to be allowed to move about alone. There were always people with him who seemed absorbed in his languid cynical talk. Marco thought that he never seemed to care much for his companions, though they on their part always seemed highly entertained by what he was saying. It was noticeable that they laughed a great deal, though he himself scarcely ever smiled.

'He's one of those chaps with the trick of saying witty

things as if he didn't see the fun in them himself,' The Rat summed up. 'Chaps like that are always cleverer than the other kind.'

'He's too high in favour and too rich not to be followed about,' they heard a man in a shop say one day, 'but he gets tired of it. Sometimes, when he's too bored to stand it any longer, he gives it out that he's gone into the mountains somewhere, and all the time he's shut up alone with his pictures in his own palace.'

That night The Rat came in to their attic looking pale and disappointed. He had been out to buy some food after a long and arduous day in which they had covered much ground, had seen their man three times, and each time under circumstances which made him more inaccessible than ever. They had come back to their poor quarters both tired and ravenously hungry.

The Rat threw his purchase on the table and himself into a chair.

'He's gone to Budapest,' he said. '*Now* how shall we find him?'

They sat silent for a few minutes because there seemed to be nothing to say. 'We are too tired and hungry to be able to think well,' Marco said at last. 'Let us eat our supper and then go to sleep. Until we've had a rest, we must "let go".'

'Yes. There's no good in talking when you're tired,' The Rat answered a trifle gloomily. 'You don't reason straight.'

The meal was simple, but they ate well and without words. Even when they had finished and undressed for the night, they said very little.

'Where do our thoughts go when we are asleep?' The Rat inquired casually after he was stretched out in the darkness. 'They must go somewhere. Let's send them to find out what to do next.'

'It's not as still as it was on the Gaisberg. You can hear

the city roaring,' said Marco drowsily from his dark corner. 'We must make a ledge – for ourselves.'

Sleep made it for them – deep, restful, healthy sleep. If they had been more resentful of their ill-luck and lost labour, it would have come less easily and been less natural. In their talks of strange things they had learned that the one great secret of strength and unflagging courage is to know how to 'let go' – to cease thinking over an anxiety until the right moment comes.

When Marco opened his eyes in the morning, he found The Rat lying looking at him. Then they both sat up in bed at the same time.

'I believe we are both thinking the same thing,' Marco said.

'So do I,' answered the Rat. 'It shows how tired we were that we didn't think of it last night.'

'We have both remembered,' said Marco, 'what we heard about his shutting himself up alone with his pictures and making people believe he had gone away.'

'He's in his palace now,' The Rat announced.

'Do you feel sure of that, too?' asked Marco. 'Did you wake up and feel sure of it the first thing?'

'Yes,' answered The Rat. 'As sure as if I'd heard him say it himself.'

'So did I,' said Marco.

'That's what our thoughts brought back to us,' said The Rat, 'when we "let go" and sent them off last night.' He sat up hugging his knees and looking straight before him for some time after this, and Marco did not interrupt his meditations.

The day was a brilliant one and the sun shone in through their attic window as they ate their breakfast. After it, they leaned on the window's ledge and talked about the Prince's garden. It was open to the public and they had walked round it more than once. The palace stood in the midst of it. The Prince was good-natured enough to allow quiet and well-behaved people to saunter through. It was not a fashionable promenade but a pleasant retreat for people who sometimes took their work or books and sat on the seats placed here and there among the shrubs and flowers.

'When we were there the first time, I noticed two things,' Marco said. 'There is a stone balcony which juts out from the side of the palace which looks on the Fountain Garden. That day there were chairs on it as if the Prince and his visitors sometimes sat there. Near it there was a large evergreen shrub, and I saw that there was a hollow place inside it. If someone wanted to stay in the gardens all night to watch the windows when they were lighted and see if anyone came out alone upon the balcony, he could hide himself in the hollow place and stay there until the morning.'

'Is there room for two inside the shrub?' The Rat asked.

'No. I must go alone,' said Marco.

CHAPTER 25

A Voice in the Night

LATE that afternoon there wandered about the gardens
two quiet, rather poorly dressed boys. They looked at the
palace, the shrubs, and the flower-beds, as strangers usually did, and they sat on the seats and talked as people
were accustomed to seeing boys talk together. It was a
sunny day and exceptionally warm, and there were more
saunterers and sitters than usual, which was perhaps the
reason why the *portier* at the entrance gates gave such
slight notice to the pair that he did not observe that,
though two boys came in, only one went out.

It happened that, when The Rat passed out, the *portier*
was much interested in the aspect of the sky, which was
curiously threatening. There had been heavy clouds
hanging about all day and now and then blotting out the
sunshine entirely. Just now, they had piled themselves in
thunderous, purplish mountains, and the sun had been
forced to set behind them.

'It's been a sort of battle since morning,' the *portier*
said. 'There will be some crashes and cataracts tonight.'
That was what The Rat had thought when they sat in the
Fountain Garden on a seat which gave them a good view
of the balcony and the big evergreen shrub, which they
knew had the hollow in the middle. 'If there should be a
big storm, the evergreen will not save you much, though it
may keep off the worst,' The Rat said. 'I wish there was
room for two.'

He would have wished there was room for two if he had
seen Marco marching to the stake. As the gardens emptied, the boys rose and walked round once more, as if on
their way out. By the time they had sauntered towards the

big evergreen, nobody was in the Fountain Garden, and
the last loiterers were moving towards the arched stone
entrance to the streets.

When they drew near one side of the evergreen, the two
were together. When The Rat swung out on the other
side of it, he was alone! No one noticed that anything
had happened; no one looked back. So The Rat swung
down the walks and round the flower-beds and passed
into the street. And the *portier* looked at the sky and
made his remark about the 'crashes' and 'cataracts'.

As the darkness came on, the hollow of the shrub seemed
a very safe place. It was not in the least likely that anyone
would enter the closed gardens; and if by rare chance
some servant passed through, he would not be in search of
people who wished to watch all night in the middle of an
evergreen instead of going to bed and to sleep. The hollow was well enclosed with greenery, and there was room
to sit down when one was tired of standing.

Marco stood for a long time, because by doing so he
could see plainly the windows opening on the balcony if
he gently pushed aside some flexible young boughs. He
had managed to discover in his first visit to the gardens
that the windows overlooking the Fountain Garden were
those which belonged to the Prince's own suite of rooms.
Those which opened on to the balcony lighted his favourite apartment, which contained his best-beloved books
and pictures and in which he spent most of his secluded
leisure hours.

Marco watched these windows anxiously. If the Prince
had not gone to Budapest he would be living in his
favourite rooms and lights would show themselves. And if
there were lights, he might pass before a window. The
twilight deepened into darkness and, because of the heavy
clouds, it was very dense. Faint gleams showed themselves
in the lower part of the palace, but none was lighted in

the windows Marco watched. He waited so long that it became evident that none was to be lighted at all. At last he loosed his hold on the young boughs and, after standing a few moments in thought, sat down upon the earth in the midst of his embowered tent. The Prince was not in his retreat; he was probably not in Vienna. So much lost time through making a mistake – but it was best to have made the venture. Not to have made it would have been to lose a chance. The entrance was closed for the night and there was no getting out of the gardens until the next day. He must stay in his hiding-place until the time when the people began to come and bring their books and knitting and sit on the seats. Then he could stroll out without attracting attention. But he had the night before him to spend as best he could. That would not matter at all. He could tuck his cap under his head and go to sleep on the ground. He could command himself to waken once every half-hour and look for the lights. But the clouds which made the night so dark were giving forth low rumbling growls. At intervals a threatening gleam of light shot across them and a sudden swish of wind rushed through the trees in the gardens. This happened several times, and then Marco began to hear the patter of raindrops. They were heavy and big, but few at first, and then there was a new and more powerful rush of wind, a jagged dart of light in the sky, and a tremendous crash. After that the clouds tore themselves open and poured forth their contents in floods. After the protracted struggle of the day it all seemed to happen at once, as if a horde of lions had been let loose: flame after flame of lightning, roar and crash and sharp reports of thunder, shrieks of hurricane wind, torrents of rain, gathered and rushed and burst upon the earth. It was such a storm as people remember for a lifetime and which in few lifetimes is seen at all.

Marco stood still in the midst of the rage and flooding, blinding roar of it. After the first few minutes he knew he

could do nothing to shield himself. Down the garden
paths he heard cataracts rushing. He held his cap pressed
against his eyes because he seemed to stand in the midst of
darting flames. The crashes, cannon reports and thunder-
ings, and the jagged streams of light came so close to one
another that he seemed deafened as well as blinded. He
wondered if he should ever be able to hear human voices
again when it was over. That he was drenched to the skin
and that the water poured from his clothes as if he were
himself a cataract was so small a detail that he was
scarcely aware of it. He stood still, bracing his body, and
waited. If he had been a Samavian soldier in the trenches
and such a storm had broken upon him and his comrades,
they could only have braced themselves and waited. This
was what he found himself thinking when the tumult and
downpour were at their worst. There were men who had
waited in the midst of a rain of bullets.

It was not long after this thought had come to him that
there occurred the first temporary lull in the storm. Its
fury perhaps reached its height and broke at that moment. A yellow flame had torn its jagged way across the
heavens, and an earth-rending crash had thundered itself
into rumblings which actually died away before breaking
forth again. Marco took his cap from his eyes and drew a
long breath. He drew two long breaths. It was as he began
drawing a third and realizing the strange feeling of the
almost stillness about him that he heard a new kind of
sound at the side of the garden nearest his hiding-place. It
sounded like the creak of a door opening somewhere in
the wall behind the laurel hedge. Someone was coming
into the garden by a private entrance. He pushed aside
the young boughs again and tried to see, but the darkness
was too dense. Yet he could hear if the thunder would not
break again. There was the sound of feet on the wet
gravel, the footsteps of more than one person coming
towards where he stood, but not as if afraid of being

heard; merely as if they were at liberty to come in by what
entrance they chose. Marco remained very still. A sudden
hope gave him a shock of joy. If the man with the tired
face chose to hide himself from his acquaintances, he
might choose to go in and out by a private entrance. The
footsteps drew near, passed by, and seemed to pause
somewhere near the balcony; and then flame lit up the
sky again and the thunder burst forth once more.

But this was its last great peal. The storm was at an
end. Only fainter and fainter rumblings and mutterings
and paler and paler darts followed. Even they were soon
over, and the cataracts in the paths had rushed themselves
silent. But the darkness was still deep.

It was deep to blackness in the hollow of the evergreen.
Marco stood in it, streaming with rain, but feeling nothing because he was full of thought. He pushed aside his
greenery and kept his eye on the place in the darkness
where the windows must be, though he could not see
them. He began to breathe quickly because he was waiting for something.

Suddenly he saw exactly where the windows were – because they were all lighted!

His feeling of relief was great, but it did not last very
long. It was true that something had been gained in the
certainty that his man had not left Vienna. But what
next? It would not be so easy to follow him if he chose
only to go out secretly at night. What next? To spend the
rest of the night watching a lighted window was not
enough. Tomorrow night it might not be lighted. But he
kept his gaze fixed upon it. He tried to fix all his will and
thought-power on the person inside the room. Perhaps he
could reach him and make him listen, even though he
would not know that anyone was speaking to him.

'I must speak to you. I must speak to you!' he found
himself saying in a low intense voice. 'I am outside here
waiting. Listen! I must speak to you!'

He said it many times and kept his eyes fixed upon the window which opened on to the balcony. Once he saw a man's figure cross the room, but he could not be sure who it was. The clouds were breaking and it was not long before a brilliant full moon showed herself sailing in the rift, suddenly flooding everything with light. Parts of the garden were silver white, and the tree shadows were like black velvet. A silvery lance pierced even into the hollow of Marco's evergreen and struck across his face.

Perhaps it was this sudden change which attracted the attention of those inside the balconied room. A man's figure appeared at the long windows. Marco saw now that it was the Prince. He opened the windows and stepped out on to the balcony.

'It is all over,' he said quietly. And he stood with his face lifted, looking at the great white sailing moon.

He stood very still and seemed for a moment to forget the world and himself. It was a wonderful, triumphant queen of a moon. But something brought him back to earth. A low, but strong and clear, voice came up to him from the path below.

'The Lamp is lighted. The Lamp is lighted,' it said, and the words seemed to call to him, to arrest him, to draw him.

He stood still a few seconds in silence. Then he bent over the balustrade. The moonlight had not broken the darkness below.

'That is a boy's voice,' he said in a low tone, 'but I cannot see who is speaking.'

'Yes, it is a boy's voice,' it answered, in a way which somehow moved him, because it was so ardent. 'It is the son of Stefan Loristan. The Lamp is lighted.'

'Wait. I am coming down to you,' the Prince said.

In a few minutes Marco heard a door open gently not far from where he stood. Then the man he had been following so many days appeared at his side.

'How long have you been here?' he asked.

'Before the gates closed. I hid myself in the hollow of a big shrub there, Highness,' Marco answered.

'Then you were out in the storm?'

'Yes, Highness.'

The Prince put his hand on the boy's shoulder. 'I cannot see you – but it is best to stand in the shadow. You are drenched to the skin.'

'I have been able to give your Highness – the Sign,' Marco whispered. 'A storm is nothing.'

There was a silence. Marco knew his companion was pausing to turn something over in his mind.

'So-o?' he said slowly, at length, 'The Lamp is lighted. And *you* are sent to bear the Sign.' Something in his voice made Marco feel that he was smiling.

'What a race you are! What a race – you Samavian Loristans!'

He paused as if to think the thing over again.

'I want to see your face,' he said next. 'Here is a tree with a shaft of moonlight striking through the branches. Let us step aside and stand under it.'

Marco did as he was told. The shaft of moonlight fell upon his uplifted face and showed its young strength and darkness, quite splendid for the moment in a triumphant glow of joy in obstacles overcome. Raindrops hung on his hair, but he did not look draggled, only very wet and picturesque.

The Prince looked him over with interested curiosity.

'Yes,' he said in his cool, rather dragging voice. 'You are the son of Stefan Loristan. Also you must be taken care of. You must come with me. I have trained my household to remain in its own quarters until I require its services. I have attached to my own apartments a good safe little room where I sometimes keep people. You can dry your clothes and sleep there. When the gardens are open again, the rest will be easy.'

But though he stepped out from under the trees and began to move towards the palace in the shadow, Marco noticed that he moved hesitatingly, as if he had not quite decided what he should do. He stopped rather suddenly and turned again to Marco, who was following him.

'There is someone in the room I just now left' – he said, 'an old man – whom it might interest to see you. It might also be a good thing for him to feel interest in you. I choose that he shall see you – as you are.'

'I am at your command, Highness,' Marco answered. He knew his companion was smiling again.

'You have been in training for more centuries than you know,' he said; 'and your father has prepared you to encounter the unexpected without surprise.'

They passed under the balcony and paused at a low stone doorway hidden behind shrubs. The door was a beautiful one, Marco saw when it was opened, and the corridor disclosed was beautiful also, though it had an air of quiet and aloofness which was not so much secret as private. A perfect though narrow staircase mounted from it to the next floor. After ascending it, the Prince led the way through a short corridor and stopped at the door at the end of it. 'We are going in here,' he said.

It was a wonderful room – the one which opened on to the balcony. The place was rich and mellow with exquisitely chosen beauties.

In a massive chair upon the hearth sat a figure with bent head. It was a tall old man with white hair and moustache. His elbow rested upon the arm of his chair and he leaned his forehead on his hand as if he were weary.

Marco's companion crossed the room and stood beside him, speaking in a lowered voice. Marco could not at first hear what he said. He himself stood quite still, waiting. The white-haired man lifted his head and listened. It seemed as though almost at once he was singularly interested. The lowered voice was slightly raised at last and Marco heard the last two sentences:

'The only son of Stefan Loristan. Look at him.'

The old man in the chair turned slowly and looked steadily, and with questioning curiosity touched with grave surprise. He had keen and clear blue eyes.

Then Marco, still erect and silent, waited again. The Prince had merely said to him 'an old man whom it might interest to see you'. He had plainly intended that, whatsoever happened, he must make no outward sign of seeing more than he had been told he would see – 'an old man'. It was for him to show no astonishment or recognition. The power of remaining still under scrutiny, which The Rat had often envied him, stood him now in good stead. Because he had seen the white head and tall form not many days before, surmounted by brilliant emerald plumes, hung with jewelled decorations, in the royal carriage.

'He is like his father,' this personage said to the Prince. 'But if anyone but Loristan had sent him – His looks please me.' Then suddenly to Marco, 'You were waiting outside while the storm was going on?'

'Yes, sir,' Marco answered.

Then the two exchanged some words still in the lowered voice.

'You read the news as you made your journey?' he was asked. 'You know how Samavia stands?'

'She does not stand,' said Marco. 'The Iarovitch and Maranovitch have fought as hyenas fight, until each has torn the other into fragments – and neither has blood nor strength left.'

The two glanced at each other.

'A good simile,' said the older man. 'You are right. If a strong party rose – and a greater power chose not to interfere – the country might see better days.' He looked at him a few moments longer and then waved his hand kindly.

'You are a fine Samavian,' he said. 'I am glad of that. You may go. Good night.'

Marco bowed respectfully and the man with the tired face led him out of the room.

It was just before he left him in the small quiet chamber in which he was to sleep that the Prince gave him a final curious glance. 'I remember now,' he said. 'In the room, when you answered the question about Samavia, I was sure that I had seen you before. It was the day of the celebration. There was a break in the crowd and I saw a boy looking at me. It was you.'

'Yes,' said Marco, 'I have followed you each time you have gone out since then, but I could never get near enough to speak. Tonight seemed only one chance in a thousand.'

'You are doing your work more like a man than a boy,' was the next speech, and it was made reflectively. 'No man could have behaved more perfectly than you did just now, when discretion and composure were necessary.' Then, after a moment's pause, 'He was deeply interested and deeply pleased. Good night.'

When the gardens had been thrown open the next morning and people were passing in and out again, Marco passed out also. He was obliged to tell himself two or three times that he had not wakened from an amazing dream. He quickened his pace after he had crossed the street, because he wanted to get home to the attic and talk to The Rat. There was a narrow side-street it was necessary for him to pass through if he wished to make a short cut. As he turned into it, he saw a curious figure leaning on crutches against a wall. It looked damp and forlorn, and he wondered if it could be a beggar. It was not. It was The Rat, who suddenly saw who was approaching and swung forward. His face was pale and haggard and he

looked worn and frightened. He dragged off his cap and
spoke in a voice which was hoarse as a crow's.

'God be thanked!' he said. 'God be thanked!' as people
always said it when they received the Sign, alone. But
there was a kind of anguish in his voice as well as relief.

'Aide-de-camp!' Marco cried out – The Rat had begged
him to call him so. 'What have you been doing? How long
have you been here?'

'Ever since I left you last night,' said The Rat, clutch-
ing tremblingly at his arm as if to make sure he was real.
'If there was not room for two in the hollow, there was
room for one in the street. Was it my place to go off duty
and leave you alone – was it?' fiercely.

'You were out in the storm?'

'Weren't you?' still fiercely. 'I huddled against the wall
as well as I could. What did I care? Crutches don't prevent a fellow waiting. I wouldn't have left you if you'd
given me orders. And that would have been mutiny.
When you did not come out as soon as the gates opened, I
felt as if my head got on fire. How could I know what had
happened? I've not the nerve and backbone you have. I
go half–mad.' For a second or so Marco did not answer.
But when he put his hand on the damp sleeve, The Rat
actually started, because it seemed as though he were
looking into the eyes of Stefan Loristan.

'You look just like your father!' he exclaimed, in spite
of himself. 'How tall you are!'

'When you are near me,' Marco said, in Loristan's own
voice, 'when you are near me, I feel – I feel as if I were a
royal prince attended by an army. You *are* my army.'

The sun was warm in the attic window when they
reached their lodging, and the two leaned on the rough
sill as Marco told his story. It took some time to relate;
and when he ended, he took an envelope from his pocket
and showed it to The Rat. It contained a flat package of
money.

'He gave it to me just before he opened the private door,' Marco explained. 'And he said to me, "It will not be long now. After Samavia, go back to London as quickly as you can – *as quickly as you can*!"'

'I wonder – what he meant?' The Rat said, slowly. A tremendous thought had shot through his mind. But it was not a thought he could speak of to Marco.

'I cannot tell. I thought that it was for some reason he did not expect me to know,' Marco said. 'We will do as he told us. As quickly as we can.' They looked over the newspapers, as they did every day. All that could be gathered from any of them was that the opposing armies of Samavia seemed each to have reached the culmination of disaster and exhaustion. Which party had the power left to take any final step which could call itself a victory, it was impossible to say. Never had a country been in a more desperate case.

'It *is* the time!' said The Rat, glowering over his map. 'If the Secret Party rises suddenly now, it can take Melzarr almost without a blow. It can sweep through the country and disarm both armies. They're weakened – they're half–starved – they're bleeding to death; they *want* to be disarmed. Only the Iarovitch and the Maranovitch keep on with the struggle because each is fighting for the power to tax the people and make slaves of them. If the Secret Party does not rise, the people will, and they'll rush on the palaces and kill every Maranovitch and Iarovitch they find. And serve them right!'

'Let us spend the rest of the day in studying the road-map again,' said Marco. 'Tonight we must be on the way to Samavia!'

CHAPTER 26

Across the Frontier

THAT one day, a week later, two tired and travel-worn boys should drag themselves with slow and weary feet across the frontier line between Jiardasia and Samavia, was not an incident to attract attention. War and hunger and anguish had left the country stunned and broken Since the worst had happened, no one was curious as to what would befall them next. If Jiardasia herself had become a foe, instead of a friendly neighbour, and had sent across the border hordes of soldiery, there would only have been more shrieks, and home-burnings, and slaughter which no one dare resist. But, so far, Jiardasia had remained peaceful. The two boys – one of them on crutches – had evidently travelled far on foot. Their poor clothes were dusty and travel-stained, and they stopped and asked for water at the first hut across the line. The one who walked without crutches had some coarse bread in a bag slung over his shoulder and they sat on the roadside and ate it as if they were hungry.

When the boys were well on their way along the roads, it was not difficult to keep out of sight if it seemed necessary. The country was mountainous and there were deep forests by the way – so far-reaching and with such thick undergrowth that full-grown men could easily have hidden themselves. It was because of this, perhaps, that this part of the country had seen little fighting. There was too great an opportunity for ambush. As the two travellers went on, they heard of burned villages and towns destroyed nearer Melzarr and other fortress-defended cities, or in the country surrounding the estates of powerful nobles and leaders. It was true, as Marco had said to the white-

haired personage, that the Maranovitch and Iarovitch
had fought until the forces of each side lay torn and
bleeding, their strength and their supplies exhausted.
Each day left them weaker and more desperate. Europe
looked on with small interest in either party, but with
growing desire that the disorder should end and cease to
interfere with commerce. All this and much more Marco
and The Rat knew, but as they made their cautious way
through the tortured little country, they learned other
things. The stories told of its beauty and fertility were not
romances. Its heaven-reaching mountains, its plains of
rich verdure on which flocks and herds might have fed by
thousands, its splendour of forest and clear rushing rivers
had a primeval majesty. The two boys travelled through
forest and woodland when it was possible to leave the
road. It was safe to thread a way among trees and tall
ferns and saplings. It was not always easy, but it was safe.
Sometimes they saw a charcoal-burner's hut or a shelter
where a shepherd was hiding with the few sheep left to
him. Each man they met wore the same look of stony
suffering in his face; but when the boys begged for bread
and water, no one refused to share the little he had. It
soon became plain to them that they were thought to be
two young fugitives whose homes had been destroyed and
who were wandering about with no thought but that of
finding safety until the worst was over. That one of them
travelled on crutches added to their apparent helpless-
ness, and that he could not speak the language of the
country made him more an object of pity. The peasants did
not know what language he spoke. Sometimes a foreigner
came to find work in this small town or that. This poor
lad might have come to the country with his father and
mother and then have been caught in the whirlpool of
war and tossed out on the world parentless. But no one
asked questions. Even in their desolation they were a silent
and noble people who were to courteous for curiosity.

'In the old days they were simple and stately and kind. All doors were open to travellers. The master of the poorest hut uttered a blessing and a welcome when a stranger crossed his threshold. It was the custom of the country,' Marco said. 'I read about it in a book of my father's. Above most of the doors the welcome was carved in the stone. It was this – "The Blessing of the Son of God, and Rest within these walls."'

'They are big and strong,' said The Rat. 'And they have good faces. They carry themselves as if they had been drilled – both men and women.'

It was not through the blood-drenched part of the land their way led them, but they saw hunger and dread in the villages they passed. Crops which should have fed the people had been taken from them for the use of the army; flocks and herds had been driven away, and faces were gaunt and grey. Those who had as yet only lost crops and herds knew that homes and lives might be torn from them at any moment. Only old men and women and children were left to wait for any fate which the chances of war might deal out to them.

When they were given food from some poor store, Marco would offer a little money in return. He dare not excite suspicion by offering much. He was obliged to let it be imagined that in his flight from his ruined home he had been able to snatch at and secrete some poor hoard. Their journey was a hard and hungry one. They must make it all on foot and there was little food to be found. But each of them knew how to live on scant fare. They travelled mostly by night and slept among the ferns and undergrowth through the day. They drank from running brooks and bathed in them. Moss and ferns made soft and sweet-smelling beds, and trees roofed them. Sometimes they lay long and talked while they rested. And at length a day came when they knew they were nearing their journey's end.

'It is nearly over now,' Marco said, after they had thrown themselves down in the forest in the early hours of one dewy morning. 'He said "After Samavia, go back to London as quickly as you can – *as quickly as you can*". He said it twice. As if – something were going to happen.'

'Perhaps it will happen more suddenly than we think – the thing he meant,' answered The Rat.

Suddenly he sat up on his elbow and leaned towards Marco.

'We are in Samavia!' he cried. 'We two are in Samavia! And we are near the end!'

Marco rose on his elbow also. He was very thin as a result of hard travel and scant feeding. His thinness made his eyes look immense and black as pits. But they burned and were beautiful with their own fire.

'Yes,' he said, breathing quickly. 'And though we do not know what the end will be, we have obeyed orders. The Prince was next to the last one. There is only one more. The old priest.'

'I have wanted to see him more than I have wanted to see any of the others,' The Rat said.

'So have I,' Marco answered. 'His church is built on the side of this mountain. I wonder what he will say to us.'

Both had the same reason for wanting to see him. In his youth he had served in the monastery over the frontier – the one which, till it was destroyed in a revolt, had treasured the story of the royal lad brought to be hidden among the brotherhood by the ancient shepherd. The young acolyte who had served there must have heard wonderful legends. But the monastery had been burned, and the young acolyte had in later years crossed the frontier and become the priest of a few mountaineers whose little church clung to the mountainside. He had worked hard and faithfully for his people. Only the secret Forgers of the Sword knew that his most ardent worshippers were those with whom he prayed and to whom he gave blessings in dark caverns under the earth, where arms piled themselves and men with dark strong faces sat together in the dim light and laid plans and wrought schemes.

This Marco and The Rat did not know as they talked of their desire to see him.

'He may not choose to tell us anything,' said Marco. 'When we have given him the Sign, he may turn away and say nothing as some of the others did. He may have nothing to say which we should hear. Silence may be the order for him, too.'

It would not be a long or dangerous climb to the little church on the rock. They could sleep or rest all day and begin it at twilight.

It was a long and deep sleep which nothing disturbed. So few human beings ever climbed the hill, except by the narrow rough path leading to the church, that the little wild creatures had not learned to be afraid of them. Once, during the afternoon, a hare hopping along under the ferns to make a visit stopped by Marco's head, and, after looking at him a few seconds with his lustrous eyes, began to nibble the end of his hair. He only did it from curiosity and because he wondered if it might be a new kind of grass, but he did not like it and stopped nibbling almost at once, after which he looked at it again, moving the soft sensitive end of his nose rapidly for a second or so, and then hopped away to attend to his own affairs. A very large and handsome green stag-beetle crawled from one end of The Rat's crutches to the other, but having done it, he went away also. Two or three times a bird, searching for his dinner under the ferns, was surprised to find the two sleeping figures, but, as they lay so quietly, there seemed nothing to be frightened about. A beautiful little field mouse running past discovered that there were crumbs lying about and ate all she could find on the moss. After that she crept into Marco's pocket and found some excellent ones and had a feast. But she disturbed nobody and the boys slept on.

It was a bird's evening song which awakened them both. The evening air had freshened and was fragrant with hillside scents. When Marco first rolled over and opened his eyes, he thought the most delicious thing on earth was to waken from sleep on a hillside at evening and hear a bird singing. It seemed to make exquisitely real to him the fact that he was in Samavia – that the Lamp was lighted and his work was nearly done. The Rat awakened when he did, and for a few minutes both lay on their backs without speaking. At last Marco said, 'The stars are coming out. We can begin to climb.'

Then they both got up and looked at each other.

'The last one!' The Rat said. 'Tomorrow we shall be on our way back to London – Number 7 Philibert Place. After all the places we've been to – what will it look like?'

'It will be like wakening out of a dream,' said Marco. 'It's not beautiful – Philibert Place. But *he* will be there.' And it was as if a light lighted itself on his face and shone through the very darkness of it.

And The Rat's face lighted in almost exactly the same way. 'We've obeyed orders,' he said. 'We've not forgotten one. No one has noticed us, no one has thought of us. We've blown through the countries as if we had been grains of dust.'

Marco's face was still shining. 'God be thanked!' he said. 'Let us begin to climb.'

They pushed their way through the ferns and wandered in and out through the trees until they found the little path. The hill was thickly clothed with forest and the little path was sometimes dark and steep; but they knew that, if they followed it, they would at last come out to a place where there were scarcely any trees at all, and on a crag they would find the tiny church waiting for them.

There were many stars in the sky when at last a turn of
the path showed them the church above them. It was
built of rough stone. It looked as if the priest himself and
his flock might have broken and carried or rolled bits of
the hill to put it together. It had the small, round,
mosque-like summit the Turks had brought into Europe
in centuries past, and close to it was a shed-like house,
which was the priest's.

'There is a candle burning in one of the windows,' said
Marco.

'There is a well near the door – and someone is beginning to draw water,' said The Rat, next. 'It is too dark to
see who it is. Listen!'

They heard the bucket descend on the chains, and
splash in the water. Then it was drawn up, and it seemed
someone drank long. Then they saw a dim figure move
forward and stand still. Then they heard a voice begin to
pray aloud, as if the owner, being accustomed to utter
solitude, did not think of earthly hearers.

'Come,' Marco said. And they went forward. Because
the stars were so many and the air so clear, the priest
heard their feet on the path, and saw them almost as soon
as he heard them. He ended his prayer and watched them
coming. A lad on crutches and a lad who was noticeable
for a bearing which was neither haughty nor proud but
set him somehow aloof from every other lad one had ever
seen – though, as he drew near, the starlight showed his
face thin and his eyes hollow as if with fatigue or hunger.

'And who is this one?' the old priest murmured to himself. '*Who?*'

Marco drew up before him and made a respectful
reverence. Then he lifted his black head, squared his
shoulders and uttered his message for the last time.

'The Lamp is lighted, Father,' he said. 'The Lamp is
lighted.'

The old priest stood still and gazed into his face. The

next moment he bent his head so that he could look at him closely. It seemed almost as if he were frightened and wanted to make sure of something. At the moment it flashed through The Rat's mind that the old woman had looked frightened in something the same way.

'I am an old man,' he said. 'My eyes are not good. If I had a light' – and he glanced towards the house.

It was The Rat who, with one whirl, swung through the door and seized the candle. He held it so that the flare fell on Marco's face.

The priest drew nearer. He gasped for breath. 'You are the son of Stefan Loristan!' he cried. 'It is *his son* who brings the Sign.'

He fell upon his knees and hid his face in his hands. Both the boys heard him sobbing and praying – praying and sobbing at once.

They glanced at each other. The Rat was bursting with excitement, but he felt a little awkward also and wondered what Marco would do. An old fellow on his knees, crying, made a chap feel as if he didn't know what to say. Must you comfort him or must you let him go on?

Marco only stood quite still and looked at him with understanding and gravity.

'Yes, Father,' he said. 'I am the son of Stefan Loristan, and I have given the Sign to all. You are the last one. The Lamp is lighted.'

The priest's tears and prayers ended. He rose to his feet – a rugged-faced old man with thick white hair which fell on his shoulders – and smiled at Marco while his eyes were still wet.

'You have passed from one country to another with the message?' he said. 'You were under orders to say those four words?'

'Yes, Father,' answered Marco.

'That was all. You were to say no more?'

'I know no more. Silence has been the order since I took

my oath of allegiance when I was a child. I was not old
enough to fight, or serve, or reason about great things. All
I could do was to be silent, and to train myself to remember, and be ready when I was called. When my father saw
I was ready, he trusted me to go out to give the Sign. He
told me the four words. Nothing else.'

The old man watched him with a wondering face.

'If Stefan Loristan does not know best,' he said, 'who
does?'

'He always knows,' answered Marco proudly. 'Always.'
He waved his hand like a young king towards The Rat.
He wanted each man they met to understand the value of
The Rat. 'He chose for me this companion,' he added. 'I
have done nothing alone.'

'He let me call myself his aide-de-camp!' burst forth
The Rat. 'I would be cut into inch-long strips for him.'

Marco translated.

Then the priest looked at The Rat and slowly nodded
his head. 'Yes,' he said. 'He knew best. He always knows
best. That I see.'

'How did you know I was my father's son?' asked
Marco. 'You have seen him?'

'No,' was the answer; 'but I have seen a picture which is
said to be his image – and you are the picture's self. It is
indeed a strange thing that two of God's creatures should
be so alike. There is a purpose in it.' He led them into his
bare house and made them rest, and drink goat's milk,
and eat food. As he moved about the hut-like place, there
was a mysterious and exalted look on his face.

'You must be refreshed before we leave here,' he said, at
last. 'I am going to take you to a place hidden in the
mountain where there are men whose hearts will leap at
the sight of you. To see you will give them new power
and courage and new resolve. Tonight they meet as they
or their ancestors have met for centuries, but now they
are nearing the end of their waiting. And I shall bring

them the son of Stefan Loristan, who is the Bearer of the
Sign!'

They ate the bread and cheese and drank the goat's
milk he gave them, but Marco explained that they did
not need rest as they had slept all day. They were prepared to follow him when he was ready.

The old man took a knotted staff in his hand and led
the way. It was rugged and steep with no track to mark it.
Sometimes they seemed to be walking around the mountain, sometimes they were climbing, sometimes they dragged themselves over rocks or fallen trees, or struggled
through almost impassable thickets; more than once they
descended into ravines and, almost at the risk of their
lives, clambered and drew themselves with the aid of the
undergrowth up the other side. The Rat was called upon
to use all his prowess, and sometimes Marco and the priest
helped him across obstacles with the aid of his crutch.

'Haven't I shown tonight whether I'm a cripple or not?'
he said once to Marco. 'You can tell *him* about this, can't
you? And that the crutches helped instead of being in the
way?'

They had been out nearly two hours when they came to
a place where the undergrowth was thick and a huge tree
had fallen among it in some storm. Not far from the tree
was an outcropping rock. Only the top of it was to be seen
above the heavy tangle.

They had pushed their way through the jungle of
bushes and saplings, led by their companion. They did
not know where they would be led next and were prepared to push forward farther when the priest stopped
by the outcropping rock. He stood silent a few minutes as
if he were listening to the forest and the night. But there
was not even a breeze to stir a leaf, or a half-wakened bird
to chirp.

He struck the rock with his staff – twice, and then twice
again.

Marco and The Rat stood with bated breath.

They did not wait long. Presently each of them found himself leaning forward, staring not at the priest or his staff, but at *the rock itself*!

It was moving! Yes, it moved. The priest stepped aside and it slowly turned, as if worked by a lever. It gradually revealed a chasm of darkness dimly lighted, and the priest spoke to Marco. 'There are hiding-places like this all through Samavia,' he said. 'Patience and misery have waited long in them. They are the caverns of the Forgers of the Sword. Come!'

CHAPTER 27

'It is the Lost Prince. It is Ivor!'

MANY times since their journey had begun the boys had found their hearts beating with the thrill and excitement of things. The story of which their lives had been a part was a pulse-quickening experience. But as they carefully made their way down the steep steps leading seemingly into the bowels of the earth, both Marco and The Rat felt as though the priest must hear the thudding in their young sides.

'"The Forgers of the Sword." Remember every word they say,' The Rat whispered, 'so that you can tell it to me afterwards. Don't forget anything! I wish I knew Samavian.'

At the foot of the steps stood the sentinel who worked the lever that turned the rock. He was a big burly peasant with a good watchful face, and the priest gave him a greeting and a blessing as he took from him the lantern he held out.

They went through a narrow and dark passage, and down some more steps, and turned a corner into another corridor cut out of rock and earth. It was a wider corridor, but still dark, so that Marco and The Rat had walked some yards before their eyes became sufficiently accustomed to the dim light to see that the walls themselves seemed made of arms stacked closely together.

'The Forgers of the Sword!' The Rat was unconsciously mumbling to himself, 'The Forgers of the Sword!'

It must have taken years to cut out the rounding passage they threaded their way through, and longer years to forge the solid, bristling walls. But The Rat remembered the story of the mountain herdsmen who had

banded themselves together with an oath which had been
handed down from generation to generation. The Samavians were a long-memoried people, and the fact that
their passion must be smothered had made it burn all the
more fiercely. Five hundred years ago they had first sworn
their oath; and kings had come and gone, had died or
been murdered, and dynasties had changed, but the
Forgers of the Sword had not forgotten or wavered in
their belief that some time – some time, even after the
long dark years – their Lost Prince would be among them
once more. For the last hundred years their number and
power and their hiding–places had so increased that
Samavia was at last honeycombed with them. And they
only waited, breathless – for the Lighting of the Lamp.

The old priest knew how breathlessly, and he knew
what he was bringing them. Marco and The Rat were not
quite old enough to know how fierce and full of eagerness
the waiting of savage full-grown men could be. But there
was a tense-strung thrill in knowing that they who were
being led to them were the Bearers of the Sign. The Rat
went hot and cold; he gnawed his fingers as he went. He
could almost have shrieked aloud, in the intensity of his
excitement, when the priest stopped before a big black
door!

Marco made no sound. Excitement or danger always
made him look tall and quite pale. He looked both now.

The priest touched the door, and it opened.

They were looking into an immense cavern. Its walls
and roof were lined with arms – guns, swords, bayonets,
javelins, daggers, pistols, every weapon a desperate man
might use. The place was full of men, who turned towards
the door when it opened. They all made obeisance to the
priest, but Marco realized almost at the same instant that
they started on seeing that he was not alone.

They were a strange crowd as they stood under their
canopy of weapons in the lurid torchlight. Marco saw at

once that they were men of all classes, though all were
alike roughly dressed. There were mountaineers, and
plainsmen young and mature of years. Some of the biggest
were men with white hair but with the bodies of giants,
and with determination in their strong jaws. They had
been beaten so often, they had been oppressed and robbed, but in the eyes of each one was the unconquered
flame which, throughout the years had been handed
down from father to son.

The priest laid his hand on Marco's shoulder, and
gently pushed him before him through the crowd which
parted to make way for them. He did not stop until the
two stood in the very midst of the circle, which fell back
gazing wonderingly. Marco looked up at the old man. It
was plain that he did not speak because he was excited,
and could not. He opened his lips and his voice seemed to
fail him. Then he tried again and spoke so that all could
hear – even the men at the back of the gazing circle.

'My children,' he said, 'this is the son of Stefan Loristan,
and he comes to bear the Sign. My son,' to Marco, 'speak!'

Then Marco understood what he wished, and also what
he felt. He felt it himself, that magnificent uplifting
gladness, as he spoke, holding his black head high and
lifting his right hand.

'The Lamp is lighted, brothers!' he cried. 'The Lamp
is lighted!'

Then The Rat, who stood apart, watching, thought
that the strange world within the cavern had gone mad!
Wild cries broke forth, men caught each other in passionate embrace, they fell upon their knees, they wrung each
other's hands, they leaped into the air. It was as if they
could not bear the joy of hearing that the end of their
waiting had come at last. They rushed upon Marco, and
fell at his feet. The Rat saw big peasants kissing his shoes,
his hands, every scrap of his clothing they could seize. The
wild circle swayed and closed upon him until The Rat

was afraid. He did not know that, overpowered by this frenzy of emotion, his own excitement was making him shake from head to foot, and that tears were streaming down his cheeks. The swaying crowd hid Marco from him, and he began to fight his way towards him because his excitement increased his fear. Marco was only a boy. They did not know how fiercely they were pressing upon him and keeping away the air.

'Don't kill him! Don't kill him!' yelled The Rat, struggling forward. 'Stand back, you fools! Let me pass!'

And though no one understood his English, one or two suddenly remembered they had seen him enter with the priest and so gave way. But just then the priest himself lifted his hand above the crowd, and spoke in a voice of stern command.

'Stand back, my children!' he cried. 'Madness is not the homage you must bring to the son of Stefan Loristan. Obey! Obey!' His voice had a power in it that penetrated even the wildest herdsman. The frenzied mass swayed back and left space about Marco, whose face The Rat could at last see. It was very white with emotion, and in his eyes there was a look which was like awe.

The Rat pushed forward until he stood beside him.

'I'm your aide-de-camp,' he said. 'I'm going to stand here! Your father sent me! I'm under orders! I thought they'd crush you to death.'

He glared at the circle about them as if they had been enemies. The priest seeing him, touched Marco's arm.

'Tell him he need not fear,' he said. 'It was only for the first few moments. The passion of their souls drove them wild. They are your slaves.'

'Those at the back might have pushed the front ones on until they trampled you under foot, in spite of themselves!' The Rat persisted.

'No,' said Marco. 'They would have stopped if I had spoken.'

'Why didn't you speak, then?' snapped The Rat.

'All they felt was for Samavia and for my father,' Marco said, 'and for the Sign. I felt as they did.'

Then followed a strange ceremonial. The priest went about among the encircling crowd and spoke to one man after another — sometimes to a group. A larger circle was formed.

At the end of the cavern a block of stone had been cut out to look like an altar. It was covered with white, and against the wall above it hung a large picture veiled by a curtain. From the roof there swung before it an ancient lamp of metal suspended by chains. In front of the altar was a sort of stone dais. There the priest asked Marco to stand, with his aide-de-camp on the lower level in attendance. A knot of the biggest herdsmen went out and returned. Each carried a huge sword which had perhaps been the earliest made in the dark days gone by. The bearers formed themselves into a line on either side of Marco. They raised their swords and formed a pointed arch above his head and a passage twelve men long. When the points first clasped together The Rat struck himself hard upon his breast. His exultation was too keen to endure. He gazed at Marco standing still — in that curiously splendid way in which both he and his father *could* stand still — and wondered how he could do it. He looked as if he were prepared for any strange thing which could happen to him — because he was 'under orders.' The Rat knew that he was doing whatsoever he did merely for his father's sake. It was as if he felt that he was representing his father, though he was a mere boy; and that because of this, boy as he was, he must bear himself nobly and remain outwardly undisturbed.

At the end of the arch of swords, the old priest stood and gave a sign to one man after another. When the sign was given to a man he walked under the arch to the dais, and there knelt and, lifting Marco's hand to his lips, kissed it with passionate fervour. Then he returned to the place he had left. One after another passed up the aisle of swords, one after another knelt, one after the other kissed the brown young hand, rose, and went away. Once or twice Marco spoke a few Samavian words, and the face of the man spoken to flamed with joy. The Rat had time to see, as Marco had seen, that many of the faces were not those of peasants. Some of them were clear cut and subtle and of the type of scholars or nobles. It took a long time for them all to kneel and kiss the lad's hand, but no man omitted the ceremony; and when at last it was at an end, silence filled the cavern. They stood and gazed at each other with burning eyes.

The priest moved to Marco's side, and stood near the altar. He leaned forward and took in his hand a cord which hung from the veiled picture – he drew it and the curtain fell apart. There seemed to stand gazing at them from between its folds a tall kingly youth.

'Son of Stefan Loristan,' the old priest said, in a shaken voice. 'It is the Lost Prince! It is Ivor!'

Then every man in the room fell on his knees. Even the men who had upheld the archway of swords dropped their weapons with a crash and knelt also.

Marco started forward, staring at the picture, his breath caught in his throat, his lips apart.

'But – but –' he stammered, 'but if my father were as young as he is – he would be *like* him!'

'When you are as old as he is, *you* will be like him – *You*!' said the priest. And he let the curtain fall.

The Rat stood staring with wide eyes from Marco to the picture and from the picture to Marco. And he breathed faster and faster and gnawed his finger ends. But he did not utter a word. He could not have done it, if he had tried.

Then Marco stepped aside from the dais as if he were in a dream, and the old man followed him. The men with the swords sprang to their feet and made their archway again with a new clash of steel. The old man and the boy passed under it together. Now every man's eyes were fixed on Marco. At the very door by which he had entered, he stopped and turned to meet their glances. He looked very young and thin and pale, but suddenly his father's smile was lighted in his face. He said a few words in Samavian clearly and gravely, saluted, and passed out.

'What did you say to them?' gasped The Rat, stumbling after him as the door closed behind them and shut in the murmur of impassioned sound.

'There was only one thing to say,' was the answer. 'They are men – I am only a boy. I thanked them for my father, and told them he would never – never forget.'

CHAPTER 28

'Extra! Extra! Extra!'

I T was raining in London – pouring. It had been raining
for two weeks, more or less, generally more. When the
train from Dover drew in at Charing Cross, the weather
seemed suddenly to have considered that it had so far
been too lenient and must express itself much more vigor-
ously. So it had gathered together its resources and
poured them forth in a deluge which surprised even
Londoners. The rain so beat against and streamed down
the windows of the third-class carriage in which Marco
and The Rat sat that they could not see through them.

They made their homeward journey much more
rapidly than they had made the one on which they had
been outward bound. It had of course taken them some
time to tramp back to the frontier, but there had been no
reason for stopping anywhere after they had once reached
the railroad. They had been tired sometimes, but they
had slept heavily on the wooden seats of the railway carriages. Their one desire was to get home. No. 7 Philibert
Place rose between them in its noisy dinginess as the one
desirable spot on earth. To Marco it held his father. And
it was Loristan alone that The Rat saw when he thought
of it. Loristan as he would look when he saw him come
into the room with Marco, and stand up and salute, and
say: 'I have brought him back, sir. He has carried out
every single order you gave him – every single one. So
have I.' So he had. He had been sent as his companion
and attendant, and he had been faithful in every thought.
If Marco would have allowed him, he would have waited
upon him like a servant, and have been proud of the
service. But Marco would never let him forget that they

were only two boys and that one was of no more importance than the other. He had secretly even felt this atti-
tude to be a sort of grievance. It would have been more
like a game if one of them had been the mere servitor of
the other, and if that other had blustered a little, and
issued commands, and demanded sacrifices. If the faithful
vassal could have been wounded or cast into a dungeon
for his young commander's sake, the adventure would
have been more complete. But though their journey had
been full of wonders and rich with beauties, though the
memory of it hung in The Rat's mind like a background
of tapestry embroidered in all the hues of the earth with
all the splendours of it, there had been no dungeons and
no wounds. After the adventure in Munich their unimportant boyishness had not even been observed by such
perils as might have threatened them. As The Rat had
said, they had 'blown like grains of dust' through Europe
and had been as nothing. As this was what Loristan had
planned. If they had been men, they would not have been
so safe.

From the time they had left the old priest on the hillside to begin their journey back to the frontier, they both
had been given to long silences as they tramped side by
side or lay on the moss in the forests. Now that their work
was done, reaction had set in. There were no more plans
to be made and no more uncertainties to contemplate.
They were on their way back to Philibert Place. Each of
them was thinking of many things. Marco was full of
longing to see his father's face and hear his voice again.
He wanted to feel the pressure of his hand on his shoulder
– to be sure that he was real and not a dream. The last
was because during this homeward journey everything
that had happened often seemed to be a dream. It had all
been so wonderful – the climber standing looking down
at them the morning they awakened on the Gaisburg; the
shoemaker measuring his foot in the small shop; the old

woman and her noble lord; the prince with his face turned upward as he stood on the balcony looking at the moon; the old priest kneeling and weeping for joy; the great cavern with the yellow light upon the crowd of passionate faces. But he had not dreamed them; he was going back to tell his father about them.

The Rat gnawed his finger ends a great deal. His thoughts were more wild and feverish than Marco's. They leaped forward in spite of him. It was no use to pull himself up and tell himself that he was a fool. Now that all was over, he had time to be as great a fool as he was inclined to be. But how he longed to reach London and stand face to face with Loristan! The Sign was given. The Lamp was lighted. What would happen next? His crutches were under his arms before the train drew up.

'We're there! We're there!' he cried restlessly to Marco. They had no luggage to delay them. They took their bags and followed the crowd along the platform. The rain was rattling like bullets against the high glassed roof. People turned to look at Marco, seeing the glow of exultant eagerness in his face. They thought he must be some boy coming home for the holidays and going to make a visit at a place he delighted in. The rain was dancing on the pavements when they reached the entrance.

'A cab won't cost much,' Marco said, 'and it will take us quickly.'

They called one and got into it. Each of them had flushed cheeks, and Marco's eyes looked as if he were gazing at something a long way off – gazing at it, and wondering.

'We've come back!' said The Rat, in an unsteady voice. 'We've been – and we've come back!' Then suddenly turning to look at Marco, 'Does it ever seem to you as if, perhaps, it – it wasn't true?'

'Yes,' Marco answered, 'but it was true. And it's done.'

Then he added after a second or so of silence, just what The Rat had said to himself, 'What next?' He said it very low.

The way to Philibert Place was not long. When they turned into the roaring, untidy road, where the buses and drays and carts struggled past each other with their loads, and the tired-faced people hurried in crowds along the pavement, they looked at them all feeling that they had left their dream far behind indeed. But they were at home.

It was a good thing to see Lazarus open the door and stand waiting before they had time to get out of the cab. Cabs stopped so seldom before houses in Philibert Place that the inmates were always prompt to open their doors. When Lazarus had seen this one stop at the broken iron gate, he had known whom it brought. He had kept an eye on the windows faithfully for many a day – even when he knew that it was too soon, even if all was well, for any travellers to return.

He bore himself with an air more than usually military and his salute when Marco crossed the threshold was for-mal stateliness itself. But his greeting burst from his heart.

'God be thanked!' he said in his deep growl of joy. 'God be thanked!'

When Marco put forth his hand, he bent his grizzled head and kissed it devoutly.

'God be thanked!' he said again.

'My father?' Marco began. 'My father is out?' If he had been in the house, he knew he would not have stayed in the back sitting-room.

'Sir,' said Lazarus, 'will you come with me into his room? You, too, sir,' to The Rat. He had never said 'sir' to him before.

He opened the door of the familiar room, and the boys entered. The room was empty.

Marco did not speak; neither did The Rat. They both stood still in the middle of the shabby carpet and looked up at the old soldier. Both had suddenly the same feeling that the earth had dropped from beneath their feet. Lazarus saw it and spoke fast and with tremor. He was almost as agitated as they were.

'He left me at your service – at your command,' he began.

'Left you?' said Marco.

'He left us, all three, under orders – to *wait*,' said Lazarus. 'The Master has gone.'

The Rat felt something hot rush into his eyes. He brushed it away that he might look at Marco's face. The shock had changed it very much. Its glowing eager joy had died out, it had turned paler and his brows were drawn together. For a few seconds he did not speak at all, and, when he did speak, The Rat knew that his voice was steady only because he willed that it should be so.

'If he has gone,' he said, 'it is because he had a strong reason. It was because he also was under orders.'

'He said that you would know that,' Lazarus answered. 'He was called in such haste that he had not a moment in which to do more than write a few words. He left them for you on his desk there.'

Marco walked over to the desk and opened the envelope which was lying there. There were only a few lines on the sheet of paper inside and they had evidently been written in the greatest haste. They were these:

'The Life of my life – for Samavia.'

'He was called – to Samavia,' Marco said, and the thought sent his blood rushing through his veins – 'He has gone to Samavia!'

Lazarus drew his hand roughly across his eyes and his voice shook and sounded hoarse.

'There has been great disaffection in the camps of the Maranovitch,' he said. 'The remnant of the army has gone mad. Sir, silence is still the order, but who knows – who knows? God alone.'

He had not finished speaking before he turned his head as if listening to sounds in the road. They were the kind of sounds which had broken up the Squad, and sent it rushing down the passage into the street to seize on a newspaper. There was to be heard a commotion of newsboys shouting riotously some startling piece of news which had called out an 'Extra'.

The Rat had heard it first and dashed to the front door. As he opened it a newsboy running by shouted at the topmost power of his lungs the news he had to sell: 'Assassination of King Michael Maranovitch by his own soldiers! Assassination of the Maranovitch! Extra! Extra! Extra!'

When the Rat returned with a newspaper, Lazarus interposed between him and Marco with great and respectful ceremony. 'Sir,' he said to Marco, 'I am at your command, but the Master left with me an order which I was to repeat to you. He requested you *not* to read the newspapers until he himself could see you again.'

Both boys fell back.

'Not read the papers!' they exclaimed together.

Lazarus had never before been quite so reverential and ceremonious.

'Your pardon, sir,' he said. 'I may read them at your orders, and report such things as it is well that you should know. There have been dark tales told and there may be darker ones. He asked that you would not read for yourself. If you meet again – when you meet again' – he corrected himself hastily – 'when you meet again, he says you will understand. I am your servant. I will read and answer all such questions as I can.'

The Rat handed him the paper and they returned to the back room together.

'You shall tell us what he would wish us to hear,' Marco said.

The news was soon told. The story was not a long one as exact details had not yet reached London. It was briefly that the head of the Maranovitch party had been put to death by infuriated soldiers of his own army. It was an army drawn chiefly from a peasantry which did not love its leaders, or wish to fight, and suffering and brutal treatment had at last roused it to furious revolt.

'What next?' said Marco.

'If I were a Samavian –' began The Rat and then he stopped.

Lazarus stood biting his lips, but staring stonily at the carpet. Not The Rat alone but Marco also noted a grim change in him. It was grim because it suggested that he was holding himself under an iron control. It was as if while tortured by anxiety he had sworn not to allow himself to look anxious, and the resolve set his jaw hard and carved new lines in his rugged face. Each boy thought this in secret, but did not wish to put it into words. If he was anxious, he could only be so for one reason, and each realized what the reason must be. Loristan had gone to Samavia – to the torn and bleeding country filled with riot and danger. If he had gone, it could only have been because its danger called him and he went to face it at its worst. Lazarus had been left behind to watch over them and what he knew he could not tell them, and perhaps he knew little more than that a great life might be lost.

Because his master was absent, the old soldier seemed to feel that he must comfort himself with a greater cere-monial reverence than he had ever shown before. He held himself within call, and at Marco's orders, as it had been his custom to hold himself with regard to Loristan. The ceremonious service even extended itself to The Rat, who appeared to have taken a new place in his mind. He also seemed now to be a person to be waited upon and replied to with dignity and formal respect.

When the evening meal was served, Lazarus drew out Loristan's chair at the head of the table and stood behind it with a majestic air.

'Sir,' he said to Marco, 'the Master requested that you take his seat at the table until – while he is not with you.'

Marco took the seat in silence.

At two o'clock in the morning, when the roaring road was still, the light from the street lamp, shining into the small bedroom, fell on two pale faces. The Rat sat up on his sofa bed in the old way with his hands closed round his knees. Marco lay flat on his hard pillow. Neither of them had been to sleep and yet they had not talked a great deal. Each had secretly guessed a good deal of what the other did not say.

'There is one thing we must remember,' Marco had said, early in the night. 'We must not be afraid.'

'No,' answered The Rat, almost fiercely, 'we must not be afraid.'

'We are tired; we came back expecting to be able to tell it all to him. We have always been looking forward to that. We never thought once that he might be gone. And he *was* gone. Did you feel as if –' he turned towards the sofa, 'as if something had struck you on the chest?'

'Yes,' The Rat answered heavily. 'Yes.'

'We weren't ready,' said Marco. 'He had never gone before; but we ought to have known he might some day be – called. He went because he was called. He told us to wait. We don't know what we are waiting for, but we know that we must not be afraid.'

The Rat lifted his head and looked at the bed sideways.

'Did you think' – he said slowly – 'did you *ever* think

that perhaps *he* knew where the descendant of the Lost Prince was?'

Marco answered even more slowly.

'If anyone knew – surely he might. He has known so much,' he said.

'Listen to this!' broke forth The Rat. 'I believe he has gone to *tell* the people. If he does – if he could show them – all the country would run mad with joy. It wouldn't be only the Secret Party. All Samavia would rise and follow any flag he chose to raise. They've prayed for the Lost Prince for five hundred years, and if they believed they'd got him once more, they'd fight like madmen for him. But there would not be anyone to fight. They'd *all* want the same thing! If they could see the man with Ivor's blood in his veins, they'd feel he had come back to them – risen from the dead. They'd believe it!'

He beat his fists together in his frenzy of excitement. 'It's the time! It's the time!' he cried. 'No man could let such a chance go by! He *must* tell them – he *must*! That *must* be what he's gone for. He knows – he knows – he's always known!' And he threw himself back on the sofa and flung his arms over his face, lying there panting.

'If it is the time,' said Marco in a low, strained voice – 'if it is, and he knows – he will tell them.' And he threw his arms up over his own face and lay quite still.

Neither of them said another word, and the street lamp shone in on them as if it were waiting for something to happen. But nothing happened. In time they were asleep.

CHAPTER 29

'Twixt Night and Morning

AFTER this, they waited. They did not know what they waited for, nor could they guess even vaguely how the waiting would end. All that Lazarus could tell them he told. He would have been willing to stand respectfully for hours relating to Marco the story of how the period of their absence had passed for his Master and himself. He told how Loristan had spoken each day of his son, how he had often been pale with anxiousness, how in the evenings he had walked to and fro in his room, deep in thought, as he looked down unseeingly at the carpet.

'He permitted me to talk of you, sir,' Lazarus said. 'I saw that he wished to hear your name often. I reminded him of the times when you had been so young that most children of your age would have been in the hands of nurses, and yet you were strong and silent and sturdy and travelled with us as if you were not a child at all – never crying when you were tired and were not properly fed. As if you understood – as if you understood,' he added, proudly. 'If, through the power of God a creature can be a man at six years old, you were that one. Many a dark day I have looked into your solemn, watching eyes, and have been half afraid; because that a child should answer one's gaze so gravely seemed almost an unearthly thing.'

'The chief thing I remember of those days,' said Marco, 'is that he was with me, and that whenever I was hungry or tired, I knew he must be, too.'

The feeling that they were 'waiting' was so intense that it filled the days with strangeness. When the postman's knock was heard at the door, each of them endeavoured not to start. A letter might some day come which would tell them – they did not know what. But no letters came. When they went out into the streets, they found themselves hurrying on their way back in spite of themselves. Something might have happened. Lazarus read the papers faithfully, and in the evening told Marco and The Rat all the news it was 'well that they should hear'. But the disorders of Samavia had ceased to occupy much space. They had become an old story, and after the excitement of the assassination of Michael Maranovitch had died out, there seemed to be a lull in events. Michael's son had not dared to try to take his father's place, and there were rumours that he also had been killed. The head of the Iarovitch had declared himself king, but had not been crowned because of disorders in his own party. The country seemed existing in a nightmare of suffering, famine, and suspense.

'Samavia is "waiting" too,' The Rat broke forth one night as they talked together, 'but it won't wait long – it can't. If I were a Samavian and in Samavia –'

'My father is a Samavian and he is in Samavia,' Marco's grave young voice interposed. The Rat flushed red as he realized what he had said. 'What a fool I am!' he groaned. 'I – I beg your pardon – sir.' He stood up when he said the last words and added the 'sir' as if he suddenly realized that there was a distance between them which was something akin to the distance between youth and maturity – but yet was not the same.

'You are a good Samavian, but – you forget,' was Marco's answer.

Lazarus's intense grimness increased with each day that passed. The ceremonious respectfulness of his manner towards Marco increased also. It seemed as if the more anxious he felt the more formal and stately his bearing became. It was as though he braced his own courage by doing the smallest things life in the back sitting-room required as if they were of the dignity of services performed in a much larger place and under much more imposing circumstances. The Rat found himself feeling almost as if he were an equerry in a court, and that dignity and ceremony were necessary on his own part. He began to experience a sense of being somehow a person of rank, for whom doors were opened grandly and who had vassals at his command. The watchful obedience of fifty vassals embodied itself in the manner of Lazarus.

'I am glad,' The Rat said once, reflectively, 'that, after all, my father was once – different. It makes it easier to learn things perhaps. If he had not talked to me about people who – well, who had never seen places like Bone Court – this might have been harder for me to understand.'

When at last they managed to call the Squad together, and went to spend a morning at the Barracks behind the churchyard, that body of armed men stared at their commander in great and amazed uncertainty. They felt that something had happened to him. They did not know what had happened, but it was some experience which had made him mysteriously different. He did not look like Marco, but in some extraordinary way he seemed more akin to him. They only knew that some necessity in Loristan's affairs had taken the two away from London and the Game. Now they had come back, and they seemed older.

At first, the Squad felt awkward and shuffled its feet uncomfortably. After the first greetings it did not know exactly what to say. It was Marco who saved the situation.

'Drill us first,' he said to The Rat, 'then we can talk about the Game.'

' 'Tention!' shouted The Rat, magnificently. And then they forgot everything else and sprang into line. After the drill was ended, and they sat in a circle on the broken flags, the Game became more resplendent that it had ever been.

'I've had time to read and work out new things,' The Rat said. 'Reading is like travelling.'

Marco himself sat and listened, enthralled by the adroitness of the imagination he displayed. Without revealing a single dangerous fact he built up, of their journeyings and experiences, a totally new structure of adventures which would have fired the whole being of any group of lads. It was safe to describe places and people, and he so described them that the Squad squirmed in its delight at feeling itself marching in a procession attending the Emperor in Vienna; standing in line before palaces; climbing, with knapsacks strapped tight, up precipitous mountain roads; defending mountain-fortresses; and storming Samavian castles. The Squad glowed and exulted. The Rat glowed and exulted himself. Marco watched his sharp-featured, burning-eyed face with wonder and admiration. This strange power of making things alive was, he knew, what his father would call 'genius'.

'Let's take the oath of 'legiance again,' shouted Cad, when the Game was over for the morning.

'The papers never said nothin' more about the Lost Prince, but we are all *for* him yet! Let's take it!' So they stood in line again, Marco at the head, and renewed their oath.

'The sword in my hand – for Samavia!'

'The heart in my breast – for Samavia!'

'The swiftness of my sight, the thought of my brain, the life of my life – for Samavia.'

'Here grow twelve men – for Samavia.'

'God be thanked!'

It was more solemn than it had been the first time. The Squad felt it tremendously. Both Cad and Ben were conscious that thrills ran down their spines into their boots. When Marco and The Rat left them, they first stood at salute and then broke out into a cheer.

On their way home, The Rat asked Marco a question.

'Did you see Mrs Beedle standing at the top of the basement steps and looking after us when we went out this morning?'

Mrs Beedle was the landlady of the lodgings at No. 7 Philibert Place. She was a mysterious and dusty female, who lived in the 'cellar kitchen' part of the house and was seldom seen by her lodgers.

'Yes,' answered Marco, 'I have seen her two or three times lately, and I do not think I ever saw her before. My father has never seen her, though Lazarus says she used to watch him round corners. Why is she suddenly so curious about us?'

'I'd like to know,' said The Rat. 'I've been trying to work it out. Ever since we came back, she's been peeping round the door of the kitchen stairs, or over balustrades, or through the cellar-kitchen windows. I believe she wants to speak to you, and knows Lazarus won't let her if he catches her at it. When Lazarus is about, she always darts back.'

'What does she want to say?' said Marco.

'I'd like to know,' said The Rat again.

When they reached No. 7 Philibert Place, they found out, because when the door opened they saw at the top of the cellar-kitchen stairs at the end of the passage the mysterious Mrs Beedle, in her dusty black dress and with a dusty black cap on, evidently having that minute mounted from her subterranean hiding-place. She had come up the steps so quickly that Lazarus had not seen her.

'Young Master Loristan!' she called out authoritatively. Lazarus wheeled about fiercely.

'Silence!' he commanded. 'How dare you address the young Master?'

She snapped her fingers at him, and marched forward folding her arms tightly. 'You mind your own business,' she said. 'It's young Master Loristan I'm speaking to, not his servant. It's time he was talked to about this.'

'Silence, woman!' shouted Lazarus.

'Let her speak,' said Marco. 'I want to hear. What is it you wish to say, madam? My father is not here.'

'That's just what I want to find out about,' put in the woman. 'When is he coming back?'

'I do not know,' answered Marco.

'That's it,' said Mrs Beedle. 'You're old enough to understand that two big lads and a big fellow like that can't have food and lodgin's for nothing. You may say you don't live high – and you don't – but lodgin's are lodgin's and rent is rent. If your father's coming back and you can tell me when, I mayn't be obliged to let the rooms over your heads; but I know too much about foreigners to let bills run when they are out of sight. Your father's out of sight. He,' jerking her head towards Lazarus, 'paid me for last week. How do I know he will pay me for this week!'

'The money is ready,' roared Lazarus.

The Rat longed to burst forth. He knew what people in Bone Court said to a woman like that; he knew the exact words and phrases. But they were not words and phrases an aide-de-camp might deliver himself of in the presence of his superior officer; they were not words and phrases an equerry uses at court. He dare not *allow* himself to burst forth. He stood with flaming eyes and a flaming face, and bit his lips till they bled. He wanted to strike with his crutches. The son of Stefan Loristan! The Bearer of the Sign!

'Do you want the money now?' asked Marco. 'It is only the beginning of the week and we do not owe it to you until the week is over. Is it that you want to have it now?'

Lazarus had become deadly pale. He looked huge in his fury, and he looked dangerous.

'Young Master,' he said slowly, in a voice as deadly as his pallor, and he actually spoke low, 'this woman –'

Mrs Beedle drew back towards the cellar-kitchen steps.

'There's police outside,' she shrilled. 'Young Master Loristan, order him to stand back.'

'No one will hurt you,' said Marco. 'If you have the money here, Lazarus, please give it to me.'

Lazarus literally ground his teeth. But he drew himself up and saluted with ceremony. He put his hand in his breast pocket and produced an old leather wallet. There were but a few coins in it. He pointed to a gold one.

'I obey you, sir – since I must –' he said, breathing hard. 'That one will pay her for the week.'

Marco took out the sovereign and held it out to the woman.

'You hear what he says,' he said. 'At the end of this week if there is not money enough to pay for the next, we will go.'

Lazarus looked so like a hyena, only held back from springing by chains of steel, that the dusty Mrs Beedle was afraid to take the money.

'If you say that I shall not lose it, I'll wait until the week's ended,' she said. 'You're nothing but a lad, but you're like your father. You've got a way that a body can trust. If he was here and said he hadn't the money but he'd have it in time, I'd wait if it was for a month. He'd pay it if he said he would. But he's gone; and two boys and a fellow like that one don't seem much to depend on. But I'll trust *you*.'

'Be good enough to take it,' said Marco. And he put the coin in her hand and turned into the back sitting-room as if he did not see her.

The Rat and Lazarus followed him.

'Is there so little money left?' said Marco. 'We have always had very little. When we had less than usual, we lived in poorer places and were hungry if it was necessary. We know how to go hungry. One does not die of it.'

The big eyes under Lazarus's beetling brows filled with tears.

'No, sir,' he said, 'one does not die of hunger. But the insult – the insult! That is not endurable.'

'She would not have spoken if my father had been here.' Marco said. 'And it is true that boys like us have no money. Is there enough to pay for another week?'

'Yes, sir,' answered Lazarus, swallowing hard as if he had a lump in his throat, 'perhaps enough for two – if we eat but little. If – if the Master would accept money from those who would give it, he would always have had enough. But how could such a one as he? How could he? When he went away, he thought – he thought that –' but there he stopped himself suddenly.

'Never mind,' said Marco. 'Never mind. We will go away the day we can pay no more.'

'I can go out and sell newspapers,' said The Rat's sharp voice. 'I've done it before. Crutches help you to sell them. The platform would sell 'em faster still. I'll go out on the platform.'

'I can sell newspapers, too,' said Marco.

Lazarus uttered an exclamation like a groan.

'Sir,' he cried, 'no, no! Am I not here to go out and look for work? I can carry loads. I can run errands.'

'We will all three begin to see what we can do,' Marco said.

Then – exactly as had happened on the day of their return from their journey – there arose in the road outside the sound of newsboys shouting. This time the outcry seemed even more excited than before. The boys were running and yelling and there seemed more of them than usual. And above all other words was heard 'Samavia! Samavia!' But today The Rat did not rush to the door at the first cry. He stood still – for several seconds they all three stood still – listening. Afterwards each one remembered and told the others that he had stood still because

some strange, strong feeling held him *waiting* as if to hear
some great thing.

It was Lazarus who went out of the room first and The
Rat and Marco followed him.

One of the upstairs lodgers had run down in haste and
opened the door to buy newspapers and ask questions.
The newsboys were wild with excitement and danced
about as they shouted. The piece of news they were yelling had evidently a popular quality.

The lodger bought two papers and was handing out
coppers to a lad who was talking loud and fast.

'Here's a go!' he was saying. 'A Secret Party's risen up
and taken Samavia! 'Twixt night and mornin' they done
it! That there Lost Prince descendant 'as turned up, an'
they've *crowned* him – 'twixt night and mornin' they
done it! Clapt 'is crown on 'is 'ead, so's they'd lose no
time.' And off he bolted, shouting ''Cendant of
Lost Prince! 'Cendant of Lost Prince made King of
Samavia!'

It was then that Lazarus, forgetting even ceremony,
bolted also. He bolted back to the sitting-room, rushed in,
and the door fell to behind him.

Marco and The Rat found it shut when, having secured
a newspaper, they went down the passage. At the closed
door, Marco stopped. He did not turn the handle. From
the inside of the room there came the sound of big con-
vulsive sobs and passionate Samavian words of prayer
and worshipping gratitude.

'Let us wait,' Marco said, trembling a little. 'He will not
want anyone to see him. Let us wait.'

His black pits of eyes looked immense, and he stood at
his tallest, but he was trembling slightly from head to foot.
The Rat had begun to shake, as if from an ague. His face
was scarcely human in its fierce unboyish emotion.

'Marco! Marco!' his whisper was a cry. 'That was what
he went for – *because he knew*!'

'Yes,' answered Marco, 'that was what he went for.' And his voice was unsteady, as his body was.

Presently the sobs inside the room choked themselves back suddenly. Lazarus had remembered. They had guessed he had been leaning against the wall during his outburst. Now it was evident that he stood upright, probably shocked at the forgetfulness of his frenzy.

So Marco turned the handle of the door and went into the room. He shut the door behind him, and they all three stood together.

When the Samavian gives way to his emotions, he is emotional indeed. Lazarus looked as if a storm had swept over him. He had choked back his sobs, but tears still swept down his cheeks.

'Sir,' he said hoarsely, 'your pardon! It was as if a convulsion seized me. 'I forgot everything – even my duty. Pardon, pardon!' And there on the worn carpet of the dingy back sitting-room in the Marylebone Road, he actually went on one knee and kissed the boy's hand with adoration.

'You mustn't ask pardon,' said Marco. 'You have waited so long, good friend. You have given your life as my father has –' His voice broke and he stood and looked at him with an appeal which seemed to ask him to remember his boyhood and understand the rest.

'Don't kneel,' he said next. 'You mustn't kneel.' And Lazarus, kissing his hand again, rose to his feet.

'Now – we shall *hear*!' said Marco. 'Now the waiting will soon be over.'

'Yes, sir. Now, we shall receive commands!' Lazarus answered.

The Rat held out the newspapers.

'May we read them yet?' he asked.

'Until further orders, sir,' said Lazarus hurriedly and apologetically – 'until further orders, it is still better that I should read them first.'

CHAPTER 30

The Game is at an End

So long as the history of Europe is written and read, the unparalleled story of the Rising of the Secret Party in Samavia will stand out as one of its most startling and romantic records. Perhaps the whole story would fill too many volumes to admit of its ever being told fully. But history makes the growing of the Secret Party clear — though it seems almost to cease to be history when it is forced to deal with the Bearing of the Sign by two boys, who, being blown as unremarked as any two grains of dust across Europe, lit the Lamp whose flame so flared up that there sprang forth Samavians by the thousand thousand ready to feed it — Iarovitch and Maranovitch swept aside for ever and only Samavians remaining to cry aloud in ardent praise and worship of the God who had brought back to them their Lost Prince. The battle-cry of his name had ended every battle. Swords fell from hands because swords were not needed. The Iarovitch fled in terror and dismay; the Maranovitch were nowhere to be found. Between night and morning, as the newsboy had said, the standard of Ivor was raised and waved from palace and citadel alike. From mountain, forest, and plain, from city, village, and town, its followers flocked to swear allegiance; broken and wounded legions staggered along the roads to join and kneel to it; women and children followed, weeping with joy and chanting songs of praise. The Powers held out their sceptres to the lately prostrate and ignored country. Train-loads of food and supplies of all things needed began to cross the frontier; the aid of the nations was bestowed. The story of the crowning of the King had been the wildest of all — the multitude of ecstatic people,

famished, in rags, and many of them weak with wounds,
kneeling at his feet, praying, as their one salvation and
security, that he would go attended by them to their
bombarded and broken cathedral, and at its high altar let
the crown be placed upon his head.

'The story of the coronation in the shattered cathedral,
whose roof had been torn to fragments by bombs,' said an
important London paper, 'reads like a legend of the
Middle Ages. There is in Samavia's national character
something of the medieval still.'

Lazarus, having bought and read every newspaper record-
ing the details which had reached London, returned to
report almost verbatim, standing erect before Marco, the
eyes under his shaggy brows sometimes flaming with exultation, sometimes filled with a rush of tears. He could
not be made to sit down. His whole big body seemed to
have become rigid with magnificence. Meeting Mrs
Beedle in the passage, he strode by her with an air so
thunderous that she turned and scuttled back to her
cellar-kitchen, almost falling down the stone steps in her
nervous terror. In such a mood, he was not the person to
face without something like awe.

In the middle of the night, The Rat suddenly spoke to
Marco as if he knew that he was awake and would hear
him.

'He has given all his life to Samavia!' he said. 'When
you travelled from country to country, and lived in holes
and corners, it was because by doing it he could escape
spies, and see the people who must be made to understand. No one else could have made them listen. An emperor would have begun to listen when he had seen his
face and heard his voice. And he could be silent, and wait
for the right time to speak. He could keep still when other
men could not. He could keep his face still – and his
hands – and his eyes. Now all Samavia knows what he has

done. They will go mad with joy when they see his face!'

'They have seen it now,' said Marco, in a low voice from his bed.

Then there was a long silence, though it was not quite silence because The Rat's breathing was so quick and hard.

'He – must have been at the coronation!' he said at last. 'The King – what will the King do to – repay him?'

Marco did not answer. His breathing could be heard also. His mind was picturing that same coronation – the roofless cathedral, the ruins of the high altar, the multitude of kneeling, famine-scourged people, the battle-worn, wounded and bandaged soldiery! And the King! And his father! Where had his father stood when the King was crowned? Surely, he had stood at the King's right hand!

'King Ivor!' he murmured as if he were in a dream. 'King Ivor!'

The Rat started up on his elbow.

'You will see him,' he cried out. 'He's not a dream any longer. The Game is not a game now – and it is ended – it is won! It was real – *he* was real! Marco, I don't believe you hear.'

'Yes, I do,' answered Marco, 'but it is almost more a dream than when it was one.'

'If there is no bigger honour to give him, he will be made a prince – and Commander-in-Chief – and Prime Minister! Can't you hear those Samavians shouting, and singing, and praying? You'll see it all!' His voice suddenly dropped – as if it dropped into a pit. 'You'll see it all. But I shall not.'

Then Marco awoke from his dream and lifted his head. 'Why not?' he demanded. It sounded like a demand.

'Because I know better than to expect it!' The Rat groaned. 'You've taken me a long way, but you can't take

me to the palace of a king. I'm not such a fool as to think
that, even of your father –'

He broke off because Marco did more than lift his head.
He sat upright.

'You bore the Sign as much as I did,' he said. 'We bore
it together.'

'Who would have listened to *me*?' cried The Rat. '*You*
were the son of Stefan Loristan.'

'You were the friend of his son,' answered Marco. 'You
went at the command of Stefan Loristan. You were the
army of the son of Stefan Loristan. That I have told you.
Where I go, you will go. We will say no more of this – not
one word.'

And he lay down again in the silence of a prince of the
blood. And The Rat knew that he meant what he said, and
that Stefan Loristan also would mean it. And he began
to wonder what Mrs Beedle would do when she heard
what had happened – what had been happening all the
time a tall, shabby 'foreigner' had lived in her dingy back
sitting-room, and been closely watched lest he should
go away without paying his rent. The Rat saw himself
managing to poise himself very erect on his crutches
while he told her that the shabby foreigner was – well,
was at least the friend of a King, and had given him his
crown.

The next day passed, and the next; and then there
came a letter. It was from Loristan, and Marco turned
pale when Lazarus handed it to him. Lazarus and The
Rat went out of the room at once, and left him to read it
alone. It was evidently not a long letter, because it was
not many minutes before Marco called them again into
the room.

'In a few days, messengers – friends of my father's – will
come to take us to Samavia. You and I and Lazarus are to
go,' he said to The Rat.

'God be thanked!' said Lazarus. 'God be thanked!'

Before the messengers came, it was the end of the week. Lazarus had packed their few belongings, and on Saturday Mrs Beedle was to be seen hovering at the top of the cellar steps, when Marco and The Rat left the back sitting-room to go out.

'You needn't glare at me!' she said to Lazarus, who stood glowering at the door which he had opened for them. 'Young Master Loristan, I want to know if you've heard when your father is coming back?'

'He will not come back,' said Marco.

'He won't, won't he? Well, how about next week's rent?' said Mrs Beedle. 'Your man's been packing up, I notice. He's not got much to carry away, but it won't pass through that front door until I've got what's owing me. People that can pack easy think they can get away easy, and they'll bear watching. The week's up today.'

Lazarus wheeled and faced her with a furious gesture.

'Get back to your cellar, woman,' he commanded. 'Get back under ground and stay there. Look at what is stopping before your miserable gate.'

A carriage was stopping – a very perfect carriage of dark brown. The coachman and footman wore dark brown and gold liveries, and the footman had leaped down and opened the door with respectful alacrity. 'They are friends of the Master's come to pay their respects to his son,' said Lazarus. 'Are their eyes to be offended by the sight of you?'

'Your money is safe,' said Marco. 'You had better leave us.'

Mrs Beedle gave a sharp glance at the two gentlemen who had entered the broken gate. They were of an order which did not belong to Philibert Place. They looked as if the carriage and the dark brown and gold liveries were everyday affairs to them.

'At all events, they're two grown men, and not two boys

without a penny,' she said. 'If they're your father's friends, they'll tell me whether my rent's safe or not.'

The two visitors were upon the threshold. They were both men of self-contained dignity and when Lazarus opened wide the door, they stepped into the shabby entrance hall as if they did not see it. They looked past its dinginess, and past Lazarus, and The Rat, and Mrs Beedle – *through them*, as it were – at Marco.

He advanced towards them at once.

'You come from my father!' he said, and gave his hand first to the elder man, then to the younger.

'Yes, we come from your father. I am Baron Rastka – this is the Count Vorversk,' said the elder man, bowing.

'If they're barons and counts, and friends of your father's, they are well-to-do enough to be responsible for you,' said Mrs Beedle, rather fiercely, because she was somewhat overawed and resented the fact. 'It's a matter of next week's rent, gentlemen. I want to know where it's coming from.'

The elder man looked at her with a swift, cold glance. He did not speak to her, but to Lazarus. 'What is she doing here?' he demanded.

Marco answered him. 'She is afraid we cannot pay our rent,' he said. 'It is of great importance to her that she should be sure.'

'Take her away,' said the gentleman to Lazarus. He did not even glance at her. He drew something from his coat pocket and handed it to the old soldier. 'Take her away,' he repeated. And because it seemed as if she were not any longer a person at all, Mrs Beedle actually shuffled down the passage to the cellar-kitchen steps.

Lazarus did not leave her until he, too, had descended into the cellar-kitchen, where he stood and towered above her like an infuriated giant.

'Tomorrow he will be on his way to Samavia, miserable

woman!' he said. 'Before he goes, it would be well for you
to implore his pardon.'

But Mrs Beedle's point of view was not his. She had
recovered some of her breath.

'I don't know where Samavia is,' she raged, as she struggled to set her dusty black cap straight. 'I'll warrant it's
one of these little foreign countries you can scarcely see on
the map – and not a decent English town in it! He can go
as soon as he likes, so long as he pays his rent before he
does it. Samavia, indeed! You talk as if he was Buckingham Palace!'

CHAPTER 31

His Majesty Awaits You!

WHEN a party composed of two boys attended by a big soldierly manservant and accompanied by two distinguished-looking, elderly men, of a marked foreign type, appeared on the platform of Charing Cross Station they attracted a good deal of attention. In fact, the good looks and strong, well-carried body of the handsome lad with the thick black hair would have caused eyes to turn towards him even if he had not seemed to be regarded as so special a charge by those who were with him.

'See that fine, big lad over there!' said a workman, whose head, with a pipe in its mouth, stuck out of a third-class smoking-carriage window. 'He's some sort of a young swell, I'll lay a shillin'! Take a look at him,' to his mate inside.

The mate took a look.

'Yes, he's some sort of young swell,' he summed him up. 'But he's not English by a long chalk. He must be a young Turk, or Russian, sent over to be educated.'

A good-natured looking guard was passing, and the first man hailed him.

'Have we got any swells travelling with us this morning?' he asked, jerking his head towards the group. 'That looks like it. Anyone leaving Windsor or Sandringham to cross from Dover today?'

The man looked at the group curiously for a moment and then shook his head.

'They do look like something or other,' he answered, 'but no one knows anything about them. Everybody's safe in Buckingham Palace and Marlborough House this week. No one either going or coming.'

No observer, it is true, could have mistaken Lazarus for an ordinary attendant escorting an ordinary charge. He bore himself like a grenadier, and stood by Marco as if across his dead body alone could anyone approach the lad.

'Until we reach Melzarr,' he had said with passion to the two gentlemen – 'until I can stand before my Master and behind him embrace his son I implore that I may not lose sight of him night or day. I implore that I may travel, armed, at his side. I am but his servant, and have no right to occupy a place in the same carriage. But put me anywhere. I will be deaf, dumb, blind to all but himself. Only permit me to be near enough to give my life if it is needed. Let me say to my Master, "I never left him." '

'We will find a place for you,' the elder man said, 'and if you are so anxious, you may sleep across his threshold when we spend the night at a hotel.'

'I will not sleep!' said Lazarus. 'I will watch. Suppose there should be demons of Maranovitch loose and infuriated in Europe? Who knows!'

'The Maranovitch and Iarovitch who have not already sworn allegiance to King Ivor are dead on battlefields. The remainder are now Fedorovitch and praising God for their King,' was the answer Baron Rastka made him.

But Lazarus kept his guard unbroken. When he occupied the next compartment to the one in which Marco travelled, he stood in the corridor throughout the journey. When they descended at any point to change trains, he followed close at the boy's heels, his fierce eyes on every side at once and his hand on the weapon hidden in his broad leather belt. When they stopped to rest in some city, he planted himself in a chair by the bedroom door of his charge, and if he slept he was not aware that nature had betrayed him into doing so.

If the journey made by the young Bearers of the Sign had been a strange one, this was strange by its very contrast. Now, two well-dressed boys in the charge of two men of the class whose orders are obeyed, journeyed in compartments reserved for them, their travelling appurtenances supplying every comfort that luxury could provide.

The Rat had not known that there were people who travelled in such a manner; that wants could be so perfectly foreseen; that officials, porters at stations, the staff of restaurants, could be by magic transformed into active and eager servants. To lean against the upholstered back of a railway carriage and look through the window at passing beauties, and then to find books at your elbow and excellent meals appearing at regular hours, these unknown perfections made it necessary for him at times to pull himself together and give all his energies to believing that he was quite awake. Awake he was, and with so much on his mind to 'work out' that on the first day of the journey he had decided to give up the struggle, and wait until fate made clear to him such things as he was to be allowed to understand of the mystery of Stefan Loristan.

What he realized most clearly was that the fact that the son of Stefan Loristan was being escorted in private state to the country his father had given his life's work to, was never for a moment forgotten. The Baron Rastka and Count Vorversk were of the dignity and courteous reserve which marks men of distinction. They watched over him with a gravity and forethought which seemed to encircle him with a rampart. Without any air of subservience, they constituted themselves his attendants. His comfort, his pleasure, even his entertainment, were their private care.

The night before they reached Melzarr, they slept at a town some hours distant from the capital. They arrived at midnight and went to a quiet hotel.

'Tomorrow,' said Marco, when The Rat left him for the night, 'tomorrow, we shall see him. God be thanked!'

'God be thanked!' said The Rat, also. And each saluted the other before they parted.

In the morning, Lazarus came into the bedroom with an air so solemn that it seemed as if the garments he carried in his hands were part of some religious ceremony. 'I am at your command, sir,' he said. 'And I bring you your uniform.'

He carried, in fact, a richly decorated Samavian uniform, and the first thing Marco had seen when he entered was that Lazarus himself was in uniform also. His was the uniform of an officer of the King's Body Guard.

'The Master,' he said, 'asks that you wear this on your entrance to Melzarr. I have a uniform, also, for your Aide-de-camp.'

When Rastka and Vorversk appeared, they were in uniform also. It was a uniform which had a touch of the Orient in its splendour. A short fur-bordered mantle hung by a jewelled chain from the shoulders, and there was much magnificent embroidery of colour and gold.

'Sir, we must drive quickly to the station,' Baron Rastka said to Marco. 'These people are excitable and patriotic, and His Majesty wishes us to remain incognito, and avoid all chance of public demonstration until we reach the capital.' They passed rather hurriedly through the hotel to the carriage which awaited them. The Rat saw that something unusual was happening in the place. Servants were scurrying round corners, and guests were coming out of their rooms and even hanging over the balustrades.

As Marco got into his carriage, he caught sight of a boy about his own age who was peeping from behind a bush. Suddenly he darted away, and they all saw him tearing down the street towards the station as fast as his legs would carry him.

But the horses were faster than he was. The party reached the station, and was escorted quickly to its place in a special saloon-carriage which awaited it. As the train made its way out of the station, Marco saw the boy who had run before them rush on to the platform, waving his arms and shouting something with wild delight. The people who were standing about turned to look at him, and the next instant they had all torn off their caps and thrown them up in the air and were shouting also. But it was not possible to hear what they said.

'We were only just in time,' said Vorversk, and Baron Rastka nodded.

The train went swiftly, and stopped only once before they reached Melzarr. This was at a small station, on the platform of which stood peasants with big baskets of garlanded flowers and evergreens. They put them on the train, and soon both Marco and The Rat saw that something unusual was taking place. At one time, a man standing on the narrow outside platform of the carriage was plainly seen to be securing garlands and handing up flags to men who worked on the roof.

'They are doing something with Samavian flags and a lot of flowers and green things!' cried The Rat, in excitement.

'Sir, they are decorating the outside of the carriage,' Vorversk said. 'The villagers on the line obtained permission from His Majesty. The son of Stefan Loristan could not be allowed to pass their homes without their doing homage.'

'I understand,' said Marco, his heart thumping hard against his uniform. 'It is for my father's sake.'

At last, embowered, garlanded, and hung with waving banners, the train drew in at the chief station at Melzarr.

'Sir,' said Rastka, as they were entering, 'will you stand up that the people may see you. Those on the outskirts of the crowd will have the merest glimpse, but they will never forget.'

Marco stood up. The others grouped themselves behind him. There arose a roar of voices, which ended almost in a shriek of joy which was like the shriek of a tempest. Then there burst forth the blare of brazen instruments playing the National Hymn of Samavia, and mad voices joined in it.

If Marco had not been a strong boy, and long trained in self-control, what he saw and heard might have been almost too much to be borne. When the train had come to a full stop, and the door was thrown open, even Rastka's dignified voice was unsteady as he said, 'Sir, lead the way. It is for us to follow.'

And Marco, erect in the doorway, stood for a moment, looking out upon the roaring, acclaiming, weeping, singing and swaying multitude – and saluted just as he had saluted the Squad, looking just as much a boy, just as much a man, just as much a thrilling young human being.

Then, at the sight of him standing so, it seemed as if the crowd went mad – as the Forgers of the Sword had seemed to go mad, on the night in the cavern. The tumult rose and rose, the crowd rocked, and leapt, and, in its frenzy of emotion, threatened to crush itself to death. But for the lines of soldiers, there would have seemed no chance for anyone to pass through it alive.

'I am the son of Stefan Loristan,' Marco said to himself, in order to hold himself steady. 'I am on my way to my father.'

Afterwards, he was moving through the line of guarding soldiers to the entrance, where two great state-carriages stood; and there, outside, waited even a huger and more frenzied crowd than that left behind. He saluted there again, and again, and again, on all sides. It was what they had seen the Emperor do in Vienna. He was not an emperor, but he was the son of Stefan Loristan who had brought back the King.

'You must salute, too,' he said to The Rat, when they

got into the state carriage. 'Perhaps my father has told them. It seems as if they knew you.'

The Rat had been placed beside him on the carriage seat. He was inwardly shuddering with a rapture of exultation which was almost anguish. The people were looking at him – shouting at him – surely it seemed like it when he looked at the faces nearest in the crowd. Perhaps Loristan –

'Listen!' said Marco suddenly, as the carriage rolled on its way. 'They are shouting to us in Samavian, "The Bearers of the Sign!" That is what they are saying now. "The Bearers of the Sign!"'

They were being taken to the palace. That Baron Rastka and Count Vorversk had explained in the train. His Majesty wished to receive them. Stefan Loristan was there also.

The city had once been noble and majestic. It was somewhat oriental, as its uniforms and national costumes were. There were domed and pillared structures of white stone and marble, there were great arches, and city gates, and churches. But many of them were half in ruins through war, and neglect, and decay. They passed the half-unroofed cathedral, standing in the sunshine in its great square, still in all its disaster one of the most beautiful structures in Europe. In the exultant crowd were still to be seen haggard faces, men with bandaged limbs and heads, or hobbling on sticks and crutches. The richly coloured native costumes were most of them worn to rags. But their wearers had the faces of creatures plucked from despair to be lifted to heaven.

The palace was as wonderful in its way as the white cathedral. The immensely wide steps of marble were guarded by soldiers. The huge square in which it stood was filled with people whom the soldiers held in check.

'I am his son,' Marco said to himself, as he descended from the state carriage and began to walk up the steps

which seemed so enormously wide that they appeared almost like a street. Up he mounted, step by step, The Rat following him. And as he turned from side to side, to salute those who made deep obeisance as he passed, he began to realize that he had seen their faces before.

'These who are guarding the steps,' he said, quickly under his breath to The Rat, 'are the Forgers of the Sword!'

There were rich uniforms everywhere when he entered the palace, and people who bowed almost to the ground as he passed. He was very young to be confronted with such royal ceremony; but he hoped it would not last too long, and that after he had knelt to the King and kissed his hand, he would see his father and hear his voice.

Through the vaulted corridors, to the wide-opened doors of a magnificent room he was led at last. The end of it seemed a long way off as he entered. There were many richly dressed people who stood in lines as he passed up towards the canopied dais. He felt that he had grown pale with the strain of excitement, and he had begun to feel that he must be walking in a dream, as on each side people bowed low and curtsied to the ground.

He realized vaguely that the King himself was standing, awaiting his approach. But as he advanced, each step bearing him nearer to the throne, the light and colour about him, the strangeness and magnificence, the wildly joyous acclamation of the populace outside the palace, made him feel rather dazzled, and he did not clearly see any one single face or thing.

'His Majesty awaits you,' said a voice behind him which seemed to be Baron Rastka's. 'Are you faint, sir? You look pale.'

He drew himself together, and lifted his eyes. For one full moment, after he had so lifted them, he stood quite still and straight, looking into the deep beauty of the royal face. Then he knelt and kissed the hands held out to him – kissed them both with a passion of boy love and worship.

The King had the eyes he had longed to see – the King's hands were those he had longed to feel again upon his shoulder – the King was his father! the 'Stefan Loristan' who had been the last of those who had waited and laboured for Samavia through five hundred years, and who had lived and died kings, though none of them till now had worn a crown! His father was the King!

It was not that night, nor the next, nor for many nights that the telling of the story was completed. The people knew that their King and his son were bound together by an affection of singular strength and meaning, and their love for their people added to their feeling for each other. By mountain fires, in huts, under the stars, in fields, and in forests, all that was known of their story was told and retold a thousand times.

But none knew it as it was told in a certain quiet but stately room in the palace.

It was a wonderful and intense story, that of the long wanderings and the hiding of the dangerous secret. Among all those who had known that a patriot was labouring for Samavia, and using all the power of a great mind to gain friends for his unhappy country, there had been but one who had known that Stefan Loristan had a claim to the throne. He had made no claim, he had sought – not a crown – but the final freedom of the nation.

'Not the crown!' he said to the two young Bearers of the Sign. 'Not a throne. "The Life of my life – for Samavia." That was what I worked for – what we have all worked for. If there had risen a wiser man in Samavia's time of need, it would not have been for me to remind them of their Lost Prince. I could have stood aside. But no man arose. The crucial moment came – and the one

man who knew the secret, revealed it. Then – Samavia
called, and I answered.'

He put his hand on the thick, black hair of his boy's
head.

'There was a thing we never spoke of together,' he said.
'I believed always that your mother died of her bitter
fears for me and the unending strain of them. She was
very young and loving, and knew that there was no day
when we parted that we were sure of seeing each other
alive again. When she died, she begged me to promise that
your boyhood and youth should not be burdened by the
knowledge she had found it so terrible to bear. I should
have kept the secret from you, even if she had not so
implored me. I had never meant that you should know
the truth until you were a man. If I had died, a certain
document would have been sent to you which would have
left my task in your hands and made my plans clear. You
would have known then that you also were a Prince Ivor,
who must take up his country's burden and be ready
when Samavia called. I tried to help you to train yourself
for any task. You never failed me.'

'Your Majesty,' said The Rat, 'I began to work it out,
and think it must be true that night–when we were with
the old woman on the top of the mountain. It was the way
she looked at – at His Highness.'

'Say "Marco",' threw in Prince Ivor. 'It's easier. He was
my army, father.'

Stefan Loristan's grave eyes melted.

'Say "Marco",' he said. 'You were his army – and more –
when we both needed one. It was you who invented The
Game!'

'Thank you, your Majesty,' said The Rat. 'You do me a
great honour! My mind went on working until sometimes I was afraid I might let something out at the wrong
time. When we went down into the cavern, and I saw the
Forgers of the Sword go mad over him – I *knew* it must be

true. But I didn't dare speak. I knew you meant us to wait; so I waited.'

'You are a faithful friend,' said the King, 'and you have always obeyed orders!'

The clear light of this night's splendour drew them out on a broad balcony of white marble which looked like snow. The pure radiance of the great moon fell upon all they saw spread before them – the lovely but half-ruined city, the great palace square with its broken statues and arches, the splendid ghost of the unroofed cathedral whose high altar was bare to the sky.

They stood and looked at it. There was stillness in which all the world might have ceased breathing.

'What next?' said Prince Ivor, at last speaking quietly and low. 'What next, Father?'

'Great things which will come, one by one,' said the King, 'if we hold ourselves ready.'